Katherine Garbera ~~more than one hundre~~ ~~into over two dozen l~~ ~~worldwide. She is the~~ mother of two incredibly creative and snarky grown children. Katherine enjoys champagne, reading, walking and travelling with her husband. Visit her on the web at katherinegarbera.com

Coming soon from Katherine Garbera

How to Charm a Nerd

Discover more at afterglowbooks.co.uk

THE BOOKBINDER'S GUIDE TO LOVE

KATHERINE GARBERA

First Published in Great Britain 2024
by Afterglow Books by Mills & Boon, an imprint of HarperCollins*Publishers* Ltd
1 London Bridge Street, London, SE1 9GF

www.harpercollins.co.uk

HarperCollins*Publishers*
Macken House, 39/40 Mayor Street Upper,
Dublin 1, D01 C9W8, Ireland

The Bookbinder's Guide to Love © 2024 Katherine Garbera

ISBN: 978-0-263-32277-4

0124

This book contains FSC™ certified paper and other controlled sources to ensure responsible forest management.

For more information visit: www.harpercollins.co.uk/green

Printed and Bound in the UK using 100% Renewable Electricity at CPI Group (UK) Ltd, Croydon, CR0 4YY

This book is for everyone who has found solace,
family and adventure in the pages of a book.

Prologue

"Charm, curse, confluence," Liberty Wakefield said.

"That sounds…" Serafina Conte didn't know how to describe this latest version of kiss, screw, avoid that her friend was trying to come up with to market in their store. It was bold, in-your-face.

Liberty was the most witchy of the three best friends. Their town was sold on the idea, the possibility, that they weren't just friends and business owners…but a coven of witches. It didn't help matters that Liberty had insisted they go to the top of Hanging Hill at midnight on the summer solstice and dance around. More than a few people noticed.

It had been fun, and Sera had always been a no-regrets kind of person.

Oh, who was she kidding. She'd *never* been a no-regrets person. Not once. But Liberty and Poppy were her best friends. And she'd do anything for them. Hence discussing a witchy version of this game that they could possibly create and sell in their shop. Liberty had suggested they make an oracle deck that featured forty-eight different cards inspired by their shop: sixteen cards of authors living and dead from Sera's part; sixteen cards of bakers and famous tea makers from Poppy's; and lastly sixteen cards featuring witches, wizards and magical creatures, both real and fictional, from her own. There would also be twelve blank cards the purchaser could fill in with either people they knew or celebrities or their own category.

"I'm fine with it as long as it brings more customers in," Poppy Kitchener said.

"Me too," Sera said.

The door to their shop opened and they all turned since traffic had been slow on this gray November day. Most locals had hurried home to get ready for Thanksgiving, and tourists were probably doing the same. Sera hadn't celebrated the holiday much. It was for families, and she'd never really had one. Not one of her own. She'd grown up in foster homes, and Thanksgiving hadn't been a big deal.

Poppy was British, so she didn't celebrate, but Liberty did. And they were all going to her mom's house the next day for the feast. Sera was looking forward to it, but trying to be cool in case they canceled on her. Even though she knew her friends would never do that, old habits died hard.

"Hello, are you still open?"

Sera vaguely recognized the woman standing in the doorway. But couldn't place her face. Maybe they'd gone to college together?

"We sure are. Do you need help finding something, or do you just want to browse on your own?" Liberty asked.

"Browse, I guess," the woman said.

"Would you like some tea?" Poppy asked.

"Yes. I'd love it. And I think you have some handmade journals, right?"

"We do," Sera said, getting up and going over to her corner of the shop, which was lined with floor-to-ceiling bookcases stocked with books that she chose, as well as journals she bound by hand. Something about the woman's voice was ringing bells, but for the life of her Sera couldn't place it.

"This is a selection of premade journals," she said, leading her to the display table. "What are you looking for?"

"I don't know. Something that will inspire me."

"To write? This journal has pages that I took from an old manuscript. The writing has faded, but some of the gold leaf they used to embellish the words remains. Want to look at that?"

"I'd love to."

Sera showed her the journals and stepped aside so she could check them out in private when Liberty came over, grabbed her arm and dragged her toward the back room. "OMG. That's Amber Rapp."

As soon as Liberty said the name, everything clicked. The pop singer was known for her catchy tunes and snarky lyrics about her breakups. It *was* her. "I thought she was someone from college."

"As if. What's she doing here?"

"She said she was looking for inspiration," Sera said.

"You should offer to make her a custom journal like you did for Poppy and me," Liberty said.

Sera wasn't sure. That was something private between the

three of them. But Amber did say she was looking for inspiration, and both Liberty and Poppy claimed their journals had helped them meet their goals. "Why not?"

She went back into the room where Amber was still standing at the table. When she looked up, she seemed to know they'd figured out who she was. She waited as if ready to take a selfie or sign something.

What kind of life must that be?

"I guess I'll take this one," Amber said, holding up a leather-covered journal that Sera had made a few weeks ago using a newer binding process she'd learned from her friend Ford.

"I don't know if you'll be interested, but I sometimes make special journals with an intent inscribed."

"She made one for me and Poppy and it led us to opening the store," Liberty said.

"How?" Amber sounded skeptical.

"Well, you write down an intention and then I will emboss it into the cover of the book. You fill out the journal, and when it's full, the intention becomes real," Sera said.

"Really?"

"Yes. It's worked for all three of us," Poppy said, coming over with the tea she'd made.

"Okay. I'll try it," Amber said.

Sera went to her workbench and took a piece of old parchment and a fountain pen and came back, handing them to Amber.

"What should I write?"

"Something you can believe in. I wrote, 'There is magic in

the words in this book, and they will create the life I want,'"
Sera said.

"We did the same," Liberty added.

Amber took a minute to think and wrote a version of Sera's
suggestion.

"Okay, it will take about thirty minutes for me to put this
into the cover."

"Want to have your cards read while you wait?" Liberty
asked.

"Love to."

Sera heard them move away as she went back to her workbench and carefully lifted the cardboard back under the front
cover. She placed the handwritten piece of parchment on the
inside and then closed the cover with glue and reattached the
bindings of the leather. When she was done, Amber told them
she'd enjoyed meeting them and left.

"Wow. We should have asked for a selfie," Poppy said.

"No one is going to believe she was here," Sera said. "But
I think it was probably nicer for her to just be a girl in the
shop than Amber Rapp, megastar."

"Probably. Her cards were intense," Liberty said. "So back
to charm, curse or confluence. What do we think of Merle?"

"Gross. He's my cousin," Poppy said.

"Charm," Sera said. She liked Merle, who bought a lot of
books from her on wizardry and war for his Dungeons and
Dragons campaigns. He was the dungeon master for his group.

"Great, so that leaves curse for me," Poppy said.

"Confluence, then. He's a bit too nerdy," Liberty said. "But
I'd still rock his dungeon."

They all laughed. Sera had found something she'd never had the courage to write about in her manifesting journal. *Sisters*.

One year later, Amber Rapp dropped her new album and it went straight to the top of the charts. She gave all the credit to her visit to WiCKed Sisters in Birch Lake, Maine—which just confirmed for many locals that they were indeed a coven and most likely good witches. Since then, Amber's fans had descended on the town in droves, all wanting to get their hands on the journal Amber had purchased, have tea in Poppy's shop and get their cards read by Liberty.

One

Serafina Conte wished she had magic. Not the kind that everyone thought she had, where she could make their dreams come true, but the kind where she could turn an onerous man into a toad.

To be fair, she wasn't sure what she'd do with Wesley Sitwell once he was a toad—maybe put him in a terrarium like they had for the fourth-grade class turtle and feed him dead flies once a week. That sounded perfect to her.

Except despite what Amber Rapp had told her followers, the co-owners of WiCKed Sisters weren't modern-day witches. Sera and her friends had no control over anything paranormal. She was pretty sure Amber's success had come from her own determination to release an album unlike anything she'd created before. She'd made her own magic.

But Amber wasn't taking the credit and had given it all to them. So each day before they opened the shop there was a crowd of people outside, not just younger fans but their parents and grandparents as well.

Sitting among the stacks of books that lined the back room of her shop, Sera felt at home and safe in a way that nothing else had ever made her feel. She glanced at the letter she had just received, written on very official-looking letterhead from Sitwell & Associates, Attorneys at Law.

It forbade her from attending the funeral of Ford Sitwell, being held on Saturday at 10:00 a.m. at St. Luke's Catholic Church, right in the heart of the town of Birch Lake, Maine. Could they *ban* her from church? She was pretty sure Sister Mary Edward would disagree. No one was banned from the church.

A wave of sadness rolled over her, engulfing her. Ford had treated her like she imagined a grandfather would have. He'd been kind and funny, sharing his library and the books he'd loved. Though Sera had always been well-read, he'd introduced her to authors she'd never heard of and to worlds that had dominated her dreams.

They'd talked about books and bookmaking; Ford had been a bookbinder in his twenties. Long before he'd settled down and had a family. He'd regaled her with stories of that time in his life and taught her techniques that had fallen out of use. She'd used those techniques to start making her journals and had seen the quality of her product begin to change.

Ford had been the one to tell her she was never going to produce a quality book if she kept buying the cheapest materials on the market. She'd spent every Thursday morning for the last two years visiting with him. He'd been the first man to give her a gift on her birthday, and Sera knew she'd never forget him.

It didn't matter that he'd turned ninety on his last birthday and that she'd known he wasn't going to live forever. Her entire life had been marked by the fact that she was alone. Ford had left an indelible mark as well, so it made her angry that this Wesley Sitwell, speaking on behalf of his father and brother, was now trying to keep her from saying goodbye to her friend.

"There you are. You know the shop is packed, right?" Liberty Wakefield asked, sitting down next to Sera on the overstuffed love seat that she'd wedged into this back room between the bookshelves. Liberty had a cup of her morning mud water, some kind of functional mushroom drink that was supposed to improve concentration.

"I do."

"And? What are you doing?"

"Truth?"

Liberty lifted both eyebrows at her as if to say, *Duh!*

"I'm trying to conjure a spell to turn Wesley Sitwell into a toad," Sera admitted, dropping the letter onto her lap and reaching for her own cup of Earl Grey tea.

"What's he done? Sitwell... Is he related to that old guy you visit?"

"Used to visit. Ford died yesterday," Sera said. "His funeral is on Saturday morning."

"Oh, Sera," Liberty said, hugging her.

"I can't believe he's gone."

"I'm sorry. I didn't get your relationship, but I know you liked him and he treated you like a surrogate granddaughter," Liberty said, taking the letter and skimming it. "He left you something?"

"Yeah, some old journals and books. That was our thing. But his son and grandsons are ticked and don't want me at the funeral."

"So what's their deal? Do they want the old books?" Liberty asked. "Do you want me to put a spell on them?"

"The books or the Sitwells?"

"Both," Liberty said, grinning at her.

Sera smiled at her friend, glad she'd found Liberty when they'd both been working for a national coffee chain, dreaming of something bigger. "No to the spells for now."

But the old books weren't just a box of paperbacks that no one wanted to read. The books were antiquarian and possibly valuable if they were repaired. Sera was still a bit shocked that Ford had left them to her, but he'd been showing her the techniques needed to restore them, so she suspected that had been his motivation. Last week he'd told her he didn't want her skills to get rusty when she'd mentioned that the new crowds at WiCKed Sisters meant she barely had time to do anything but make her journals.

She had asked him if she could have the old books he'd shown her in his attic. They were water damaged, and some of the pages were torn or folded over. The paper aged better because of that, and it had a nice— Well, *patina* wasn't the right word, but it looked pretty in the journals after she worked her magic on them.

"What are you going to do?" Liberty asked.

She'd never been one to cling to people. She knew most of them weren't going to be in her life for a long time. In fact, her longest relationship was with Liberty and Poppy, and she'd only known them for five years. It was probably why she loved books so much.

Books were always available. When she'd had no money, she'd gone to the library, and when she had a little bit of money, the used bookstore. Now, when she was making more money than she'd ever dreamed of, she could afford to buy new books and she had a huge stack of them piled in her bedroom next to the dresser and on her nightstand.

But this gift from Ford wasn't about money; it was special to her. He had left her books because they'd talked about stories and even read together. Books had created a bond between the two of them. But apparently his family wanted her to give the books back, and they were sending Wesley to discuss the issue.

"I'm not sure. I mean, I don't have any family, so I'm not entirely sure how I'd feel if a stranger—"

"You weren't a stranger to Ford. You were family to him," Liberty said. "Seriously. Do you want me to deal with the toad?"

Yes, because she hated confrontation, but she knew she couldn't ask Liberty to do this for her. There was a part of Sera that wished she were more like Liberty. Her friend spoke her mind and didn't worry about it. If she hurt someone's feelings, she'd apologize for it later. But she never held her tongue.

"Thanks. I've got it. I'm more concerned about how I'm going to keep up with the demand for journals," Sera said, changing the subject so she could get ready for her day and not worry so much about Wesley Sitwell.

"Are you running low?" Liberty asked with a note of concern in her voice.

And that concern was justified. The Amber Rapp thing meant customers wanted to have tea in Poppy's shop, get their cards read by Liberty and then write a message to themselves that Sera put into the cover of a handmade journal. They wanted the full ritual in the hopes of bottling some of Amber's success. If they didn't have journals, that would affect everyone.

Sera wasn't about to let down her friends. They were her found family.

"Yes, because I make them all by hand… I might need to hire someone else," Sera said. It was nice to have something practical to discuss rather than Ford's family.

"I think we should talk about hiring staff to run the register. That way we don't have to ring up customers. I'm sure Poppy would agree."

"Probably. She mentioned she was hiring two new servers for the tea shop," Sera said. She sent a message to Poppy in their group text, telling her they wanted to hire more staff and asking if she was going to be back in Birch Lake on Friday for dinner.

Poppy texted back a thumbs-up.

"That's taken care of. I guess that means Merle is going to be running the tea shop today," Liberty said. "I know he's Poppy's cousin, but he gets on my nerves."

"He's okay. Just a little nerdy…and that's saying something, coming from me," Sera said with a laugh.

"You're a bookworm, not nerdy," Liberty said. "He is full-on nerd."

"Why does that bother you?" As a tarot reader, Liberty

herself wasn't considered normal by everyone's standards—
but something about Merle always seemed to throw her off.

She shrugged. "I don't know. Probably because he's kinda
hot and weird as hell."

"I thought that was your type," Sera said with a grin.

Liberty shot her the bird and then got up to take her mug
to the sink. "Want me to draw a card for you before you go
meet the old guy's grandson?"

Did she?

"Yes, but only tell me if it's a good one."

Liberty shook her head. "All the cards are neutral, neither
good nor bad. You know that, right? Life isn't good or bad."

Maybe. Sera wasn't convinced. "Yeah, sure. But remember
that time you drew the tower and freaked?"

Liberty had a bunch of different decks, some themed for
Samhain or to specific areas of interest. But her everyday carry
for tarot was the original Rider-Waite tarot deck.

"Only because my mom was supposed to fly that day,"
Liberty said.

"That's what I'm afraid of. What if you draw something
that says 'outlook not good'?"

"These are tarot cards, not a Magic 8 Ball. You know you
can handle yourself. You didn't con anyone out of anything.
You met a nice old man who liked books and you went to
his house for the last couple of years to talk with him. Where
was the grandson then?"

Liberty had a point. The letter made it sound like she didn't
deserve the books that Ford had left her. Her old thought pro-
cesses and behaviors were making her believe it. She wasn't

the orphan girl being shifted from foster home to foster home with nothing to call her own.

She had become friends with Ford, and she was going to miss their weekly chats about the classics in the library of his large Victorian house, which had seen better days. She hadn't become friends with him in the hopes of getting anything.

They'd connected over a love of stories—he'd turned her on to the author Dodie Smith's *I Capture the Castle*. As much as she appreciated their shared fondness for books, what she had really come to cherish was their unexpected friendship.

In her heart, she felt sad at the thought of never speaking to him again. Ford had made her feel like she belonged in a way she'd only ever found with Liberty, Poppy and the books on her keeper shelf.

She wasn't going to let Wesley or anyone else take that from her. She'd been writing her own story since she'd been old enough to realize reality sucked. She'd been fourteen when she'd accepted that she'd cast herself as the best friend instead of the leading lady. When she'd turned twenty-one and met Liberty and Poppy, she'd seen in them something she'd never found in herself.

They were the leading ladies of their lives.

Something Sera had promised herself she'd become. Something she'd inched closer to when she'd gone in with her friends on this shop. Something she was going to have to *be*, because she wasn't about to let Sitwell & Associates take Ford's gift to her.

Wesley Sitwell wasn't sure what he'd expected Grandpa's twenty-six-year-old "friend" to look like, but it wasn't that girl. Serafina Conte. She was bustling around behind the counter under a sign that read Words Are Magic.

Her thick, dark, curly hair had sprung free from the ponytail at the small of her neck. The hair band had popped while he'd been watching her. He didn't know why he was obsessed with her hair.

Except *maybe* he did. His first crush had been Emma Watson as Hermione Granger, and Serafina Conte was giving him all the Hermione feels.

From a distance, her eyes were deep brown and she had thick eyebrows that furrowed as she ran from the counter to her back room and returned like a windup toy that his brother, Oz, had broken one of the legs off of when they were kids, spinning in a silly, constant circle.

But there was nothing silly about this woman. She wore a blouse probably more suited to a woman Grandpa's age. It had a bow and puffy sleeves, and she'd paired it with faded jeans and some chunky-heeled platform boots. The jeans hugged her curves, showing off her near-perfect ass, which might have explained his grandfather's obsession with her.

She had a slightly rounded face, and if she'd been wearing lipstick, she'd worried it off long before he'd entered the shop. Her face was earnest when she spoke to her customers. Still, Wes didn't trust her.

Grandpa, who'd had the same friends for most of his life— namely his chess buddies Hamish and Ronald, though the latter had died last year—had suddenly developed a close association with this woman.

Wes wasn't the type to stalk Reddit for conspiracies, but that didn't mean he overlooked something this obvious. When a hottie started a friendship with a much older man, it raised a huge red flag. Not that Ford had been an easy man to influence, but to suddenly leave a small fortune in books to this woman…there *had* to be more to it than met the eye.

Or he wanted there to be. Wes didn't want to face the fact that he and Grandpa had fallen out. Wes had broken the partnership they'd formed when he'd left college and started his book repair business. The problem with Grandpa was that he refused to budge; everything always had to be his way. And Wes… Well, he was just as stubborn as Ford.

Ford had been the one to foster Wes's own love of books, so Wes always believed he would inherit them. Books had been his way out of a troubled childhood. His mom left, taking Wes and his twin until his dad agreed to a divorce, nearly bankrupting both his dad and grandpa before returning Wes and his twin.

His dad hadn't handled the situation well, and to say he hadn't been father of the year was an understatement. Wes had always been the one least like him. Wes had his mom's looks, and that had engendered… *Hatred* might be too strong a word for what his dad felt when he'd looked into Wes's blue eyes and watched as, over time, the white-blond hair Wes had been born with turned to a rich honey blond that matched his mother's.

Grandpa had left a note specifying that a box of curated antique books and journals were to be given to Serafina Conte. His dad hadn't really been bothered by Grandpa's bequest for the sake of the books—the old man never understood Wes's choice to follow in Ford's footsteps. But his dad didn't like the fact that the woman, any woman, might have manipulated

Ford the way his ex-wife manipulated him. He'd agreed to Wes's request to use the family letterhead to send her a letter insisting she return Grandpa's books to them. The truth was most of the old books Grandpa had needed repair.

Which was why Wes was here.

He was the one Ford had trained and he had always assumed Grandpa would give the books to him. Wes had hoped repairing the books would fix the damage he'd done when he'd told Grandpa he was forging his own path.

But it hadn't.

Instead, Serafina Conte, who probably thought the books were worth money, like his dad did, had gotten them. That was a little too sus. Wes wasn't leaving Birch Lake until he had the books back. Then he'd fix them. He might suck at relationships, but he was good at repairing broken things.

Who the hell was she? And why the fuck had Grandpa left the books to her?

"Sorry, folks. That's all the journals I can make for today. Come back tomorrow and I'll have more for you."

She stood on a step stool near the counter, and though there were some rumbles of disappointment, most of the customers didn't seem too upset to have to leave. As the shop emptied, Wes stayed to the side of the doorway.

The shop was lined with books, some newer editions but mostly secondhand titles. Nothing on the shelves had the same pedigree as the books his grandfather had left her. But she did have a few titles that would sell for a hefty price at the online auction house he ran as a sideline to make ends meet. Repairing old books was a specialist skill, but it didn't exactly rake in the big bucks.

"Can I help you find what you're looking for?" she asked, coming up next to him.

Up close, her eyes weren't brown but more of a greenish hazel. Her hair looked like every sex dream he'd had back in the day, and her mouth… Fuck him, he couldn't stop staring at it.

She reached up, pulling her hair back, which made his eyes drop to her chest and the way her shirt pulled tight across her breasts. It wasn't just her ass that was perfect.

"So?" she asked.

"I believe I've found what I'm looking for."

"Those are great books and a bit of a steal," she said with a playful grin that went straight to his dick.

"They definitely are, but I'm not here for the books, Serafina Conte. I'm here for you."

"For me?" she asked, a bit startled. Then her eyes narrowed. "Sitwell?"

"Indeed. Expecting me?"

Her mouth tightened in a frown.

"Not really. Are you here to deliver some extra threat if I show up at the funeral?" she asked. "I checked with the church and you can't ban me from attending. Also, I think Ford would be disappointed to know you tried to."

"Then you didn't know Ford very well."

"To be fair, I've only known him for a couple of years," she said. "Not the lifetime I assume you've had with him."

"Exactly, so why did he give you that box of books?" Wes asked. "What exactly did you do with him for two years?"

The smile left her face as she glared at him. "What do you think we did?"

"I wouldn't be asking if I knew," he said.

"But you have some idea," she retorted.

"I do."

She just stared at him, as if daring him to say what he was thinking. He hadn't been this irritated by a woman in a very long time. He wasn't sure who she thought she was dealing with. "Were you fucking?"

She opened and closed her mouth a few times and then turned and walked away from him without another word.

Two

Fucking?

She hated that he'd rattled her. When she'd seen him standing across the store, it had been hard to keep from looking at him again and again. He was ticking all her boxes, or had been until she'd realized who he was.

Also, what was wrong with her gut? She had been getting turned on watching his long fingers as he'd run them along the books on the shelf while he waited for her.

Sex. As if that were the only reason Ford would want to spend time with her. Shaking her head, she walked away from Wesley Sitwell. Trying very hard to ignore the fact that he didn't look like the evil toad demon he actually was.

His face reminded her of Ford's. But where Ford's hair had thinned and turned gray, Toad Sitwell's was thick, a rich honey blond that almost made her fingers tingle with the thought of touching it. His jaw was strong and his nose sort of Romanesque, much like Ford's had been. But where Ford's eyes had radiated a kind intellect, there was only suspicion and accusation in the younger Sitwell's blue eyes.

He wore a tweed overcoat with the collar up at the back. He'd opened it when he entered her shop and she noticed he had on a formfitting black cable-knit sweater and a pair of matching pants underneath. His chest didn't look overdeveloped, which normally she liked in a guy, but this time was a mark against him. In fact, she didn't like the firm line of his jaw or his mouth either. No matter that the deep timbre of his voice conjured an image of a man—not him—reading to her by a crackling fireplace after they'd had sex.

She wasn't sure why she was dwelling on his clothing except it gave her an extra few minutes to think of what she was going to say.

But really, did she owe this man a response?

"As if the only reason your grandfather would spend every Thursday morning with me for the last two years was so I could hook up with him," she said. "Grow up, Sitwell. Women can have friendships with men—even older men— without having sex with them. I'm not sure where you're from or who you—"

"I'm sorry."

She blinked a few times, and then let his apology sink in. Then she gave him a tight smile and admitted to herself that she was floundering again. He had thrown her with his apology. To be fair, it was something Ford would have done if he'd said something to hurt her feelings.

Having any of Ford's relatives think she'd conned her way into his life using sex was preposterous. She wasn't the kind of woman anyone expected to trade on her looks to get things.

He'd literally just seen her wild hair break a ponytail holder.

"Sure," she said.

She walked back behind the counter, glancing around the shop, which was quiet but not empty. Two teenagers, who she knew were homeschoolers, had obviously heard the exchange, and both were trying to be cool as they pretended to study a book they'd picked up from the shelf.

She smiled at them, trying to hide her unease.

God. This was turning into a really crap day. As soon as she was behind the counter, she reached out and rubbed her fingers over the jade stone that Liberty had charged for her during their last new-moon ritual. It was meant to bring knowledge and resolve difficult situations. The fact that her last difficulty had been whether or not she should renew her Netflix account or switch to a new streaming service wasn't lost on her.

He walked to her and stood on the other side of the counter. "Can we start over?"

"Sure."

No, she thought, but she still had customers in the shop, so she wasn't going to kick him out. But she wanted to. She glanced toward the tea shop, but Poppy was out of town and Liberty was on her dais reading cards, so Sera had to handle Toady Sitwell on her own.

"*I'm* sure that's not exactly a yes," he said dryly.

"Then you're smarter than you seemed earlier," she said. Then, not liking how snarky she was being, she took a deep breath. But that was how she felt right now. She didn't want to make nice with this man. How could he be related to Ford?

"I guess I deserve that."

"You do," she said.

"I just want to ask some questions," he said.

She raised both eyebrows at him. "Yeah, right. I received your letter, so I'm not falling for that."

"Yeah, about that... I should have waited until I met you before firing off that letter," he said. "I was pissed, so I know it wasn't very..."

"Nice?"

He just shrugged. It was apparent he wasn't backing down from his position, so why the half-assed apology?

"Sorry, Conte, I don't know you. Grandpa was ninety. The first time he mentioned you was about two weeks ago."

Though a part of her knew that Ford and his son and grandsons weren't particularly close and that it shouldn't bother her, it still did. She remembered Ford's face last week when they'd been talking, the way his blue eyes had crinkled when he'd laughed at her reaction to reading a Victorian Sampler she'd found on his bookshelf. The old, printed selection of erotic short stories had been bound and printed in 1885. She'd pointed out that it had been a little shocking to realize the people in the old-timey photos had been horny, which had amused him.

And making Ford laugh had made her smile. She still couldn't believe he was gone. Until she'd received the letter, she hadn't known. "How did he die?"

"Hamish, his—"

"I know who Hamish is. I guess Ford didn't show up for the daily chess game. What was the cause of death?" Sera had learned early on to stand up for herself. She might be the best friend in the story of her life, but she wasn't a friend who people walked over.

Wesley leaned against the counter and sighed, and for the first time, she saw some genuine emotion on the man's face. He seemed sad that his grandfather was gone, which didn't fit with what Ford had told her. Maybe this grandson at least had some regret for the long years of estrangement.

"Grandpa had a stroke while he was sleeping. Hamish went to check on him and found him in his bed."

He'd probably died in his sleep; that was how he'd wanted to go. He'd told her more than once that he knew he was on borrowed time and that he'd done everything he had wanted to. Sera had felt that perhaps Ford was still hanging on so she could meet him but hadn't felt brave enough to tell him. Now she wished she had.

"I'm glad it happened that way," Sera said.

"Me too," Wesley said.

"He spoke of you," Sera said, offering an olive branch. Ford had a lot of regret for the way he'd treated his son and grandsons after they'd been returned to the family. It had been an eye-opener for her on the dynamics of family relationships that she'd never experienced.

"Did he?"

She simply nodded.

"I mean, I think you're Wesley, right?"

"Everyone calls me Wes," he said, holding out his hand.

"Serafina Conte," she said.

She took his hand and goose bumps spread up her arm and warmth spread down her body. His mouth curved into a welcoming smile, and for a minute she was captured by his blue gaze and couldn't think. Then she pulled her hand back as she heard the two teenagers giggle.

She wiped her hand on the side of her jeans, but she could still feel his palm against hers.

"You seem almost normal now," she said, not at all like the dude who'd asked her if she had been hooking up with his grandfather or who'd sent the very cold letter from Sitwell & Associates.

"By *normal*, do you mean not a douchebag asking about your sex life?"

"Yeah, that. Sort of sets an odd tone," she said. She was starting to feel almost like there was more to Wesley Sitwell than she'd originally thought.

Given she'd thought very little of him, that wasn't really saying much.

"Definitely. Like learning your grandpa has a twenty-six-year-old girl 'friend,'" he said.

She shrugged. "Probably better than meeting at the funeral. Hope you learned not to jump to conclusions."

"Some habits die hard."

"Like trying to intimidate people with formal letters?"

"No, that's not a habit. I *was* hoping the letter would discourage you from keeping the books," he said.

"I'm not giving them up," she said, refusing to give ground on this.

It was as if Ford had given her controlling shares in his company or something. They were acting like him leaving her anything was unreasonable.

"I can see that. Can we get some coffee? I'd like to know more about why Grandpa left you those books."

That was the first reasonable thing he'd said since she'd met him. But she wasn't ready to be reasonable. "I can't while my shop is open."

"I heard you say you were out of journals," he pointed out.

"I still sell books and I have to prepare the journals for tomorrow," she said, which was the truth. She needed to have at least fifty for the next day, but that wasn't realistic. She'd probably end up with half a dozen or so.

The teenagers finally decided on what they wanted, the latest in a graphic novel series that had been made into a hit show on one of the streaming services. Wes stepped to one side as she checked them out, putting their books into a paper bag stamped with the WiCKed Sisters logo.

"Is there anything else?" she asked. Because she would really like him to leave. She needed time to deal with Ford's death, she still had journals to prep and she wanted to sit on her chair in the back room. Alone. "I have to get back to work."

"What about a drink after work? Just to talk and figure out where we can go from here."

A drink. One drink to learn more about Ford's grandson. There was something about him.

It's just one drink.

Funny, but that thought almost sounded like Ford's voice in her head. It was the least she could do for her old friend.

"Sure."

"Do you ever answer any other way?"

"Sure," she said, even though it really didn't make sense. She saw a smile tease the corner of his lips.

"I'll meet you here at six," he said, turning to the door and then stopping at the books that she'd caught him look-

ing at earlier. He ran his finger over the spine of the one clos-
est to him. A leather-bound edition of Thomas Hardy's *Far
from the Madding Crowd*. "This book is worth more than you
have it marked."

Then he buttoned up his wool coat and walked out the
door. She didn't look away until he'd walked past the stone
statue in the middle of the park and out of her view.

"Who was that?" Liberty asked, coming through the book-
lined passageway that connected her part of the shop to Sera's.

"Wesley Sitwell."

"The toad?"

"Yes."

"He's cute."

"Was he?" *Liar.*

"So you thought so too. What did he want?"

Sera wasn't entirely sure. To insult her, to find out who she
was, to make her doubt she deserved the books his grandfather had left her. Whatever it was, she wasn't going to allow
him to win. Not on this. Ford had once remarked that the
Sitwells were lost in their bitterness and distrust, and Sera
hadn't understood what he meant. But seeing Wesley helped
clarify things.

Wes got as far as the other side of the huge park in the
middle of Birch Lake's town square before he stopped walking and ducked behind the side of a building. He leaned back
against the wall. He'd fucked up when he'd pissed her off.

Now the books might never be his. One more screwup
when it came to Grandpa.

The January breeze blew around him, making him wish

he was back in his shop. God, he almost hated this place. He loved his grandpa, but that relationship had been hard-won. He and Oz were sent up here every summer to work for Grandpa and give his dad a break from parenting.

It had always felt like some sort of punishment to come here. Until he'd gone to college. Then his arrogant ass got a lesson in real life. It had been Grandpa who'd offered him a second chance when he'd lost his scholarship and Dad had stopped paying his tuition.

Grandpa had stepped up, paid for Wes's education at a local college in exchange for working with him over the summers. And those three summers they'd worked together had been good. But then the arrogant asshole Wes was deep down had stirred to life and fucked things up.

The books meant something. Wes wished he'd taken the time to come up and see Grandpa before he'd died. His father didn't really care about Grandpa's estate. He'd put it succinctly in a terse text to Wes and his brother.

There's nothing I want in Birch Lake.

His father and grandpa had never really gotten along after everything happened with the divorce. Wes didn't know what was between the two of them and figured he never would.

He left his spot in the alley and started walking up the cobblestoned street closed to car traffic, leading him away from WiCKed Sisters.

Oz would never let Wes live it down if he'd seen him with Serafina. Close up, he noticed that she had a gap between her two front teeth, and her lush mouth was tantalizing.

The Bookbinder's Guide to Love   35

The part of WiCKed Sisters that she ran had been lined with bookshelves and smelled of paper and leather, which meant the sweet hint of lavender had to have been Serafina's perfume.

He'd been thinking about sex since he'd seen her. It was her hair, that mass of curls flying around her face, making her seem like she was wild. And then the old-fashioned blouse paired with jeans that were trendy and molded to every one of her curves.

He couldn't get her out of his mind. She was a mass of contradictions. Was that why Grandpa had been meeting with her? Maybe Wes could use that as an excuse for why he'd blurted out his argumentative statement.

His phone pinged. He was tempted to throw it into the nearest trash can.

He really needed to be back in his own shop, working on repairing the leather-bound editions that had come from a recent estate sale. He thought better when he was repairing damaged books. Life made sense when he was in the past fixing things.

His phone went off again. Oz wasn't going to stop.

He picked up.

"About damned time."

He could easily picture his brother sitting in his corner office, insulated from the people below him scurrying on with their lives. Oz had been following in their father's footsteps practically from birth. He was as methodical and results-based as their father had always been.

"Emergency?" Wes asked.

"Did you get your books back, nerd?" Oz asked.

"Fuck off."

"So no. Dad told me he let you use our letterhead."

"Yeah. So?" Even to his own ears he sounded defensive.

"Let's hope she doesn't follow up and find out we're tax attorneys."

"She already called the church and will be attending the funeral."

"For fuck's sake, you told her she couldn't."

In retrospect, probably not his best idea. "Was there a reason for this call?"

"Just checking on you. You and Grandpa *were* close for a while," Oz said.

"Yeah. I'm fine."

"Sure you are. I had my assistant get in touch with the funeral home. We need to send a suit over for Grandpa to be buried in."

"I'll do that. I'm sticking around Birch Lake."

"For how long?"

"For as long as it takes," he said.

"What about your business?"

"It's fine. The auction house is online and I source books from estate sales. Since when are you a mother hen?"

The wind gusted around him and he hurried his pace toward his car.

"Since you started sending letters on our letterhead," Oz said, pausing. "Be careful."

"Sure." Borrowing Serafina's word.

"That means what, exactly?"

"It's deliberately vague, Oz—take the hint."

There was silence on the line.

"So is that good or bad?" Oz asked.

"Depends on how you look at it. I'm not sure about Ms. Conte," he told Oz.

"What about her?"

Wes remembered the way she'd looked when she spoke of Ford. There had been affection on her face, so there was clearly something between the pair of them. But what?

In a way, Sera was like an old book he'd found in a box tucked in an attic somewhere. Her cover was obscured, hiding who she was. But he would use patience and skill and coax the truth from her. Repairing cracks, discovering what was hidden within her pages.

"Why Grandpa gave her one box of books. She owns a bookshop, but there's something more to it," Wes said.

"Maybe he did it to piss you off," Oz said.

"There's a good chance of that," Wes agreed. He could feel his defenses going up and needed to end this before Oz reopened old wounds. "Bye."

He disconnected the phone, shoving it into his pocket. This wasn't just about books.

He'd come in hot and hard for Serafina but had backed down when he'd seen her reaction. She wasn't going to give in to him. He needed to do this differently. Shove his wounded pride out of the picture. But that had never been easy. He'd have to show her he wasn't the dick he'd been in her store.

She was going to take a lot of persuasion.

He drove to Grandpa's house on the outskirts of town. In its heyday, the big Victorian mansion had no doubt been splendid, but the decades had taken their toll and it looked worn and tired. Maybe he'd do something about the house while he was in town.

Wes parked in the circle drive. He still had a key to the house on his key ring, even though he'd been stubborn about coming back. He unlocked the door, and as he stepped inside he was hit with the smell of dusty old books. Which reminded him of his grandpa.

He closed his eyes. He wouldn't be able to talk to Ford ever again. Tears burned and he rubbed his eyes hard with the heels of his palms.

He went upstairs and got the suit for Grandpa to be buried in. Stepping into the bedroom, he couldn't help the wave of grief hitting him again.

Three

Sera sat at a long wooden worktable at the back of the shop, next to the door that led to the storage area. She had the paper ready, which she used to make herself until she'd found a supplier who made 150 gsm paper of good quality. She had already made the signatures, which were formed from several sheets of A4-sized paper that had been folded over. A signature was a group of sheets folded in half, to be worked into the binding as a unit.

After she folded them, she pressed them using a stack of old heavy books to make them flatter. She even had a book press, which she used later in the process, once all the signatures were put inside the cover.

But the next step for the signatures was to punch and bind them together. A4-sized paper, once folded in half, made an A5-sized journal, which was the perfect size.

Sera had started making journals for herself. As a way to tell her story. There was nothing constant about her life, and for a while she'd been obsessed with Anne Frank, as well as a series of fictional diaries about women in history. So she'd started writing about her life. Her foster mom Tawdra hadn't had money to buy fancy journals but had tons of printer paper, so Sera watched a YouTube video and learned how to make her own journal. The covers had been infinitely harder at first. But later she'd found cardboard in the recycling and used that.

She shook her head, remembering how crude that first journal had been. But when she'd taken it to school, other kids had noticed, and soon she'd started taking orders and custom-making journals for her classmates. Nearly every time she made more journals, she felt like she was back in that bedroom she'd shared with Milly at Tawdra's, and then she looked around, seeing how far she'd come.

The Sera in that bedroom wouldn't have thought this was possible. But Tawdra had always been nice to her and even gave her some space in the garage as a workshop once she started making money.

She had learned how to do French binding, and that was her standard go-to. At first, she hadn't covered the spines of the books, so the French binding, with its fancy X design, had looked prettier. Each of her journals was fifty-four pages long, which required nine signatures, with a kettle stitch at the bottom to attach each signature. This stitching and binding was almost automatic for her at this point, so she made quick work of them.

She was working faster than normal. Part of it was that feeling of everything falling apart. She knew the feeling well—it had happened each time she'd learned she'd be leaving one foster home and moving to another. She had coping strategies. But she hadn't had to use them since she'd been eighteen.

Ford's death and the unexpected gift of books had rattled her. Wesley—with his hidden smile, tall frame and that brooding look in his eyes—had also sent her for a loop. She'd been trying to ignore that he hadn't looked like an asshole. In fact, until he'd revealed himself, she'd been checking him out.

Liberty came over as she was finishing the last one, placing a cup of Earl Grey tea next to her elbow and leaning back against the bench.

"I know you said not to draw a card," Liberty started. "But I did."

Of course she had. Sera looked over at her friend as she pushed the last of the bound pages aside and reached for her cup of tea.

"And?"

"Like I said, you know cards aren't good or bad."

"Which means this one is bad. Great. What else can happen? Ford died, his hot grandson is an asshole and now what?"

"His grandson *was* hot. Is hot asshole your type?"

"No, definitely not," she said. But a quick look back at her dating history revealed that she didn't always make smart choices when it came to guys.

She did want to grab Wesley by the lapel of his oh-so-proper wool overcoat and kiss him. Partly to shock and partly just to prove to herself that he wasn't as attractive as her imagination was trying to make him. "And if it was, is it better than hot weird?"

Liberty lightly punched her in the arm. "That's not my type."

"Sure."

"So do you want to know what I drew?"

"Yes."

"The Moon."

Great. The *hidden enemies* one. But as Liberty mentioned, it wasn't necessarily bad. Though it was hard to see the good in that card.

"What did you ask when you pulled it?" Sera wanted to know. She needed more details before she freaked out completely. Her stress level was getting higher, and no matter how many times she'd rubbed the jade stone next to the register, it seemed to keep ratcheting up.

She knew it was the fact that Wesley Sitwell had been in her shop making accusations, apologizing and confusing the ever-loving hell out of her.

"Should Sera worry about the toad?"

Great. And the cards had pretty much said yes.

"Well, I'm fucked, then. Does it mean there's more that Sitwell is keeping from me?"

"I'm not sure, but I thought you should know," Liberty said. "If you want to take the afternoon off, I can handle the shop. I only have one reading left today and that's not until five, and Merle can help out."

"Is this a ploy to get me out of here so you can flirt with Merle?"

"If I wanted to flirt with him, I'd do it in front of you," Liberty said with a laugh and then hugged her.

Sera hugged her friend back, for just a moment letting down the steel wall she kept around her heart, allowing Liberty to comfort her. Then she straightened and nodded. "I think I will take the rest of the afternoon."

She left the shop, got in her restored '79 MGB convertible, which was damned cold in winter, and drove through Birch Lake, feeling like she had no destination in mind, but her heart knew otherwise. She turned outside of town and headed up the hill toward Ford's house. She wasn't sure what she'd find until she saw a car parked in front of the house.

Wes hated being at his grandfather's house alone. He needed to do something. He got up and walked to the stairs that led to the attic. Up there he knew that his grandfather had stored old books sometimes. Maybe there was a volume from the 1680s in desperate need of Wes's hands.

Because his hands needed something to do. His mind was a jumble right now that resembled those curls on Serafina Conte's head. Those curls he wanted to wrap around his fingers as he leisurely kissed her until neither of them were thinking of books or the past. He wondered if he'd feel that gap between her teeth when he pushed his tongue into her mouth.

Was she really a witch? Was that why he was still thinking about her though he'd left her over an hour ago?

Don't be an ass. Of course she wasn't a witch. She just had that witchy vibe. Normally that wasn't a turn-on. He dealt with a lot of modern "witches" in his online bookstore. Rituals and practices of witchcraft were fairly common today. He couldn't keep any of the old pamphlets or booklets in stock. They always fetched high prices at auction.

The attic door had an old-fashioned handle with a skeleton key that was kept on a nail on the wall next to it.

He unlocked it, hitting the light switch and hearing the mechanism flicker on before he started up the stairs. It was dusty but not overly so, as if someone had been up here recently. He caught the faint scent of lavender.

Serafina.

Of course. Had she been up here digging around looking for something to steal? Joke was on her—everything up here was junk. Stuff that was broken and in need of repair. Maybe that was why he'd always been more comfortable up here.

There were boot prints in the dust on the floor in a chunky pattern. They stopped in front of a box of photo albums. He pulled the first one up—and then dropped it.

His and Oz's baby album. He wasn't sure he wanted to go down that path. The past held no interest for him. Not unless it was an old book he could repair and sell for profit. He pushed the album aside and pulled out two more books.

One was a magazine from 1780 that still had a letter tucked inside. He sat down and read it. It was from one of his ancestors in England who thought this issue of *Ladies Household* might be useful. He set it to one side to bring downstairs later. Then his fingers brushed ripped leather. He ran his finger over it, cursing as he got a splinter from the wood board.

This is what I'm looking for.

He pulled the book from the bottom of the box, ignoring the pain in his finger. The doorbell rang. The tune was one his grandpa had liked as a teenager. Wes walked to the attic window that overlooked the front of the house.

He saw an old convertible with a ragtop sitting next to his car. It looked like one of those old British racing models.

He opened the window. "Be down in a minute."

A figure stepped back from under the gable that covered the front porch, curly hair flying around her head. She frowned up at him.

Seemed a little time apart hadn't softened Serafina's attitude toward him. Fair enough.

It was just...this place. Birch Lake wasn't full of happy childhood memories, and this house wasn't either. Something about not getting to talk to his grandfather before he'd died was making him edgy.

He walked out of the attic and downstairs, leaving the old book on a side table in the hallway. He opened the door, noticing she'd put on a wool tweed blazer before coming here. It hugged the curves of her waist, ending at the top of those hips of hers, the ones he really had a hard time not staring at.

He had to stop this attraction he felt for her. It would be so much easier if she wasn't his type, but Serafina Conte was ticking all his boxes.

"Hello. I thought we were meeting at your shop later," he said.

"Right. Well, I finished up early, so I'm here to pick up my box of books," she said.

"I don't know where it is," Wes said. "Want to come in and try to find it?"

"Thanks," she said, stepping inside the foyer and rubbing her hands together as if she were cold. "I didn't know you'd be here."

"Obvs."

She rolled her eyes. "I guess we could talk now."

"I thought you had to work," he said dryly.

"I do. I need to get back, but...I had Liberty draw a card for me and she got the Moon. And then I started panicking because you want my books, and the Moon is all about hidden enemies."

"What's the Moon card?"

"It's a tarot card from the Rider-Waite deck."

"Of course it is," he said. Maybe she *was* a witch. His assistant, Hazel, drew cards at the different moon phases, but she really didn't share any of that with Wes. He was too practical for that sort of nonsense. He'd never seen any influence over his life except his own hot-tempered, stupid decisions. A card or interference from the universe had never been anything he'd given credence to.

"I guess you don't believe in spirits and the influence of the world around us."

"Nope. Though one time Oz and I did use the Magic 8 Ball to decide if we should get Pokémon Diamond or Pokémon Pearl. Does that count?"

She shook her head and laughed. It was such a light, tinkling sound, for a minute he forgot he was in this place. The one spot he didn't want to be and found himself once again thinking about her mouth. That laughter had to be some sort of spell, right? It wasn't anything he had ever heard in his place. "No."

"Was Grandpa into all that?" he asked. Maybe she'd used her tarot cards to influence him.

"Ford was too practical for that. But he always had a few books to recommend to me since he knew I was."

"Like which ones?"

"*The Book of English Magic* comes to mind," she said. "It was interesting, but it's a modern book pretending to be an antique, and I prefer older tomes."

"Me too. And I like the word *tomes*. Hardly anyone uses it."

"I do own a bookshop, you know."

He could almost fool himself into thinking she was flirting with him. If he'd met her at an estate sale, he definitely would have been flirting with her. Since the moment their hands had met, a low hum had been running through his body. He'd done his best to ignore it, but now that she was here and close to him, it was hard to ignore the heat creeping through his skin and the blood pounding from his ears to his dick.

"Yeah, I've been to it. So what else did you two do?" he asked. He still wasn't entirely sure of that relationship. How much time could she spend talking about books? Maybe it was his own attraction to her making him want to poke holes in what was probably an innocent relationship. He wanted there to be something about her he could point to and say, *Got ya, you were using him.*

He was jealous. Not that he was ever going to admit it to her. He'd been the one to walk away from Grandpa, but Wes had never thought Ford would find someone else to teach his bookbinding craft to. It had been their thing.

"He showed me bookbinding techniques and different ways to make covers. He knew a lot about bookmaking."

"I know about that. What else did he share?"

"Yeah, he'd worked as an apprentice in a shop in London

when he was eighteen," she said. "He got up to a lot of adventures there."

Adventures.

The old man had been an apprentice in a bookbinding shop? This was news to him.

FFS. There might be more to why Ford had left her the books than Wes wanted to deal with. When he looked at her now, he wasn't seeing a sexy, grown-up Hermione but something more. A real woman who had formed a bond with his grandpa. Something Wes had left an opening for.

Maybe she could give him some of the closure he was looking for. Of course, she'd never be able to tell him why Grandpa had bailed him out in college or helped him start his business. Or if he'd ever forgiven Wes for pushing him away and ignoring him. But she would be able to give him some insight into Ford Sitwell, and maybe that would bring the answers he needed.

Trusting her instincts had never felt so difficult. She'd always been able to sum up a person in a few minutes, but Wesley wasn't cooperating. Typical of her exchanges with him so far. But this couldn't be blamed on him. This mistrust was all on her.

And maybe a little bit on Liberty, who'd kept harping on about how he looked, and Sera's own traitorous thoughts, which kept stirring up images of him reading to her without his shirt on. Not helpful. In the bookshop with his open overcoat, she'd been limited to admiring his thick hair, which was begging for her to run her fingers through it. If there was a God, then it would at least be greasy or feel gross, but she could already tell from her spot across from him at the kitchen table that it wasn't.

She was making do with a cup of Lipton's because he didn't have Earl Grey. Which made her feel bougie to even think. When she'd first started changing her energy from best friend to leading lady, she'd stopped apologizing for liking things. Stopped settling for good enough and okay because she was a foster kid, stopped feeling she should just be grateful for small things.

She *was* grateful, but it was also okay to want something she liked.

"You're staring into that tea like it's going to show you the future. I mean it's a tea bag, so there's no leaves in the bottom, right?" he asked.

He kept bringing up witchy things. Maybe he'd heard the gossip around town that she, Liberty and Poppy were a coven and had used magic to lure Amber Rapp into their store. Amber hadn't helped the matter by sharing a similar sentiment with her followers.

"Uh, no. Are you afraid of me?" she asked, because that could totally work in her favor. Since she'd gotten here, she still hadn't been able to figure out why she'd come. Her gut had gotten her this far and then gone mysteriously quiet.

He threw his head back, laughing in a way that made his entire face light up, and she felt that tingle go through her again.

"No. Are you afraid of me?" he asked.

"Witches aren't afraid of men," she said with a wink.

He leaned back in his chair, crossing his arms over his chest, which was covered in that cable-knit sweater that fit him very nicely. He playfully glared down his nose at her. "Now?"

This reminded her of Ford making her laugh and joking with her. She just shook her head and took another sip of her tea.

"So you're not a witch, but everyone thinks your journals will grant a wish. Tell me about that."

"You could check out Amber Rapp's socials," she said. Talking about the journals wasn't something she wanted to do with him. Everything about the process was so personal, it made her feel vulnerable to think about telling him. And Wesley, no matter how charming he'd been a minute ago, wasn't her friend. She was pretty sure after the funeral, when he realized she wasn't giving up anything Ford had left her, she'd never see him again.

Getting personal wasn't happening.

"I'm not on social media," he said.

"What? Why not?"

"Just not my thing. I'm more of a real-world kind of person."

"We all live in the real world—you're not special," she pointed out.

"Didn't mean it that way. Oz calls me a nerd."

"Are you?" She was curious about who Oz was despite herself. Everything Wesley revealed was just a little more tempting. It wasn't the way his hands held the mug or the easy way he laughed at himself. But those things didn't hurt.

"Probably," he said. "I am much more at home in my workshop repairing old books."

She groaned.

"What?"

"Nothing," she said, pretending to look at her watch, because how could he like being in a workshop? She wanted to have nothing in common with this man. Not even the connection to Ford since it seemed none of the Sitwell men got along.

But that one fact had made him likable. Sort of. "I should be getting back to the shop. Are we still meeting for a drink or you good now?"

"I'd still like to meet for drinks. I want to know more about Grandpa's last few years."

She was tempted to ask him why now, but she caught a hint of sadness on his face and stopped herself. She might not understand his emotions when it came to his grandfather, but it was clearly more complicated than she knew.

"Sure. You can buy one drink and I'll answer a few questions. Sound good?"

"Thanks," he said, walking her out to the hallway.

She noticed the ruined old book, which had been in a box in the attic, on the hall table. She'd tried to read it, but the foolscap pages were fragile and she didn't know medieval French. "Be careful with that."

"Thanks," he said dryly. Aside from the moment when he'd lost his temper and accused her of seducing his grandfather, he consistently used sarcasm when he was upset.

"It's just that I know Ford wanted to have someone repair it," she said. "He was going to call them this week."

It hurt to think of the things that would go undone. Maybe she should call to have the book repaired, but for who? Ford was gone and couldn't enjoy the bound manuscript that had been in his wife's family for generations. It had somehow gotten lost in the attic decades earlier.

"He called me about it," Wesley said.

"Why?"

"That's what I do, remember? I deal in old books. Repair, value and sell them."

Of course, he'd just said that. She'd been too busy trying not to think about his mouth and what kind of kisser he might be. That explained his anger with her about the books. But it didn't explain why Ford had given them to her. She had thought maybe Ford had been hanging on so she could continue to be his friend, but what if there was more to it? What if she had been meant to meet Ford so she could learn from Wesley?

Four

Sera drove away from Ford's house and his disturbingly sexy grandson. She wasn't sure where to go. Back to the workshop so she could start getting ahead on the journals seemed the smartest thing, but she didn't feel like working.

She was sad, needing to cry about Ford's death, but she'd decided to wait until she was home later. She always had a hard time with goodbyes and had created a ritual for herself to accept them and embrace new opportunities. But where was she going to find another ninety-year-old man who wanted to talk books with her?

It didn't help that she was attracted to Wesley Sitwell. She wanted to keep him firmly in toad territory, but that wasn't happening. For some reason she kept thinking about his mouth and the way it looked when he'd formed the word *tomes*.

Tomes.

Ugh. She was such a fucked-up word nerd getting turned on by a big vocabulary. But there it was.

And she wanted to hate him, but that wasn't happening. She would do better to keep her mind on Ford. Sera pulled her car into the parking lot of a coffee shop where she'd first met Ford. She'd been out exploring the area around Birch Lake trying to figure out where she'd want to buy a house and had gone into the coffee shop to do some online research.

It had been crowded on a Saturday morning and Ford had offered her the seat opposite him at his table. Sera had always felt like she had good instincts when it came to people. That day had proved her right once again.

He'd been reading *Their Eyes Were Watching God* by Zora Neale Hurston. She'd read it at seventeen, living in Florida, scared of the future. Janie's story of sexual awakening and strength throughout her life, even in a hurricane, had given Sera hope.

She'd mentioned she liked the book and Ford started a conversation. It was the first time she'd talked books with anyone other than her college professors. It had been invigorating. She and Ford didn't view the story the same way, which had been one of the things she'd loved about him.

He always challenged her to look deeper. She'd reread the book and then come back the next week to talk about it again.

She entered the coffee shop, taking off her coat, noticing the table she and Ford usually occupied was empty. She put her coat over her usual chair—before going to order a café au lait.

"Hey, girl. Surprised to see you today. Is Ford meeting you?" Lily, the woman who owned and ran the café, asked.

Sera swallowed against the lump of emotions in her throat. "Ah, no. He passed away yesterday."

"I'm sorry to hear that. I really liked him. Are you okay?" Lily asked while she was making Sera's coffee.

No. She wasn't okay. But Sera wasn't going to tell Lily that. She just smiled sadly. "It was a shock but maybe it shouldn't have been. Ford just seemed ageless more than old to me."

"That's a nice way of putting it." Lily gave her a comforting look. "Do you want anything to go with your coffee?" she asked.

Sera ordered a butter croissant, which Lily made fresh every morning, and then took both to her table. She almost wished she could have had one more conversation with Ford. But the truth was she wouldn't have asked the questions that were on her mind now. Because she would have had no way of guessing he would leave her anything in his will.

Why had he?

That was really what Wes had been asking her in all the different ways he could since she'd received his douchey letter that morning.

Sera had no idea.

Talking about books played into Ford's agelessness. Reading, for Sera, had always been an escape into a life that was different from her reality. On the pages of books, she could be a daughter or a sister, an adventurer or a spy. But her discussions with Ford had shown her how to bridge that fantasy life into reality.

The shared experience of the books they'd discussed had given them a deep friendship. But why would her friend leave her books that his grandson wanted?

Ford wasn't a man who'd done anything on a whim. In some of their conversations they'd talked about family. He'd made her feel comfortable sharing that she didn't have one. There were times when she'd been conflicted about her biological parents, both of whom had died in a meth fire in their trailer while Sera had been in day care. It was complicated, and as a foster child she'd often pretended she was a lost princess or something else. Anything other than her reality.

Ford hadn't judged. Had just shared that all parents made mistakes and told her of the ones he'd made. She listened as he'd talked about watching his son treat his grandsons poorly after they'd been returned and his divorce had been final.

Ford said he'd always been a live-and-let-live person, but he should have intervened for the family's sake. Instead, he watched his son treat his grandsons coolly and saw how it shaped the men they became.

They were distrustful and put work above relationships. Above family.

Sera took a sip of her café au lait, leaning back in her chair and finishing her snack. Had Ford left her the books to somehow help Wes?

Stop. Ford didn't have to want something from her to leave her a gift. She was the leading lady in her life, and she didn't have to justify why a dear friend might give her something. That was old thinking and she hated that she still fell into it. That was foster-care Sera trying to figure out how she had to pay back everything given to her.

She drove back to WiCKed Sisters and parked behind the shop. When she entered, she heard Liberty's voice, and as she walked into the shop, she saw her friend had Merle cornered near the tea café, which was empty, as it was almost closing time.

"Help," Merle said, looking over at her. He was tall, at least six-five, and lanky. He had thick brown hair that was shaggy and in need of a cut, but the look suited him. He always wore jeans and some kind of branded comic T-shirt or sweatshirt, depending on the season. Never the big movie-franchise comics, the more obscure ones.

"With what?" she asked, putting her bag on the counter and walking over to them.

"He won't say if he wants to curse, charm or confluence me," she teased, but there was a look in her eyes Sera recognized. There was more to her teasing Merle than just trying to needle him.

"Leave Merle be. Did the boxed card decks come in today?" she asked. "I was hoping they would before Valentine's Day."

"They did," Merle said, stepping around Liberty toward Sera. "I was opening the stock boxes in my free time…and looking for the new D&D book I asked you to order."

Despite her initial hesitation about the game, she was excited to see it.

Liberty moved between the two of them as they walked to the stockroom. They kept boxes just off the loading dock and then sorted the stock for their different lines of business and moved it into their own stockrooms.

Merle was a godsend who helped when Poppy was out of town, and he was more organized than the three of them, so he had already sorted and labeled all the boxes.

Liberty lifted one of the Charm, Curse, Confluence boxes and read from the back of it.

"'The game is simple. You are given three choices and each player has a limited number of charm, curse or confluence cards to be played during each session. The cards are made up of modern and historical authors, magicians and witches, bakers and tea makers. It also doubles as an oracle deck. Let the cards guide you to your destiny.'

"So, Merle," Liberty said, "Charm, curse, confluence with Poppy, Sera and me?"

"Liberty, for fuck's sake," Merle said, reaching around her toward the stack of boxes. "I hope your game sells, but I just want the book I ordered."

He looked over at Sera and she smiled at him.

"Your book should have been in the box from the distributor."

"I didn't see it. Maybe it'll show up on Friday. The game books are here," he said, pointing to the boxes.

The room smelled of new books, paper and binding. Sera closed her eyes, inhaling deeply.

Sera would never have dreamed that she'd be a part of something like this, and some of the ickiness left by the Sitwells and that letter fled. With Liberty and Poppy, she'd created this—the store, the cards. Liberty's drawings were really good, and the printer had gotten the gold foil she'd added right too.

"I like it. I think my drawings are okay, but maybe next time we should hire someone else?"

"Your drawings make the deck, Liberty," Merle said, coming to stand behind her and look over her shoulder. "Everything you make is charming. I'll watch the shop while you two take care of your stock."

He turned and walked away, and Liberty shook her head, watching him until he disappeared. "He vexes me."

"So you're going to hex him later?" Sera said with a laugh. "You know me so well."

Wes sat at the large kitchen table that had seen better days. The book from the attic was in the center, and he started carefully disassembling it. His mind felt freer than it had since he'd woken to the news Grandpa had died. While he took the old cover off, he reached into his bag of tools to find the solution used to separate the leather from the board.

Sera was on his mind as he put the solution on and peeled the leather away. Life would have been easier if she'd been someone else. But then, Wes knew life wasn't about being easy.

His never had been.

While he'd gone to therapy and knew he was the probable source for his own rough road—something he freely acknowledged—this time it seemed Grandpa bore a bit of the responsibility too.

Maybe Grandpa would say, *If he'd wanted those books, he should have visited or called more often.*

Fair enough.

It didn't change the fact that Wes hadn't been able to. That dogged determination he'd always grudgingly admired in his father was also one of his core traits.

It was easier to see it in Oz and his dad because who wanted to look inward and acknowledge the very same thing in himself?

While his fingers moved over the old book and skills that he'd learned from Grandpa came into play, Wes's mind reminded him of all the mistakes he'd made.

He had started to call Grandpa a number of times but had

stopped, not wanting to be the one to apologize. Why was saying sorry so hard for him? Plus, as old as Ford had been, Wes had thought Grandpa was too stubborn to die.

Even I can't dodge death.

Wes glanced over his shoulder toward the stool near the counter, where Grandpa had often sat as he taught Wes how to repair books. His voice had sounded so strong and clear, as if the old man was in the room with him.

Was this more of Serafina's magic?

More likely his own mind trying to find a way to get some closure when there was none to be had.

He'd fucked up and waited too long to make things right.

A smart man would learn from this, Wes thought.

He was going to give himself props for apologizing to Sera so quickly. But then, he hadn't done it simply because he'd behaved like an ass. He'd also done it because he was still hoping to get back those books.

He also knew Hamish had her box. Wes should have told Sera, but no, he was still playing games.

To what end?

Grandpa had taken the play out of Wes's hands by giving those books to Hamish.

He looked at the leather as it came off the board. While he knew the steps to repair an old book like this, he was still struggling to find the right steps for himself.

Maybe Sera was the key to that. Ford had left her those books knowing Wes would seek her out. He might not have spoken to Grandpa for the last few years, but his grandfather had known him better than anyone. Had he put the books between them so Wes would finally grow up? Not that Grandpa had ever called him out on the immature way Wes let his temper and stubbornness rule his life. Part of him wanted to change, but another part had no idea how.

He stretched his back as he finally got the old leather free. That box of books had unhinged Wes from the path he'd been on. Some small piece of him had always believed he deserved the things Grandpa had shown and given him. As if he'd been owed something because of his childhood.

Which, he knew, was privileged compared to so many. He had a roof over his head, food in his belly and his own room to sleep in. He hated that he was fixated on the lack of emotional support and love he'd felt growing up. Grandpa had stepped up when Wes had needed him, and Wes hadn't seen it as an olive branch.

He'd just taken and then behaved like his father. Behaved in a way he'd always hated. Like the man he didn't want to be.

The alarm on his phone pinged. It was time to leave and go meet Sera. Wes walked to the door, grabbing his coat and keys on the way. He had to figure out how to be like that piece of old leather, how to set himself free.

Which meant he had to let go of the possessiveness he felt toward those books. He had to find peace with Grandpa's decision. He also had to genuinely apologize to Sera. Find a way to make up for that dumb letter he'd sent and the resentment that had motivated him to do it.

The Bootless Soldier tavern sat at the end of the cobble-stoned main street anchoring it in the town. When Sera, Poppy and Liberty had been looking for the right location for their shop, they'd spent a lot of time sitting at a corner table drinking hard cider and debating if they should pay the higher rents on the main street or take a chance on the more mystical side street, which didn't get as much foot traffic.

Liberty had always been determined they should go with their current location and her friend had been right. But there was a traditional part of Sera that liked the old colonial architecture here. Their building had the same style, but the surrounding ones weren't the same.

She shook her head. She was standing outside the Bootless Soldier, hesitating because she wasn't sure what she wanted to happen when she met Wes again.

Her love of Ford made her want to help his family, but her own need to keep being her strongest self made her...well, *not* want to. But that went against an ingrained niceness she couldn't shake.

This thing with Wesley had her reverting back to her old self already. Being fearless was way harder than she wanted to admit.

She needed to go into the tavern. She'd said she'd have one drink, and she was a woman of her word. She'd have her drink, wish him luck in life and then leave.

There. She had a plan.

Except that plan wasn't anything like what she'd written in her journal this morning. And it didn't take into account how hot Wes looked when she entered the tavern. He saw her and stood up, waving her over.

She hesitated. Why did he have thick blond hair and an easy smile?

She'd always vaguely resented the fact that people didn't

look the same on the outside as they were on the inside. She knew that well.

In the second foster home she'd been sent to, the mom, Nina, had been so pretty, and her house had been really nice. Sera had a bedroom that was just for her; she hadn't had to share. But Nina had been exacting, and when Sera hadn't fit the mold of what Nina thought a daughter should be, she'd been verbally abusive. After a few weeks, she asked for Sera to be moved to another home.

How could Sera know if Wes was like Nina? Pretty on the outside and rotten inside.

Maybe she should take him at his word. This afternoon she'd seen another side to him. He wanted to know more about his grandfather and her.

Okay. She'd tell him, give him the gift of knowing his grandfather in the last two years. Surely that would be enough for her to feel she'd made some amends for Ford with his grandson, and then she could have her books in peace. All she had to do was ignore his mouth with those firm lips and try not to let her eyes linger on his intense blue eyes. Sure, that was so easy to do.

Maybe he'd say something jerky. That would make everything even easier.

"Hey. I wasn't sure you were going to show up," Wes said.

"I said I would."

She shrugged out of her jacket, hanging it on the back of her chair as she sat down across from him.

"That's right," he said, a note of resignation in his voice.

"You thought I wasn't a woman of my word?" she asked. What did he expect from her?

"I thought maybe you'd figured out I was just trying to manipulate you into giving me the books back. And then you'd ghost me for a little bit of revenge," he said.

"Yeah, you weren't subtle about that."

He shook his head. "Well, I'm not going to be subtle now. I've decided to stop trying to take something Grandpa wanted you to have. And to make up for being a dick, I thought I'd offer to help out in your shop for a couple of weeks."

She leaned back in her chair, looking down her nose at him in a way she'd seen Poppy do when someone was being difficult. She hoped she was carrying off some of Poppy's British attitude.

"Why would you do that?"

"Just for the reasons I stated, and I heard you say you were out of journals again today. If you can't keep up with demand, it'll be hard on you and your customers."

"So you just thought you'd volunteer?" she asked. She'd read all about not looking a gift horse in the mouth, but this one seemed like it might be a horse of the Trojan variety.

"Sort of…"

"I knew there had to be more to it," she said, signaling the waiter and ordering a glass of white wine. She needed to get her drink and leave before she fell for anything Wes offered.

"Not like that. I was hoping if I helped in your shop—and I'm very good at bookbinding—that maybe you'd tell me more about Grandpa," he said. "A few weeks for a few stories. I fucked up that relationship, and you don't owe me any information about him…but I'm hoping it will help me let him go."

Wow.

She hadn't expected that kind of honesty from Wesley Sitwell. She needed time to think about what he was asking. He wanted her to tell him about his grandfather. Her heart felt broken. Having always prided herself on rolling with the punches, she was having a hard time dealing with losing Ford. He'd just always treated her...like she mattered. She didn't owe him thanks or anything; she was just a friend. Sera treasured him more than she'd let herself admit.

Some tears burned the backs of her eyes and she blinked to clear them. Ford had been family to her. A girl who had never had a clue about her own.

She'd always wanted to know more about her own, but there was no one she could have asked. And Ford had been important to her. Also, she *could* use another set of hands making journals.

"If I agreed, you'd be a freelance worker for me. I can't just have you working in exchange for stories. I was planning to hire someone to help, so you could fill in while I interview or train an apprentice to be a full-time employee. Would you agree to that?"

"Sure."

She smiled. "Also, I'm going to have to see your bookbinding skills. I'm not doubting you, but the journals have to be made a certain way. My product is an extension of who I am."

"That's fine. Whatever you need from me, I'll deliver," he said.

His energy changed when he said that. She could see he was sad, and almost lost. Was it because of Ford's death, or something else?

She'd never really found a man in real life who lived up to the men she fantasized about. Sex was her way to find closeness, so she kept her emotions on a tight leash when it came to the men she sort of dated. But Wes was different.

His emotions...she sort of got them. Or was she just seeing something in him she wanted to see? He was complex, like every human being was.

Well, fuckity fuck. She didn't want to relate to him. But she'd been lost so many times, and she *did* relate. It made him seem more real to her. Not that toady person who accused her of sleeping with his grandfather and forbade her to go to the funeral.

Seeing him this way touched a part of her she hadn't realized was there. Some vulnerable part she'd never acknowledged until today when she'd learned Ford had died and felt the impact of his loss.

Sitting across from him, she didn't feel as lost as she'd felt in the coffee shop earlier that afternoon. She felt like Wes saw her and she was definitely seeing him.

Her eyes dropped to his mouth. She wanted to know if he tasted as devilishly good as he looked. But he was talking about working for her. So that put him into off-limits territory. And she still wasn't sure she trusted him.

Which of course just made her hungrier for a kiss.

"Sera?"

"Hmm...?"

"You're staring at my mouth."

Oh, Sera. Be smart. Just ignore the chemistry. But that wasn't where she was right now. She felt edgy and like taking a risk. Who knew? This might be the exact thing they were both looking for. The attraction wasn't one-way and maybe it was what they needed to clear the air and move forward. "Only fair since you were staring at mine earlier."

He leaned across the table. The heat in his eyes made her shiver in the best way possible. He put his hand on hers. It was big and hot, and she wanted to feel it on her body. "I was imagining how it would feel under mine."

"Me too."

Five

"Wow, didn't think that would shut you up," she said, sitting back and taking a sip of her wine.

He took a long swallow of his beer, trying to give himself time to think, but now that she'd mentioned kissing him, he couldn't stop thinking of how her body would feel pressed against his. He groaned.

She just smiled.

"So tomorrow you can come by the shop in the afternoon and show me your binding skills. I use six signatures in all the journals and then use a French kettle stitch to bind them together. Because of the nature of the journal Amber purchased, I cover them in a stiff cardboard and then cover that with fabric or leather to give the buyer two different price points," she said.

"Moving on already?" he asked.

"You clearly needed a few minutes to stop thinking about hooking up," she said.

"You said kissing," he reminded her.

"Excuse me, then. Maybe I read you wrong," she said.

"You didn't," he admitted. Against his better judgment, she had him fantasizing about what it would be like to pull her into his arms and bring his mouth down on hers. Not a soft kiss, but one with all that pent-up passion—part lust, part resentment. To take what he wanted and stop feeling.

"Before you got here, I decided to stop being a douche-bag and make amends. Somehow sex with you seems like a complication."

She reached up and pulled her hair into her hands as if she wanted to put it up. But then she shook her head, letting the curls fall free around her shoulders. Her face was slightly flushed and she chewed her lower lip, drawing his eyes to her mouth. The very thing he was trying not to dwell on.

Those lips.

He groaned. Sex wasn't emotional for him. Instead he used it when he needed a release. His own history prevented him from sleeping with anyone he might have an actual connection with. Just watching the impact of that on his father made him afraid to risk having a serious relationship with a woman. Fucked-up, right? But there it was. And no matter how much he wanted to deny it...

He liked Sera.

There were no two ways about that. He wanted something from her that no one else could give him. Something that could help him come to terms with his grandfather's death. The books Grandpa left her were his in his mind. If he couldn't have them, maybe learning from her would soothe something inside him. So fucking that up seemed dumb. Yet here he was, getting hard watching her play with her hair and stare at him.

She'd probably asked him something he needed to respond to. But he wasn't going to do it. He didn't care; right now he was following the path toward sexual fantasy, and once he went there, he'd be giving up the chance to get any information about Grandpa.

It wasn't Sera who would make it impossible. It would be him. Wes sucked at anything after hooking up. He did okay in the flirting and the teasing and the actual fucking, but once it was over...he had to get away. He had to be the one to leave. He'd been to enough therapists to know he had issues and that pattern wasn't healthy, but it worked for him. Usually. But with Sera...

"Dude."

"Hmm?"

"I'm going to pay for my own drink. See you tomorrow," she said, turning to get her wallet from her purse.

He covered her hand on the table with his. "Please don't. Sorry. Damn, that seems like all I'm saying to you. Grandpa's death has me messed up. I don't know why I'm acting like this."

She turned her hand under his, her fingers, which were cold, wrapping around his and squeezing.

"That's fine. I shouldn't have said 'Come work for me' and then 'I want to kiss you' right after," she said. "I know better. Ever since your letter arrived and Ford passed, I've been off too."

Somehow just knowing that neither of them were at their best helped. "I can do French binding and kettle stitches. Whatever you want, I can probably do it."

"Good," she said. "Tell me about the last time you talked to Ford. Why is it you weren't talking?"

He pulled his hand back and shoved it into his hair. A habit he had tried to break, but this day seemed to be one for bringing out all his insecurities and the silly things he did to deal with them.

"Two weeks ago, I got an email asking me if I had time to repair a book," Wes said. "Just a few lines typed, as if it were a formal business letter, because Grandpa always used proper format in emails and texts."

"And you said yes?"

He finished his beer, wishing it was whiskey, but getting wildly drunk wasn't something he was allowing himself to do anymore. "Nope. I didn't respond."

She sat up straighter. "Why not?"

"I was mad at him," he said.

"What for?" she asked.

"Never mind that." There was no way he was going to tell her about him being an asshole or the stubbornness he and Grandpa had shared. They were essentially strangers, and tonight, there was nothing good that would come from sharing that story. So he was going to keep it to himself. Just tucked away with all the other arrogant moments he regretted. And there were more than a few.

"When was the last time you talked to him?" he asked.

"Last Thursday. He'd loaned me a Victorian Sampler. I thought it was going to be poetry, but it turned out to be erotica. It wasn't bad either," she said with a laugh.

"I think I read that volume when I lived with Grandpa. Thin and bound in green?"

"Yes. The gold leaf has faded on the cover. It looks so indiscreet. When Ford gave it to me, I was shocked when I realized what I was reading," she said.

"Did you like it?" he asked. He'd been surprised at how turned-on he'd been when he'd read it.

She flushed and smiled at him. "After I got over the fact that the people in those black-and-white photos weren't as proper as I'd always thought...yeah, I did. You?" she asked, her face flushed and confidence in her voice. Inviting him to share his reactions.

"I did. It was quite a sexual awakening," he said. "What did Grandpa say about it?"

"Just that people aren't any different today than they've ever been. We might have different ways of doing things, but our needs are still the same," she said. "I think he was right. I mean, that book wasn't any different than porn on the internet."

He shook his head as some of the shame that lingered over the fact that he hadn't answered his grandfather's email waned. He was starting to see what Ford might have liked about Sera. She was different. She looked at the world in a way that was unique and interesting.

She wasn't judging him, but then, she didn't know the entire story. For right now, it was nice to be here in Birch Lake again and not feel like he'd let Grandpa down. And her story about the Victorian Sampler reminded him of his grandfather's sense of humor. It almost made Wes feel like he was with the old man again.

No matter that he'd just decided kissing her would be stupid, talking about Victorian erotica and remembering those long-ago stories had brought his mind straight back to it. Every interaction with her was stronger than the one before it. Sex with her wasn't ever going to be just about release; he wouldn't lie to himself about that. But he also couldn't deny how much he wanted more of her. It was going to take everything he had to resist Sera's undeniable magic.

Sera knew she should get up and walk out of the tavern before she did something she might regret. But Wes had intrigued her from the moment she'd laid eyes on him. Regret seemed inevitable at this point.

She was trying to force him to make sense. He'd been pretty wretched when he'd accused her of sleeping with Ford, but seeing him tonight, she realized part of that had been anxiety and grief. She was a stranger to him and a friend to the grandfather he'd just lost. Which person was he?

The real man, unfortunately, was something more complex, and she wished that didn't make him more appealing. He was sort of like a one-of-a-kind rare book. The type she was always hoping to find but hardly did. She wanted Wes because of how complex he was and all the things that made him complicated. He wasn't sticking around Birch Lake. There was no chance he'd break her heart after one night.

"Oh, woman. Don't talk to me about porn," he said. "I'm hanging on here by a thread and thinking of…things I decided I wasn't going to."

"Like kissing me in that dark hallway in the back of the tavern that leads to the bathrooms?"

Because that was what she was thinking. Pushing him against the black walls, putting her leg between his, rubbing her pussy against his thigh and kissing him until she came. That was it.

She didn't know if maybe Liberty had put a spell on her or if it was just her own body needing a connection after losing the one man she'd let herself care about and rely on, but there it was. She wanted a good, hard fuck with Wes.

He was trying to be cool. She knew he regretted how things were with Ford before he died, and there was a part of her that wanted to give him closure. But she needed something different.

Was it wrong to put herself first?

Liberty and Poppy would both say no. Wes was like Earl Grey tea. It was okay for her to have something she wanted.

But was it okay to take it at his expense?

He groaned again and stretched his legs under the table, one of them brushing against hers, sliding between them. The feel of it made her tingle. She rubbed her calf against his just to see what he did. He kept his leg there, shifting. Was he turned on too?

She took a deep breath. "What if for tonight we just say screw it? Pretend we don't know each other, go back to my place and then tomorrow we can go back to normal?"

If he said no, she'd respect that and she would find someone else to take home. Now that she'd made the connection between her need to get laid and the loss of Ford, she wasn't going to be able to sleep alone.

She had no problem being alone most of the time. But not tonight.

"Can you do that?"

"I have no fucking idea, but I don't want to be alone tonight," she said. "Unlike you, Ford was all I had other than my friends Liberty and Poppy. He was the only man I let myself care about. I miss him—I feel alone. I don't like it."

"Okay. Let's go," he said. He signaled the waiter and paid for their drinks. "Where do you live?"

"One block from the shop. You can leave your car in the public lot overnight." Snow was falling as they stepped outside and she pulled her coat closer, reaching back to free her hair from her collar. Wes's hands were there first; he leaned in close, and she felt the warmth of his breath against her cheek a moment before his mouth was on hers. He pulled her against him right there under the tavern lights.

His mouth was warm and his tongue slowly seduced her with long, languid sweeps into her mouth. She put her hands on his shoulders, then reached up, shoving her fingers into his thick hair, which, as she'd suspected, felt soft and luxurious.

She turned her head as she pushed her leg between his thighs and he lifted his between hers. She felt him right at her center as she moved her hips forward, going up on tiptoe. She didn't know if this was the smartest decision she'd ever made, but it felt like the best one.

She eventually pulled her head back because making out in front of the tavern wasn't what she wanted. She wanted him naked, under her, with the fire in the background. She wanted to come as long and hard as possible.

"Let's go," she said, taking his hand and leading him up the street.

He threaded his fingers through hers. After a stretch of silence, he asked, "Why was Grandpa the only man in your life?"

She shrugged. "I'm kind of turned-on and enjoying it. I don't want to talk about...that kind of stuff."

"What kind?"

"Wes. Damn. I just stopped thinking of you as a toad. Don't make me go there again."

He tugged her off balance and into his arms. "A toad? Was my kiss slimy?"

"Not at all. It made me wet and hungry for more, but I don't want to have sex against the side of a building in winter while talking about your dead grandfather. It's cold," she said.

"I'll keep you warm," he said, kissing her again. But with their heavy winter coats, she couldn't get close enough. Wes kissed her hard and deep, lingering in a way she felt all the way to her core.

"I'm counting on it. No talking until we get to my place," she said.

"Not even about how I can't stop thinking about you being wet?" he asked.

She couldn't help smiling at the way he said that. "How does that make you feel?"

"Hard. But I've been in a state of semi-erection since I showed up at your shop."

She put her hand down between them, stroking him through his jeans. He *was* hard, making her wetter, and she almost rethought sex against the side of a building. "Good to know," she said. "I thought you were hot, until I figured out who you were."

"Hopefully I'm doing the right things to change your opinion," he said.

"You're getting there."

★ ★ ★

Sera's house was a small New England cottage that was nestled on a residential street one block from WiCKed Sisters. He kept her hand in his and his mouth shut, as she'd asked him to. He didn't allow himself to dwell on anything other than the fact that she didn't want to be alone.

He wanted to know more about her, which was dangerous and stupid because he was hoping to do something altruistic with her. Trying to make amends for how he'd acted and figure out a way to be at peace with Grandpa.

But as usual nothing was straightforward.

Her front door had a wreath with three bells hanging off it. "Tell me again you're not a witch."

She threw her head back and laughed. "It's a new moon tonight. Are you worried I might put a spell on you?"

If she was going to cast one, then he was pretty sure she'd done it with her voice and words back in the tavern. He hadn't realized it then, but he was definitely under her spell.

There was no answer to that as she used her phone to unlock her front door. He just followed her inside. Her house smelled of lavender—not surprising with how he'd smelled it on her all night—and cinnamon. He toed off his shoes and then took off his jacket, noticing she was doing the same. There was a light on at the end of the hall.

Wes took her into his arms once she had her coat off. "Is this what you were picturing back at the tavern?"

He pulled her against him as he leaned back against the wall. Sera's arms were around his neck, her skin was soft and her breath warm as she exhaled. Her thighs between his legs. Her mouth was on his neck, warm and wet, sucking at the skin there as her hands pushed into his hair. He cupped her ass and lifted her up until he could rub the ridge of his cock against her.

Her mouth moved lower, her hands going under his sweater and shoving it up to his armpits. Her hands were cold as she rubbed them over the hair on his chest. Wes tried to slide his hand under her blouse but the buttons and the way it was cut made that impossible. Women didn't usually make him this desperate, but there was something about Sera, from the moment he'd seen her, that had him hungry for more.

He undid them and then she shrugged out of it, stepping back and pulling his sweater up over his head. He couldn't take his eyes off her breasts in the creamy lace bra. Her skin was pale and the figure above her jeans was full and curvy.

Wes put his hands on Sera's waist and pulled her back to him, lowering his head to drop kisses at that spot between her breasts. She reached between them, undoing her jeans first and then his. He felt her shimmy in his arms until her jeans were at her feet.

He pushed his down and then stopped.

Fuck. "I don't have a condom."

"I'm on the pill," she said. "And I don't have sex that often."

"I do, but I'm healthy," he said even as he worried about having sex without a condom. He was taking a chance; as much as he didn't really love a rubber, the pill didn't protect against STIs.

But at this moment he really didn't want anything but Sera naked under him.

"So…are we good?" she asked.

He freed his cock and lifted her off her feet. She wrapped

her legs around his hips and her arms around his shoulders. Her breasts were soft and cushiony against his chest as her mouth met his. He cupped her butt, loving the feel of it in his hands. A part of him wanted to make this last beyond tonight.

But that wasn't what she'd asked for. She wanted something quick and hard, just enough to make her not feel alone. She did *not* want to start something with a toad. Luckily, he didn't take too much offense at that.

He turned so she was between his body and the wall, shifting his hips until the tip of his erection was at the entrance to her pussy. She was wet and hot, and he groaned as he entered her in one long thrust.

She shifted around him, sucking his tongue deeper into her mouth as her hips rose toward him. God, she felt good. Better than he'd thought. He'd had bar sex before. It was quick and sometimes satisfying, but this was *more*.

This was Sera. A woman who should hate him. A woman who achieved something that was lost to him—with this town, with his grandfather. A woman he should have been jealous of, who should have made him frustrated with her ability to do what he hadn't been able to. But instead he shut down his mind and just let himself feel—her pussy around his cock as he continued driving into her, until she tightened on him and tore her mouth from his, crying out.

"Now."

He drove into her harder and faster, feeling every nerve ending in his body reaching for orgasm. Her moans echoing through the silence of the hall, driving him closer to the edge. And then she bit his lower lip and he came. He thrust into her until he was empty.

Bracing himself against the wall, he held her and then turned and slid slowly down to the floor, still cradling her. She rested her forehead on his shoulder and didn't say anything.

He tried to keep his mind still. For once it was easier than expected. Just sitting on the floor in her lavender-scented hallway near her felt like enough. *He* felt like enough.

Wes knew the feeling wouldn't last. It rarely did. But for this moment there was no past where he was the reason why his father was broke, no present where he'd let spite keep him from saying goodbye to his grandpa. No future...

Well, two out of three wasn't bad.

He felt her tense as if she was going to get up. "Stay. Just for another minute."

She nodded against him. He looked down at her and realized he hadn't touched her hair when he'd kissed her. He stroked his hand over it. It was softer than he'd imagined it would be.

Six

That was exactly what she'd needed and also something she hadn't expected. Sera wasn't going to do a debrief in her head while he was in her hallway and half-naked under her. She had to get up, but they were on the floor and she wasn't graceful.

This was precisely why she always had a plan before she acted. Now she had to try to climb off him and walk away with a semblance of control. Except she felt her thighs rubbing together as she shifted around. She loved her healthy body, but she had no clue how he felt about cellulite.

Not that it mattered.

He'd been a lay to get her mind off her loss, so she wasn't alone. That was it. He might still work for her. Or tomorrow she might just say no and send him on his way.

"Thank you."

She turned her head and saw that his eyes looked wet, like he'd been crying.

He might have needed a release too.

God, this man. He stirred emotions she wasn't—couldn't be—interested in. Emotions she was safer without. So she fell back on being sassy, which was her default when people like Wes threatened her heart. People who were only in her life temporarily. She wasn't even sure he wasn't just staying because of what she could do for him. "Sure."

He gave her a weak smile and then shook his head.

"I don't know how to act around you."

"I don't know how to act around you either," she said. "I'm also not sure how to get up off your lap and not have it turn into a comedy routine."

He shifted out from under her and stood up, tucking his penis back into his pants and offering her his hand. Something fluttered in her stomach and she realized how endearing she found the realness of Wes in this moment.

Once she was standing next to him, she didn't know what to do. Getting dressed seemed the first order of business. But also, what to do with him? The hallway was only faintly lit from the table lamp she'd left on in the living room.

"You can wash up in the powder room. I'm going to use the master bath," she said, walking away from him.

It had been a long time since she'd brought a man home. This was an old behavior she'd hoped she'd moved past. Hooking up when she felt lonely. And it was ridiculous that she felt lonely now. The shop was doing well. Her friendship with Liberty and Poppy was stronger than ever. Her own self-worth felt like it was taking shape. But clearly something was still not there.

Accepting that she was never going to be perfect no matter how much therapy and growth she had. There were always times when her past came back to challenge her, and she just had to keep pushing forward.

She washed between her legs before pulling on a pair of leggings and a sweater that said I Read and Drink Wine and went back out to the hallway. She heard the toilet flush and then waited for Wes.

He came out and leaned against the doorjamb, watching her with those eyes of his that always seemed guarded.

"So I should go, right?"

She shrugged. Clearly, she didn't want him to leave or she would have just said yes. What the hell was going on with her? Why was this man messing with her in ways she really didn't understand?

"Probably," she said at last.

"Yeah, cool. So see you tomorrow," he said, sitting to put on his shoes and then shrugging on his jacket. He fastened it while she watched. The way he adjusted the collar was the same as Ford used to do.

His eyes were a bit red. *Grief.*

"Wait. Do you want to stay and…talk about Ford?" she asked, throwing him a lifeline against her better judgment.

"You just made me put my coat on," he pointed out.

"I know. It's just… Well, you have some of his manner-isms and I can tell you were crying."

He shrugged. "Turns out I'm not dead inside."

"Hot cocoa or something stronger? I have some Baileys left over from Christmas. I'm not too sure if it's still good or not."

"Cocoa would be great," he said, taking his jacket and shoes off again and then following her down the hall into her in-timate little kitchen.

She put two mugs of tap water into the microwave and then pulled out packets of Swiss Miss. "I've got regular or mini marshmallows."

"Got to be marshmallows," he said.

She tried to ignore him as he sat at her table, but it was hard. Her body was still pulsing, and she remembered how he'd felt inside her. Maybe that was why she hadn't let him leave. She'd never been one to cling to a lover. Sex was just something she needed, something she used. That was it.

Normally.

But nothing about this day had been normal.

She pulled a can of Reddi-Wip from the fridge and turned, holding it up toward Wes. "Want some?"

He nodded, pulling the journal on the table closer to him. "Can I look in this?"

She appreciated that he'd asked. "Sure. I use it as a planner."

She finished making the hot cocoa and brought it over to him. His long fingers were skimming the journal, flipping the pages carefully. He stopped on a Thursday. She'd printed off a picture of Ford and herself on sticker paper and put it in the journal. Just a selfie she'd taken when they'd been outside the coffee shop, about to head home.

He was smiling and looking devil-may-care, the way he did when she'd finished reading a new book he recommended and they had a really good discussion about it. She reached over and touched the photo.

She was going to miss him.

Her eyes burned and she blinked, not sure she wanted to cry in front of Wes. It was one thing to acknowledge they were both grieving, but crying was something she had always done alone.

"What was he smiling about?"

"We'd debated the merits of Tolkien, one of his favorites," she said.

She had even jotted down some of the discussion under it.

"You were good friends."

Wes seemed surprised to have figured that out.

"We were. Hamish told me he was glad Ford had found me because he was sick of listening to him talk about books," Sera said, smiling a little.

She had felt like she and Ford were kindred spirits, the kind that Anne Shirley used to wax on about in *Anne of Green Gables*. It was a relationship she'd never expected to find, and wasn't sure she ever would again.

Seeing Grandpa's smiling face just reinforced the fact Wes had been a jerk over the last few years. He was tired. He was unsure. He wanted to stay in this cozy cottage of Sera's, even though it made his skin feel too tight and itchy.

He should have declined the cocoa. He should have declined the fuck too, but he was so glad he hadn't. She'd satisfied something inside that he hadn't realized had been empty for too long. Another thing he planned to ignore. When he got home, hopefully the leather would be ready for him to start working on that manuscript so he could stop thinking.

But it was going to be a long time before he again felt the way Sera'd made him feel as he'd moved inside her. The cries she'd made when she came and the way she'd put her head on his shoulder afterward had made him ache for more from her and from himself. He had started to let go, and then in the bathroom hadn't been able to stop the tears or the hurt and pain.

He preferred not to experience any of the three.

He brought his mug closer and had to stop. There was whipped cream covering it. He looked over at Sera, who was delicately sipping hers. He took a sip, trying to be chill and get into whatever vibe it was she was going for.

But she kept blinking, and he knew she was struggling not to cry. She missed her friend.

He wanted to tell her it was okay to let go, but just as he'd spent a few extra minutes in the bathroom crying by himself, he suspected she wanted the same. He had no good reason to stay, except…he didn't want to leave. Which should have been the impetus for him to get off his ass and out of her house.

When he finished the cocoa, he'd go. He closed the journal, not wanting to see any more glimpses into Sera's life with his grandfather. Or her life in general. His stomach was tight, and adrenaline was starting to rush through him. It felt like he was about to do something dumb.

So instead, he looked at the journal's binding. The fabric glue she'd used to adhere it to the cover had come undone, probably from repeated use. He pulled the journal closer again, opening the cover and leaning over it. If she'd used a different binding…

He reached into the pocket of his coat; he had a thin piece of leather that he'd been trying to match to the old book he'd taken apart earlier.

He took it out.

"What are you doing?"

"Fixing this."

But he stopped as she pulled the journal toward her. "Don't. I like it this way."

"I can make it better," he said. That was what he did. When his emotions got to be too much, he fixed things.

"I *like* it this way," she said. "But thanks."

"It will continue to degrade if you leave it. The fraying on the fabric—"

"Will continue. It's a shabby-chic journal. When I put the burlap on the cover here, I deliberately pulled out a few strands so it would start to do this."

She lifted both eyebrows at him as he looked up at her.

"I wasn't mansplaining."

"Maybe a smidge. But I get it. I'm the same way when I see an old book in a shop with a torn cover. I want to try to fix it. Sometimes the charm in a book is that it's tattered."

She touched the cover with a look of fondness in her eyes. As if she related to the journal in more ways than just the words inside it.

"Just in books?" he asked.

She tipped her head to the side and her hair dipped away from her face, those curls looking ethereal in the light from the kitchen. "Everything seems a little more interesting when it's been lived-in."

Maybe, he thought. "Lived-in and worn are two different things."

He took a huge swallow of his cocoa, trying to finish it quickly. He needed to get out of here.

"It's not worn-out yet," she said. "But the fact that you

thought of using the binding tells me you're going to ace the interview tomorrow."

"That's nothing."

"What is something that rattles you, then?" she asked.

"Dealing with Grandpa's friends," he said, remembering how the funeral director had asked him if anyone wanted to speak at the service. Hamish had already said yes, and Wes knew his father would probably not have anything to say. Did she? He really wanted to make up for telling her she couldn't attend the funeral. He got why she hadn't trusted him.

"Um...I know I was a dick about the funeral, but do you want to speak at his service?"

Her eyes widened. "I guess that spell I put in the cocoa worked."

He smiled as he knew she wanted him to. She used humor to divert him when he asked anything too personal. "You don't have to."

She blinked again rapidly and then stopped as a tear rolled down her face and she rubbed her eyes. "I'd like to. Thank you for asking."

"You're welcome. I think Grandpa would like you to."

Wes might not have spoken to his grandfather in a long time, and part of it *had* been spite—his family was really good at spite. But another part had been embarrassment and fear. What if Grandpa was happy that Wes had left? Like Wes's dad had been when he had moved out.

He stood up. "Thanks for the cocoa. I'll see you tomorrow."

He walked down the hall toward her front door, putting his coat and shoes on, aware she'd followed him. He turned back before he opened the door. There was so much he felt like he should say, but he didn't really have the right words, so he just nodded at her and then walked out. He shoved his hands in the pockets, noticing the snow had stopped and the sky was starting to lighten as he walked away from her house.

He didn't know much about new moons or witchy magic, but he felt lighter as he walked away. Staying for Grandpa and not to get the books had been a smart decision.

Sera texted Liberty and Poppy after Wes left. She wasn't sure what to say, so she just asked if they could talk.

Both said yes, and a few minutes later she was sitting in her favorite overstuffed armchair with her phone propped up against a stack of books, talking to her friends.

"What's up?" Poppy asked. "Sorry about Ford and that his family are a-holes. Is there anything I can do?"

"I already offered to put a spell on them," Liberty said. "But she's handling it. How'd drinks go with the hot toad?"

"Um…yeah, about that… I sort of hooked up with him."

"For revenge?" Liberty asked. "Revenge sex is the best."

"Not revenge, Lib. Sera's not like you. Why?"

Sera sank deeper into the chair and pulled her Disney Hercules blanket off the back of it and wrapped it around her. "Sort of to not be alone and think about Ford's death and sort of… Well, he *is* hot."

"That's all fine," Poppy said. "Which you know. So what's actually up?"

"He asked me to speak at the funeral," she said.

"Oh," Poppy said. There was concern and affection in her

voice. Poppy always seemed the most in tune to everyone else's feelings out of the three of them.

"How the mighty have fallen," Liberty added. "He sent her a dicky letter telling her not to attend."

She was glad Liberty caught Poppy up on that part. But she wasn't sure why this was making her off balance. She liked Ford. She was definitely going to journal about him and his impact on her life. She would never forget Ford and planned to do something on her own to memorialize him. Something that would fit their relationship.

But talk at his funeral? "I've never even been to a funeral."

"I have. It's not great," Poppy said. "When my grandfather died, they had a few friends speak about him. It was nice for my nan and my mum."

"I haven't been to one either. What is she supposed to say?" Liberty asked Poppy. "That's what you want to know, right?" she asked Sera.

"Yeah, but also, do you think I should do it?" Impostor syndrome was nothing new to her. She'd always been different and outside of everyone else. Except here with these two, and with Ford.

"Do you want to?" Poppy and Liberty asked at the same time.

She didn't know. "Our friendship was sort of quiet. He was so private, I'm not sure he'd want me to share much about him."

"If you do it, I think you should talk about how he influenced your life. You know, the way he showed you how to bind books and the way he gave you advice," Poppy said.

"I like that idea," Liberty said. "If you do it, do it for yourself. Like, show those Sitwells that Ford was important to you."

She liked the way that sounded. "Thanks. Also, Wes might start working for me temporarily while I find someone to help with the bookbinding."

"He is?" Liberty asked. "Are you sure about that?"

"No. But he wants to know about Ford, and I need an experienced pair of hands to help out," she said. "I've been very impulsive tonight. Can we blame the new moon?"

"New moon is for new beginnings. Maybe that's what's driving you," Liberty said. "I'll do your cards tomorrow and see if hiring Wes is the right thing to do."

"It sounds logical to me, but I think having your cards read can't hurt," Poppy said. "I'll make him some tea when he comes and read his leaves too."

"Thanks," Sera said, feeling better having talked to her friends. She'd felt alone in the pub, but she'd known she wasn't. She had all of this feminine energy and sisterhood in her life.

They hung up a few minutes later and Sera stayed in her chair, pulling a book off the top of the stack next to her. She held it close and then looked down at it. She'd dog-eared the page to mark where she'd left off. Something she'd never done to a library book. There was a freedom in marking the page in her own way.

Her gaze lifted to take in her surroundings, her own place. She hadn't just found sisters in Birch Lake; she'd found a home, and she was finally starting to find herself too. Was sleeping with Wes a mistake? Only time would tell. But tonight, with grief sitting so close to her in this empty room, she'd needed him like she needed these books.

She shook her head as she opened the cover and skimmed the first page, but her mind was too busy. She wasn't really interested in reading.

She went to the planner on the table and opened it up. She'd saved the letter Wes had sent and put it in between the pages. Writing was what she needed to do—not about Ford, because that was still too much. She had no idea where else to start but with Wes.

His presence in her life reminded her of when a new social worker would get her case. He had an agenda and something he wanted from her, just like the social workers. Sera knew she was only a number to them. A kid who needed to be placed and then monitored to make sure she stayed out of trouble. There had been no investment in her as a person.

She was leery of allowing her attachment to Ford to transfer to Wes. She didn't know him. He'd been estranged from Ford for at least the two years she'd known the older man.

As much as he said he didn't want the books, she knew he still did. They were his grandfather's, and whatever had happened in that relationship wasn't over yet.

She would do her part in helping him know the gentle side of his grandfather. But that was it. And no more hooking up.

She wrote that last point in big letters at the bottom of the page.

Once was okay, but if she let him become a habit, it would be trouble. There were moments when she saw something in him that made her long for something more. She didn't know what it was. She wasn't comfortable thinking of a family or anything like that. As close as she was with Liberty and Poppy, she still kept part of herself private.

And she knew that wouldn't change. There was no way she would ever let anyone see that deeply into her. She might be changing into the leading lady, but that didn't mean she had to give all of herself to the world.

Some leading ladies were quiet and private. And she had better reason than most to keep herself that way.

She felt better about tomorrow. When Wes came back, she'd be professional. She needed his help and he'd offered it. Maybe he'd give her some closure about Ford as well. She could help repair their bond and then move on.

Seven

Wes had always been a night owl and luckily his business suited that tendency, so when he woke at eleven, he dived into work emails. He'd hoped it would be a distraction from thinking about Sera.

He'd fucked up last night.

He'd known it at the time, but his arrogant side thought he could have her and still be all chill about the books and Grandpa. But he wasn't. He should have just ignored that sweet, tempting mouth of hers and the images she'd planted firmly in his mind of the two of them hooking up in the hall. But he hadn't.

Actually, hooking up with her in her hallway had exceeded the images in his head. Which he was trying not to dwell on…and failing. He had to be his best self today.

Wes rarely felt his best self in Birch Lake.

He shoved his coffee mug away and got up to go. Wes stared at the snow falling in the overgrown but dead-looking backyard. God knew he wasn't the only thing that was a mess here. The house showed more signs of age than it had when he'd lived with Grandpa.

Ford might not have been the best grandfather in the world, but he'd always been there for Wes. Only now that he was back here and Grandpa was gone, Wes could see he hadn't been a very good grandson. It had somehow seemed easier to pretend all the blame... Hell, he'd never really thought all the blame was Grandpa's.

More like the blame, if there was any, belonged to them being Sitwells. Their family sucked at talking things out. They were all stubborn as fuck and never apologized.

Perversely, Grandpa dying was like him getting the last move in a chess match that ended in a stalemate. Why was their family this way? Why was Wes?

He wanted to make a promise to himself not to let something small and petty come between himself and his dad or Oz, but he probably would. And then would he be in this situation again? Left with a bunch of regret and unresolved shit when they died?

He hoped not. But hope wasn't enough. Yesterday he'd decided to stop trying to take the books back from Sera. And maybe he needed to also decide to stop being stubborn with his family. But how? He had no idea how to change a lifetime of behavior.

He'd start with the books.

And maybe he'd text Oz more often.

He started to write a message to his brother but then felt lame. Oz would probably ask what was wrong, assuming

Wes was in trouble. That was truly the only time they communicated.

He tossed his phone aside and moved around the kitchen until he was back at his makeshift worktable. He'd practiced making signatures and binding journals last night so he'd be ready for his interview with Sera today.

He had no idea how she was going to feel about him today. Last night he'd respected her wishes and done what she'd asked him to. But this morning she might not feel the same. Hell, he didn't. Not that he wished he'd stayed with her.

Oh, who was he kidding—he totally wished he'd stayed at her place. It was warm and cozy, unlike Grandpa's house, filled with ghosts and drafts and regrets.

Thinking was getting him nowhere, so he pulled the paper he'd been practicing on toward him. He wasn't sure if she used one hole in the center of her signature to bind it or three. He'd seen it done both ways. Last night he'd tried one stitch and the papers slid too much, so he suspected she used more. He had one last stack of papers that he'd punched with three holes spaced a third apart down the crease. He took the binding thread he'd found in Grandpa's study and the stitching needle Wes kept in his bookbinding kit.

Interlacing his fingers, he cracked his knuckles and stretched his arms before he started working on the signature, which was the easiest part of the process. Then he set it with the others he'd made the night before. French binding was a pretty stitch, so he wasn't surprised that was what Sera used.

She liked pretty things. He'd realized that when he'd been in her house. Of course, she had functional items, but they were also decorative in a distinctly feminine way that suited her. His fingers moved almost without thought as he remembered the stacks of shelves, full of not just books but small knickknacks; some he had recognized as items from stories he'd read.

Her house was a reflection of her. It was her private domain, and she'd invited him into it. Why had she brought him back there?

He wanted to think it was because she'd relaxed her guard around him, but was it more?

Or was it simply that she hadn't wanted to be alone, as she'd said? Why would it be more?

He finished the stitching and looked down at it. Saw a few places where he'd pulled too tightly and then loosened the stitches to match. The cover was the tricky part because Sera left them unfinished so her customers could have an intention enclosed in it.

He'd watched Amber Rapp's video last night where she talked about WiCKed Sisters. Sera's journal had apparently changed Amber's life. The entire visit had. But the power of words had been the strongest.

Wes had spent his entire adult life repairing and buying and selling books, and he knew words could be powerful, but he'd never taken the time to write. He remembered Sera's planner, and before he could talk himself out of it, he pulled the bound signatures toward himself and opened to the first page.

Using the Montblanc pen Grandpa had gifted him when he graduated college, he wrote down the date and then paused. He was in his grandfather's house in a town he wasn't sure he wanted to be in, so he started writing to Grandpa. Saying what he should have said when he'd received the email.

★ ★ ★

The shop was busy, which was to be expected, and Sera spent the morning making journals. She couldn't help staring at the spot where Wes had stood the day before.

A local writer stopped in to order some research books. They chatted for a while and Sera appreciated that the author used her independent bookstore instead of a large online chain. She also had to order books for a young moms' group who came in with their three-to-five-year-olds and had tea in Poppy's shop while their kids read a new book from Sera's shop.

She was always happy to see readers, and becoming friends with a writer was sort of a dream come true. There were moments when she couldn't believe this was her life. She was proud of everything she'd made happen.

Liberty had a lot of clients booked for the morning. Poppy was back, so when she had a lull at the tea shop, Sera went over to visit.

"I love the business we've been getting, but I'm tired," Poppy said. They were both sitting at one of the smaller tables toward the back of the tea shop so they could see their clients if they were needed.

"Me too. I put an ad up for a bookbinder and for an apprentice in case Wes doesn't work out. Once I get more help, I think it will be better. Merle mentioned you were hiring staff too?"

"Yes, I am. I asked around at the local culinary school and they're sending over a few kids who need a part-time job. I don't want to discuss too much without Liberty, but I want to hire retail staff for the three of us too. So we can concen-

trate on the things we love, which was what we wanted when
we started."

Sera agreed with Poppy and suggested the three of them
have dinner at the tavern to discuss it later. She was glad to
have something business-focused to think about. As much
as she hated to admit it, she was nervous for Wes to come in
later that afternoon. She wasn't going to pretend she didn't
feel good after sex with him the night before. But it did complicate matters.

As much as she wanted to be all cool about it, her emotions had never really behaved the way she wanted them to.
While sex had made her feel connected for a short while,
she'd been lonely in her bed last night, hugging a pillow and
crying about Ford.

She still hadn't decided if she'd speak at his service or if
she'd just write something in her journal. The words were
for her. Ford wasn't going to hear them, and his family didn't
really care about her. Hamish might appreciate them, but the
truth was she would be speaking about her friendship with
Ford surrounded by people who couldn't care less about her
and her grief.

"Liberty and I talked this morning, and we are going with
you to Ford's funeral," Poppy said. "Merle's going to watch
the shop while we're gone."

Shocked, she could only stare at Poppy with her pretty
gray eyes and kind smile. Sera blinked to try to keep from
crying. This meant more to her than almost anything else. It
was as unexpected as Ford's bequest. She wasn't alone. Mentally she knew it, but old fears and thought patterns were always lurking.

"Really?"

"Yes," Poppy said. "Liberty said the only black things she owns are a see-through blouse and her witchy robes. So I'm not sure how she'll be dressed. I have a proper dress—"

Poppy broke off as Sera leaned over and hugged her friend tightly. "Thank you."

Poppy hugged her back just as fiercely. "No problem. Also…if you want me to read whatever you write about Ford so you don't have to do it, I will."

Sera sat back in her chair; she hadn't thought of that. "Okay. I'm not sure if I want to share my thoughts at all."

"Whatever you decide. We've got you," Poppy said.

"I was determined to go because Wes had told me not to, but the more I think about Ford, the more I want to be there for him. I was afraid, though."

Poppy nodded. "I would be too. But Wes'll have his family there, and you'll have yours. I mean, you did say he wasn't so mean last night…and you did hook up, so where does that leave things?"

Her family. She let those words settle around her like a warm scarf. "Ugh. I have no idea. You know I really stink at being impulsive. Like, I do better with a plan."

"We can't all be Liberty, unfortunately," Poppy said with a wry smile. "I guess you'll have to see how today goes, right?"

"Yes. I really do need his help, and if he's even a tenth as good at bookbinding as Ford always said he was, then I'll be lucky to have him."

"Ford talked about him? What did he say?" Poppy asked.

"Just odd stories every now and then about how bookbinding had given him a way to talk to the grandson he hadn't known how to connect with."

She thought about those times. Only twice had he mentioned *the grandson*. He'd never used Wes's name. But Ford said working together in silence had given them a chance to bond. He claimed that was the magic of books.

She'd thought at the time he'd brought it up to show how the two of them were connected. But now she wondered if he'd had another reason. Maybe he'd wanted her to know there was someone else he'd shared his skills with. Or maybe he'd just wanted to talk. Wes had admitted he had frozen out his grandfather.

Ford had turned to her because he'd been alone too. She had to be there for him—he was a part of her family.

Sera was at her workbench when he entered WiCKed Sisters. She looked up when the door opened, and his breath caught in the back of his throat as he took her in. Her hair was a riot of curls around her head and shoulders, and she half smiled when she saw him, giving a little wave.

He smiled back and realized he'd been right about today. They were both nervous. Neither of them knew what to expect from the other. Sex could be both cold and impersonal as well as very intimate and personal. But they were strangers despite it. There were no two ways about that.

They'd both lost someone who they had been close to. Wes at a critical point in his life. So how did they move forward? Maybe if they could both find a way to let go of Ford, it would help. Speaking of which, resisting each other would go a long way to making things easier. But he had no idea how he was going to keep his hands off Sera if she reached for him again.

It wasn't lost on Wes that bookbinding was once again giving him a path forward when he wasn't sure where to go. He didn't love this part of books. He preferred repairing old, worn ones to creating something brand-new, but he could do this, and he was determined to.

He hadn't written much in the journal back at Grandpa's house, but what he had written had made him sure of working for Sera temporarily.

"Hope it's okay I'm a few minutes early," he said.

"One of my foster moms said on time was late," Sera said with a laugh. "Come on over here and I'll show you what I'd like you to do."

He walked over to her. As he got closer, the scent of lavender was stronger. Today she wore a full-length skirt made out of tulle. She had on a formfitting scoop-neck, long-sleeved T-shirt that she'd tucked into the thick satin waistband. His eyes got as far as her breasts, and he wanted to linger, but he kept moving.

He remembered the way her breasts had felt against him last night as he'd been inside her and his blood felt hotter, his cock heavier, and he turned his attention to the workbench to get his mind back in the game.

But his body was slow to follow. She was so close that an errant strand of her hair brushed against his shoulder as she stepped next to him to pull the supplies forward.

Closing his eyes, he took a deep breath, which just made him hornier as all he smelled now was lavender, and he re-

membered last night when the sweet smell on her skin mixed
with the scent of sex.

Damn. Now he was thinking of sex and how tight she'd
been on his cock when she came.

"Wes?"

"Sorry. I need a minute," he said.

"Sure. You okay?"

No. He wasn't okay. But then, had he ever been? Something about Sera made him want to reveal these doubts and
hear what she had to say. But he wasn't about to start telling
her that. *Get. Your. Shit. Together.*

"Yes. Being this close to you makes it hard to focus on anything other than you," he said. He might be arrogant and an
ass most of the time, but he was always honest.

"Oh. Yeah, I guess last night wasn't my best idea."

"Hell, woman, it was a great idea."

She smiled. "It was pretty good, but it's making today a bit
awkward. Should we start over?"

"Nope. I'm not pretending we didn't hook up. I can be
chill...or at least pretend to be. I just wasn't prepared for how
gorgeous you were going to look today."

"Were you expecting me to be more troll-like?" she asked.

Fuck. "I didn't mean it that way. You always stop me in
my tracks. I thought I was ready for it but my memories don't
do you justice. There's something so wild about your hair
that I forget, or the way your lips are that shade of brownish
pink I can't tear my eyes from. In my mind's eye I've memorized every feature, and I'm cool with it. But then I'm standing here and see a small scar under your eye I didn't notice,
and..." He shrugged.

FFS, now he'd gone too far. So far being his normal self around Sera hadn't worked. This new dude without a filter was in control and Wes wasn't sure if he liked it or not.

She flushed a little bit and licked her lips.

"I fell off the bed and hit my face on the nightstand when I was three. My parents were still alive then and they freaked out, but we didn't have insurance, so they didn't take me to the doctor until the next morning. I couldn't have stitches and it healed just fine, but I have that tiny scar."

He reached up to touch it. She'd been so matter-of-fact telling him how she'd gotten it, but her eyes held a hint of sadness and the timbre of her voice had dipped. He wanted to know more about her past.

Until college, he'd always assumed everyone's family was perfect and his was the only one that was messed up. But as he'd gotten older, he'd come to understand that every family had something shitty they had experienced. It didn't mean there wasn't love, just that everyone dealt with something.

"I'm sorry."

"It's okay," she said, but there was a tremble in her voice. She took a deep breath and then said, "So…um…about the journal. If you work for me, I'd have you making signatures in the morning and then binding in the afternoon."

She explained how she made the signatures—three holes, as he'd suspected—and then left him to bind six of them to-gether. He was aware of her watching him as she worked, but she went to ring up two customers before he finished. She then inspected the binding and nodded. "I just learned the kettle stitch from Ford before Christmas."

"Yeah? It was the first one he showed me. What do you

think of my work?" he asked, more than a little nervous. He wanted her to be impressed, but it had been a long time since he'd made anything new.

"You'll do. I know we said it was temporary, and I was thinking a few weeks, but would you be able to do six?" she asked.

"I would need a week off during that period. I have a big auction I need to get prepared for," he said. "Would that work?"

She agreed it would and told him she could accommodate his other work if he needed more time off. She had a contract she'd printed off the internet, which they amended and then initialed and signed. For the next six weeks, Sera was officially his boss.

Eight

After they signed the contract, Sera felt a little like she owed him a story about Ford but had no idea what he wanted to know. She had promised him stories and she had a lot of them, but she wasn't really sure, now that she'd agreed to do it, that she wanted to.

There it was. The nugget of truth she had hidden even from herself.

Those stories of Ford were personal. Something that belonged to her and her alone. After a lifetime of sharing everything, she wanted to keep them just for herself.

But she'd made a deal with Wes. There was also that niggling feeling Ford wanted her to do this.

"I have two hours left in the shop. Normally I work over here making signatures or binding journals, but I have to stop if a customer needs me," she started.

"That makes sense. Which one do you want me to do?" he asked.

She chewed her lower lip for a second while she was thinking and then realized what she was doing and stopped. "Were you naturally fast, or did you do that just to impress me?"

"Um…both. I am that fast since I practiced all night," he said.

She could picture him working all night on making signatures, his hair mussed as he labored to impress her. There was no other way to take that, right? It turned her on to think of him working on something just for her. If she'd been there, she knew it would have turned more physical. She just couldn't be next to Wes without remembering his fingers on her skin.

The scent of his cologne mingled with the aroma of paper and books. Honestly, she wasn't sure she could keep things just business between them.

"Hearing about Ford must be really important to you," she said. "And I get it. So why don't you do the binding. I can do signatures at the register even."

"No problem. Do you have a room where I can put my jacket?" he asked.

"Yes. I'll give you a tour after we close, but for right now, through that door is my storage room. Just put it on the couch back there. There's a tiny bathroom in the back corner behind the bookcases in case you need it," she said.

While Wes went to put his stuff down, a couple entered the shop holding hands, and she was struck at the way they didn't say anything, squeezing each other's hands before drifting apart to browse. That kind of connection always made her envious.

She hadn't seen it that often growing up, but when she did…that was what she wanted. Family she was slowly finding for herself. But that one-to-one connection eluded her. Most of that was on her.

She had limited all her nonplatonic interactions to hookups. She liked sex but also liked her distance. She hadn't intended for it to be that way. But after her first sexual encounter, she'd felt...nothing. She'd thought it would be more magical, like in the romances she'd read. But the guy, Paul, had been nice and cuddled with her after. And all she could think was she needed distance.

She'd spent hours journaling about the relationships she wanted to bring into her life, but once the opportunity presented itself, she ended up having mindless sex in her hallway and then hiring the guy instead of dropping her guard and getting to know him.

Part of that was on Wes. He'd started things with his ass-y letter, but the other part was all her. And it wasn't even Ford's death that brought up her barriers. Her default setting was arm's length for anything that felt too intimate—too real.

She heard the sound of Wes's boots on the hardwood floor before she felt him standing behind her. "Love your back room. Do you need more paper over here?"

She turned, noticing the flecks of gray in his blue eyes and how thick his eyelashes and eyebrows were. "Sure."

The side of his mouth kicked up in a half grin as he went to get her the supplies she'd need to make signatures. Surreptitiously she rubbed the crystal next to the register. Watching Wes move was both soothing and arousing. He had a long, easy gait and his body was all fluid movement. Sort of like those animals she saw on the Discovery Channel when she wanted to feel more outdoorsy without leaving her house.

When he turned and their eyes met, she couldn't help but feel the predator stir in both of them. No matter that they had the trappings of civilization. Both of them wanted something carnal from the other. She'd thought she'd satisfied that need the night before. That a onetime bang in her hallway would be enough.

Maybe if he'd been the asshole his letter had portrayed him to be it would have been. There was something palpable between them when their eyes met and she shivered with longing. Needing him again.

How was this possible?

She'd always been able to control her lust. Last night should have set her up for at least six weeks of not wanting anyone.

Wes had been good, but he'd awakened some kind of craving in her for more. And if it had been any other guy…maybe— maybe she'd let herself indulge in it.

But it was *Wes Sitwell*. With his thick blond hair, cable-knit sweater and long fingers that had moved over her body with the same reverence he used to touch the books in her shop. He stirred something inside that was foreign and scared her. Sera had never let herself be scared by anything once she'd become an adult. She took care of herself.

So how was she going to do that with Wes, who she'd promised to share stories with? Who she wanted to lead into the back room and kiss him until they were both naked?

"Excuse me?"

She broke her stare with Wes and turned to her customer. "How can I help?"

"I noticed you have some early-edition Beatrix Potter books but didn't see *The Tailor of Gloucester*," the woman said.

"It's my husband's favorite story and I wondered if you'd be able to check your sources to find one for me."

"I sure can. Is it a surprise?" she asked, as the woman had kept her voice low.

"I'd like it to be. We've been looking for a while and haven't found it," she said.

"Jot your details down here and I'll start searching," she said. "I'll be in touch either way."

"Thanks. Also, do you have any of the intention journals left?" the woman asked.

Sera allocated a certain number for each morning and stuck to it, but now that she had Wes working with her, she might be able to offer more later in the day.

"Normally I ask that you come between ten and twelve to get them. Would that work for you?" she asked.

"It will," she said. "We're spending the night in town."

"Perfect. I will say it gets pretty crazy in the morning," Sera warned her.

"We saw the crowds earlier. So we decided to wait until they died down. We're having tea in about twenty minutes, so I thought I'd see if you could do a journal while we're waiting," she said.

Sera wanted to because she liked this lady and there was the possibility of a nice commission if she found the rare Potter title the woman wanted. But Sera had an innate sense of fairness, and she couldn't let this woman buy a journal when she'd sent people home earlier in the day.

"I can tomorrow," she said, sticking to her policy.

The woman nodded. "Can't wait."

Her husband came up and slid his hand into hers as he set

some books on the counter and the playing-card-sized box of Charm, Curse, Confluence on top of it.

"Did you find anything?" he asked his wife.

She shook her head but picked up the box. "What is this?"

"Looks like fun for our next dinner party. They have famous figures from history as well as pop culture figures from today."

Sera rang them up, glad for the excuse to ignore Wes while she did so. After the couple moved on to the tea shop, she texted her friends in the group and told them they'd made their first game sale.

Wes tried to keep his attention on his work, and once his hands were busy, he found his balance, despite the fact that he wasn't fixing an old tome. He had always felt like his value was in finding something and repairing it, breathing new life into something with history.

That feeling of being in flux was back. Part of it was Sera. He'd somehow managed to convince himself he could be in the same room as her and not want her. He was going to be mature and the kind of man Grandpa wanted him to be. Not turn into some lust-driven horndog the moment he saw her.

His body either hadn't gotten the memo or didn't care. And honestly, Wes wasn't sure he minded. He liked looking at her. And the sound of her voice when she spoke to her customers drew his ear.

She had a dusky tone, stirring him further. His fingers were mindlessly doing the French binding and then the kettle stitches of Sera's journals. He thought he could probably complete one every fifteen minutes or so.

But only if he wasn't thinking about putting Sera on the workbench in front of him and then pushing his hands up under that frothy skirt of hers and...

"Wes?"

"Yes," he said, glancing over his shoulder at her.

"What is it you do? You said you run an online auction house, but do you stock books too?" she asked, coming over to him.

He steeled himself against the scent of lavender, which was fast becoming one of his turn-ons.

"I have some. Mostly I look to see what I think I could use in my online bookstore and then auction stuff that's a higher value," he said. "Why?"

"My customer is looking for a specific Beatrix Potter book—*The Tailor of Gloucester*—and I thought you might be the man to help with that," she said. "I could even refer her to you if that's how you work."

"Nah, I can sell to you and you can sell to her. I do that a lot," he said. "I'll text Hazel and have her start a search."

He finished the binding stitch he was doing and then reached into his back pocket for his phone, his elbow accidentally brushing her breast.

He glanced up at her. "Sorry."

"It's fine. I was standing a bit close," she admitted and then moved a few inches farther away from him, leaning back against the workbench.

He sent the text to Hazel and she thumbs-upped it. "She's on it."

"Seems like we're a bit slow now. My part of the bargain is to help you get to know Ford like I knew him. But I'm still not sure where to start," she said. She turned and began working on folding signatures.

Now that she asked, he wasn't sure what he wanted to know either. Starting at the beginning seemed the best place. "How'd you meet him?"

"I was in the coffee shop near his house. It was really busy, there were no free tables, and I hadn't gotten a to-go mug so was about to just ditch my coffee when our eyes met and he gestured to the empty seat at his table. I sat down and he continued reading his book and I fumbled in my bag for my e-reader and he said—"

"'Those contraptions will never replace real books,'" Wes finished, mimicking Ford's voice.

She laughed. "God, you sound just like him."

"He hated technology. I guess that's why I was surprised to get the email from him," Wes said.

She heard the regret in his voice. But she didn't want to bring Wes down. "He did hate it. But I got him to agree that changing the font on a book for ease of reading was a good thing."

"How long did that take?" Wes asked wryly.

"Almost a year and a half," she said with a smile. "He was stubborn about everything."

"Yeah, that's sort of a Sitwell trait," he admitted. "So after that you just started meeting?"

"Yeah, but it was more organic. I pointed out that sometimes the only way to read an older, out-of-print book was on an e-reader. And he said, 'Name a book you can't get and I'll bring it to you next week.'"

"Which one did you pick?"

"A specific edition of *The Scarlet Pimpernel* by Baroness Orczy," she said. "He brought it and I loved it. But he included a couple of Alexandre Dumas books as well. Of course, I'd heard of him, but had never read any of his books. He's a good writer, but *The Man in the Iron Mask* wasn't really my thing. However, I loved *The Three Musketeers.*"

Wes nodded slowly. "I never talked books with him."

"Why not?"

"Oz—that's my twin—and I used to be sent to stay here every summer so my dad could have some downtime from being a single parent, and Grandpa used to leave us to our own things. Mostly we played on our Game Boys or outside on our bikes. He seemed to not really want us here, but we were too young to go anywhere else. We just kept to ourselves and only saw him at dinner, which he insisted we eat together."

"That sounds…sort of sad. Didn't you talk at dinner?" she asked.

"No. He put the news on and we were encouraged to think about current events," he said.

In his mind were those long-ago summer nights and that lonely table. All he'd wanted to do was get back to his game, or his laptop when he'd been older and brought one. He hadn't been interested in anything his grandfather had to say. Not then.

But he was now, and he was so envious of the time Sera had spent with Grandpa. It was time Wes could have had for himself if he'd been able to let go of his pride and just reach out. But that hadn't been an option for him.

★ ★ ★

Sera knew pretty early on that all families weren't built the same. Being in the foster system, she'd been placed in three different families growing up, and her last foster mother, Tawdra, had been great. Her husband worked for a software company and traveled most of the time, so he hadn't really been a part of their everyday life. Tawdra had been a good foster mom, giving Sera the space she needed to grow and try new things.

"Was your brother...? What does Oz stand for, or is that his name?" she asked because she'd never heard that name before.

"Oscar. And he's grouchy just like the character on *Sesame Street*," Wes said.

"Good to know." Wes could be a bit prickly, so that tracked for his brother. She wondered what their dynamic was like; it seemed as if they were close, which intrigued her, as from Ford's stories she wouldn't have expected that.

"Ford wasn't really prickly about much. Though Hamish and he did have a big, heated argument last summer about an illegal move in chess and it lasted for three weeks," she said. She'd never seen Ford that way, and now that she was remembering it, there had been a bit of Ford in Wes when he'd first come into her shop yesterday.

So much had happened in a day, even though it felt like a lifetime since they'd first met. Just one day. She'd learned Ford was dead, she'd thought about using some of Liberty's spell books to turn Wes into a toad, and then she'd fucked him instead and hired him.

Yeah.

That might be why it felt like a lifetime.

"Sounds like Grandpa. He and Hamish might have known each other all their lives, but they fell in and out a lot."

"Why do you think that is?" she asked. "I like Hamish and I looked up the move he made… It was legal, but Ford didn't want to hear it."

"Please tell me you didn't try to convince him he was wrong," Wes said.

"I did," she admitted. It hadn't gone well. Actually, it gave her a little insight into how Wes and Ford might have fallen out. Ford could be very stubborn, and she'd almost backed down but hadn't. Ford and Hamish were both old men; they didn't have time to let petty grudges dominate their moments together. One thing Sera had always been aware of was the time she got with the people she cared about. It was finite.

"I told him yelling at me wasn't going to change the facts and he'd clearly been misinformed."

"Did that work?" Wes asked as he finished the binding of one journal and started to gather six more signatures to start another one.

"Sort of. I could tell he didn't like it, but the rules were written clearly in one of his own books. So he changed the subject and then the next week he and Hamish were on friendly terms again," she said.

She'd had very little exposure to anyone of the grand-parental age when she'd been growing up. She'd only seen them in movies and on television, and usually they were boozy socialites who spoiled the kids like Rory Gilmore's grand-mother, or just warm and fuzzy. So she'd never really thought about what it would be like to be old.

She'd always dreaded turning eighteen, when she'd age out

of foster care and be on her own. But she'd never thought beyond it, beyond the present, until she'd met Ford.

He was alone by choice. He had that big house of his that had seen better days and his grumpy friendships, but for the most part he was happy with his books. And Sera admitted that was the first time she'd seen her future. Ford gave her something she wanted to aspire to.

She would be happy to live by herself in her old age, see Liberty and Poppy and just read books and putter around her home. For the first time, she'd let herself see the future and actually knew where she wanted to be. She saw it with WiCKed Sisters too.

Amber Rapp had catapulted them forward in a way that Sera wouldn't have thought to dream. She was a small dreamer. She was trying to change that. But when she tried to think big about other parts of her life, it felt...*she* felt like she wasn't worthy of it.

She felt like smaller was more what she could achieve.

"Thanks," Wes said quietly.

"You're welcome. I'm not sure it helps to hear the stories. It might put your mind at ease about the actual basis of our relationship."

He stopped working and moved toward her, putting his hand on her shoulder. A shiver of awareness went through her as she turned her head to look at him.

"I never really thought you and Grandpa had hooked up. I just said that because I was mad."

"At me?"

"At Grandpa's death and myself. I am really sorry I said it."

She smiled at him. This was the first time she'd seen him

sincere. He'd been close a few times in the tavern and at Ford's house, but this was different. His eyes were clear and those stress lines she could always see around his mouth and eyes weren't there.

"You're forgiven," she said.

Speaking of Ford's death reminded her that Liberty and Poppy were coming to the funeral with her on Saturday. "So, can I bring guests to the funeral?"

"Guests?"

"Liberty and Poppy. I was thinking more about your offer to speak as well…" She trailed off.

"They can come. As you know from calling the church, no one is banned from a funeral," he said. "Are you going to say something about him? I think Dad and Oz might benefit from hearing some of those stories."

"I'm going to write something, and is it okay…? Poppy offered to read it for me. I think I might cry if I tried to do it myself," she said.

Wes's mouth flattened and he just nodded a couple of times. "Of course that's fine. I shouldn't have made you feel like you didn't deserve to be there. You and Grandpa were genuine friends. I can see that now."

"I'm glad. I know you were hurt. I still don't know why he left me the books, but I'm glad he did because I wouldn't have met you otherwise."

"Me too," he said.

They worked quietly together for the rest of the afternoon; he shared some tips he'd learned when he worked with Ford.

Wes was showing her another side to her friend.

Nine

Wes woke to a knock on his bedroom door the next morning. He opened it and found his twin standing there.

"Hey. Dad is making breakfast. We're here until the funeral tomorrow," Oz said.

"Why?" he asked.

"Dad wants to go through the house and mark things for the estate sale," Oz said. "I'll be working from the dining room. Saw you had your stuff settled in the kitchen."

"Yeah," Wes said, still struggling to wake up. He had been planning to stay in the house. But the last thing he wanted to deal with today was his father, who was bound to ask questions about the books. Fuck.

"Didn't want you coming down to us," Oz said.

"Thanks. Appreciate that."

"Did you get your books back?"

Wes rolled his eyes. He almost wished he hadn't involved his father and Oz in this to begin with. But he had. He'd been so ticked that Grandpa had left books to a twenty-six-year-old woman that he'd actually asked his dad for a favor.

And his dad had unfortunately delivered.

"I'm working on it."

He pushed his way past his brother and headed down the stairs, where he could hear his father in the kitchen.

"Dad."

"Son. You don't have crap for groceries. I'll order some and you and your brother can Venmo me your share."

"Okay," Wes said.

He went to get a cup of coffee and then leaned against the counter and took a deep breath. "Oz mentioned you want to go through the house, mark things for sale. I'm planning to stay here for the next six weeks."

"Why?"

"I'm getting to know Grandpa's friend and trying to figure some stuff out."

"What stuff?" his dad asked.

Emotional stuff he knew his father didn't want to talk about. "Book stuff. Also, Sera and her friends are attending the funeral."

His father shook his head. "Now she's Sera. What's going on?"

"She and Grandpa were friends, like he was with Hamish," Wes said, going to sit at the kitchen table, where he had been working on repairing the book. He was careful to keep his coffee cup out of the way of the pages.

"Really? That seems a bit unlikely since he was so crotchety. I thought you said she used him to get the books you wanted."

"Yeah, about that. I might have jumped to conclusions, Dad. The books aren't even worth that much," Wes said.

"Then why did you send a letter on our letterhead?"

His dad came and sat down across from him. Wes started to get his back up, hearing in his father's question some kind of accusation, but then he just let that go. His father wasn't any better at interpersonal relationships than he was. Maybe he was curious. Maybe he wasn't.

What could Wes say? He'd gone to his dad and not Oz to ask about the letterhead because he knew Dad and Grandpa were usually fighting about something. He took a deep breath.

"Because I fucked up with Grandpa and I saw his gift to her as a final way of telling me he hadn't forgiven me."

His dad leaned back in the chair, pushing it up so it was balanced on the back two legs. "Yeah, the old man did like to always have the final word."

"Yeah, something he passed on."

His dad almost cracked a smile. "What happened between you two?"

Wes put his head down, staring at the cream on top of his coffee as if that was going to make it any easier to find the words. It didn't.

"I was an ass. I mean, he was bossy, but I was an ass, and I told him I didn't need his advice," Wes said. He could still remember Grandpa standing there in the shop where they'd been working together, watching him with that cold, icy Sitwell glare. Wes had known he'd gone too far, but he was twenty-four and an adult, goddammit. Wes still believed he'd had to stand on his own to get his business to where it was today. But surely there had been a better way to do it.

"Oz and I had a showdown like that," his dad said.

"You did?" he asked. His brother and father had always seemed like two peas in a repressed pod.

"Yeah. And like Grandpa, I told him it was my way or the highway," his dad said.

"How'd you get past that? And why didn't you tell me?" he asked.

"It wasn't any of your business, Wes."

His dad was right. They weren't a sharing bunch. "How'd you sort it out? I never did with Grandpa."

"Oz came in the next day with a business plan to open up a competing law firm, showed me the clients he'd be taking. He gave me the option to be his partner or his competitor," Dad said. "And you know me—for a split second I thought, *Fuck you*. But then…"

"You didn't," Wes said.

"Yeah." His dad sat the chair back on four legs, putting his arms on the table.

The old man looked like he wanted to say more. A part of Wes wanted to hear him say he regretted the way he'd raised them, but Wes suspected those weren't emotions his father would ever admit to. Wes got it. He hated feelings. They made life more complicated than he was comfortable with. If growing up with his dad had taught him anything, it was that talking about what he felt wouldn't resolve anything. Wes had gotten into the habit of keeping his feelings shoved way down, telling himself life was safer that way.

"Glad you sorted it out. Grandpa died before I could," Wes admitted. "I need some time before we clean out the house and sell it."

His dad took a long swallow of his coffee. "Six weeks, you said?"

"Yeah."

"Okay. We can do that. I'll mark some of the stuff I'd like to keep," he said. "You and Oz should do the same. When you move out, I'll hire a company to come in and value it and sell it, and we can split the proceeds."

"I'd like to keep the library," Wes said.

"We'll have it valued and I'll deduct it from your share," his father said, more comfortable now that he was talking about numbers. His father was a big one for balanced ledgers, and Wes wondered if in some ways that was how his father found peace, the way he did by repairing old books. His father often treated him and definitely Oz like they were business partners first, sons second. His father had said more than once that he liked ledgers because numbers didn't lie.

Wes didn't ask, just told his dad he had to get to work and went upstairs to shower and change. Sera had told him to make his own hours, but he wanted to get out of this house and away from the feelings being with his father and brother always stirred in him.

A little bit of it was shame, and regret, and anger.

Sera sat on the couch in her back room thinking about the spell Liberty had emailed them all last night. It was a conjuring spell for bringing the thing you desired most into your life. She had written it in her journal but hadn't put anything under it. She'd gotten in early today because she had wanted to get everything ready for Wes to work while she was running the shop.

But that hadn't taken long. A part of her had just wanted to be out of her house and in the shop. She was excited to see Wes.

Which was unexpected. She'd spent last night remembering him in her house and feeling all those sexy feelings again. A part of her wanted to just write the emotions down to lust.

Lust was something she'd never had an issue with expressing. There was nothing too emotional tied to it. Though a good fuck did make her feel relaxed in a way nothing else ever did.

And Wes had certainly been that. But working beside him yesterday at the bench had stirred up longings that weren't sexual. He'd talked quietly about books, recommended she switch to the Coptic stitch for binding and shared his experiences and techniques.

He hadn't been preachy or mansplainy. It had reminded her of the conversations she'd had with Ford. She saw a lot of Ford in Wes. And yet there were things about Wes that were very distinct. Like the scent of his aftershave. And the way his long fingers moved as he assembled journals—watching made her skin tingle, wanting to feel those fingers on her again.

"Hiya. Why are you hiding out back here?" Liberty walked in with her cup of mushroom mud with Poppy behind her carrying a cup of Earl Grey. They both squeezed into the seating area around her. Last night at the tavern, they'd agreed to hire three retail workers to handle the cash registers and look into hiring a manager for the entire shop.

"Just enjoying a moment of calm before the rush," Sera said. She wasn't ready to share her thoughts on Wes. Not yet. She was still trying to figure out if the changes in him were real or part of a scheme. It was hard to reconcile the angry letter she'd first received with the man who'd stood next to her making journals.

She suspected they were both real. Which made it harder to figure out if she could trust him with her feelings. And she was having *feelings* regardless of whether she wanted them or not.

Emotions that weren't lust. That felt like caring and affection and comradery.

Of course, that could all change after the funeral.

"Did you write down your thoughts about Ford?" Poppy asked.

"I did. I'll email it to you later," she said. "Are you sure you both want to come tomorrow?"

"Yes," they said at once.

"We're not letting you go alone," Poppy added.

"Thanks," Sera said as someone knocked on the back door. "That'll be Wes."

"I still can't believe you hired him," Liberty said.

"I need the help and he wants to know more about his grandfather. This is a win-win."

"Win-win? Since when do you use terms like that?" Poppy asked.

"Since I'm not sure how else to describe it," Sera said, getting up to open the back door.

Wes stood there in his wool coat with the collar turned up and he handed her a bakery bag as he stepped inside. "Brought croissants. I think you said they're your favorites."

"Thanks."

He glanced past her and noticed her partners sitting on

the couch. "Sorry, didn't think to bring some for everyone. I will next time."

She had no doubt he would. Wes was making an effort, and as much as she was leery of trusting him, a part of her realized it was down to her. It wasn't all on his end. Trust always started with herself and she'd never really been good at it. Her therapist put it down to being abandoned as a child.

But Sera suspected it was more than that. She hated to get her hopes up about a person and be disappointed. It was easier to treat everyone as a stranger until they barreled their way into her life the way Liberty and Poppy had.

And in a quieter way, Ford had.

It was really only his death that made her realize how much she cared for him. Cared about him.

"Morning," Wes called as he took off his coat and put it on the peg near the door.

"Morning," Poppy said. "I like scones, for future reference, and Liberty likes anything supersweet with a sugary glaze on it."

"Noted," Wes said.

Wes went to the electric kettle she kept on the counter and turned it on. Poppy just smiled as she got up and waved goodbye. Liberty gave Sera a look and shook her head, mouthing the words *be careful* before she left.

Be careful.

Her entire life had been careful. She hadn't really taken the time to acknowledge that before, but standing in her back room, she knew it was true. She'd been careful and it had paid off, but she hadn't been careful with Wes.

She wasn't entirely sure if that was a mistake or not. A part of her liked the butterflies in her stomach, that feeling of not knowing what was coming next. Maybe she couldn't be impulsive with anything or anyone else. But with Wes it felt like the only way for her to be.

She ate her croissant with him and he mentioned a book of poems by Edna St. Vincent Millay. She told him she'd always wanted to read them but hadn't found a hard copy that spoke to her. Ford had declared it shouldn't be read on her e-reader. If she wasn't going to use the e-reader, then she wanted to feel the weight of the book.

Talking to him felt natural and easy, like neither of them was trying. She did her best to ignore that he remembered little details about her. Things that few people had ever remembered about her.

Then she went out to start her day. She told herself she was happy because she had someone to replenish her stock of journals, but another secret part of her knew she was happy because Wes was in her shop with her. Working and smiling at her. She tried not to read into how much she was looking forward to seeing him. She knew they had six weeks together. So she wanted to be present for every one of the days and make the most of them.

She wasn't entirely sure what she felt for him and didn't really want to linger on defining it, if it was just a transfer of affection she'd held for Ford or something new and different.

But the butterflies in her stomach and the excitement in her step as she headed into work were telling her it was the latter.

Oz showed up at lunchtime as Sera was telling a group of customers she'd reached her allotment of journals for the day. She smiled at his brother and then looked over at Wes, seeming to realize they were related. He and his twin weren't identical but they looked like brothers.

"Oscar?" she asked.

"Serafina?" he countered.

Wes rushed to her side, not sure why his brother had come to the store. Also not really sure what Sera would say since Wes had sent that nasty letter to her on letterhead from his dad and Oz's firm. She might be out for blood.

"What's up?" he asked his brother.

"Just wanted to see the famous Serafina Conte."

"Oz…"

"Famous, am I?" Sera asked, stepping around him. "That's news to me."

"Well, there aren't many women who make my little brother come asking for a favor," Oz said.

Wes groaned. Oz was definitely here to needle him. Wes could see it in his brother's eyes. And Sera didn't know how his twin could be. "No. Get out, Oz."

"So he asked you for a favor?" Sera pushed Wes to the side. "It was for the books, wasn't it?"

Wes shook his head. Then just turned and walked back to the workbench. There was no stopping either one of them.

"It was for the books. Which I assume you didn't give him," Oz said.

"Nope."

He heard the smile in her voice, and that made him smile too. His stomach tightened as he thought about the last time he'd heard that note in her voice. It had been yesterday when she'd worked next to him and he tried to forget his arm had brushed her breast. Now she was talking to his brother and who knew how that would go.

But Wes had a feeling it would be interesting to see. Oz was the most rational, straight-thinking person Wes knew. His brother only did things after taking time to consider all outcomes.

Leaving his brother and Sera alone was probably not his best idea.

Sera moved to the register to take care of a paying customer and Oz drifted over to Wes. "Why are you really here?"

"I was curious about her," Oz said.

"And?"

"I can see why you're sticking around Birch Lake for six weeks," he said. "Is it for her?"

Wes shrugged.

"Wes?"

He glanced up. He didn't really know if he was staying because of Sera. "I just need some time to process everything with Grandpa's death. She's helping me do that in a way."

"You don't have to justify it to me. This is just not like you. Even Dad said you seemed different, and he hardly notices anything that's not involved with money," Oz said.

"I know. It's not like me. But I was a douche to her and to Grandpa, and I don't know how to fix it," he said.

"You seem to be making it up to her," Oz said. "And Grandpa's dead."

"I know that."

"So…"

"Remember that summer when Mom sent us that post-card?" Wes asked his brother. They'd been sixteen, and suddenly, after ten years of not hearing from her, the postcard had shown up.

"Yeah. What's that got to do with anything?" Oz asked.

"I saw you reading it before bed… I know you wrote her back," Wes said.

"Again, what of it?"

"I'm not like that. I write a person off. I did that with Grandpa too. Except he really cared about me, and I shouldn't have, but I didn't know how… Fuck, I sound like a sap. Never mind."

Oz crossed his arms over his chest. "Mom said she wasn't sure why she'd sent the postcard, that she was glad we were doing okay. I didn't write back to her after that, and she never wrote again. I'm not sure it really helped. I think she was doing it for her and not for us," Oz said.

Wes could believe that. Their mother hadn't ever done anything that wasn't for herself. "That sounds like her."

"Yeah. So, are you doing this for you or for her?" Oz asked, nodding toward Sera.

Wes looked over at Sera, smiling as she talked to another one of her customers under a sign that said Words Are Magic. Was he doing this for himself? Yes. He had always put himself first and he wasn't really sure what he could give her. He hadn't seen it from this point of view until Oz brought it up.

Wes had painted himself in some kind of noble light, like he was finally opening himself up and getting closure with Grandpa, but what was in it for Sera? He was helping her with the journal making, but did she have another reason for asking for his help?

Had she originally agreed to his idea with an ulterior motive, to get back at him or to seek something from his family? Or was it simply that she wanted to talk about the friend she'd lost?

Definitely the second—she wasn't trying to get back at him.

Oz stood silently next to him, but Wes didn't know the answer so just shrugged. His brother stayed a few more minutes, chatting about nothing in particular, and then left. Sera drifted over to him after.

"Why was he here?" she asked.

"Curiosity." Wes really hoped she'd let that be enough, but he knew her by now, or was starting to. She couldn't let a one-word answer lie.

"About?"

He knew she wasn't flirting with him, that it was just the way she talked and her innate curiosity, but after a lifetime of functional conversations where he limited himself, this felt intimate. "You and me."

"I don't understand," she said.

"Neither do I." Oz had shown up because Wes was staying in Birch Lake, the one place neither of them had ever wanted to be. After Wes's falling-out with Grandpa, he'd crashed with Oz for a few days and vowed never to come back.

So his brother was curious about the reason for the change of heart. Oz had one small conversation with Sera and had seemed to find an answer to a question only he knew.

But one conversation with Sera was all it seemed to take for the Sitwell men to be intrigued by her. First Grandpa, then himself and now Oz.

Sera had upended everything Wes believed about himself and was making him question it all.

Ten

The day of the funeral was clear, crisp and sunny. Sera stood outside the church in her long red wool coat, which she'd worn because Ford had complimented her on it. She thought it was too loud, and he said she should take more chances.

Be bolder.

His advice had usually fallen on deaf ears, but today she thought he'd appreciate the coat. She knew he was gone and that whatever lingered of his spirit was in her heart and in her mind. But somehow, she hoped her gesture would reach him. Poppy slid her arm through Sera's left one and Liberty took her right.

"I'm not sure what will happen when I enter a church, being a Wiccan and all. So if I combust, take my dust back to my mother."

Sera laughed as she knew Liberty intended, but then turned and kissed her friend on the cheek. "I'm putting some of your dust into a special journal."

"Good. I'll be back to haunt you both," Liberty said.

"I haven't been to church in years. I'm not even sure I remember what to do," Sera said.

"Well, I'm Anglican, so I sure don't know, and Liberty will be with us in spirit if things go poorly," Poppy said. "So we'll have to wing it."

Winging it was pretty much the story of her life. It was sweet that neither of her friends pointed out that she was hesitating. Sera knew once she went in the church and saw Ford in his coffin, it would be final.

The last few days had been weird because she hadn't seen Ford as she usually did and yesterday afternoon she'd had a cry in the back room until Wes came in. He'd noticed her teary eyes and offered her a handkerchief that he'd found in Ford's stuff. Then he'd started talking about a video he'd watched that morning on faster binding techniques. Comforting her. She wasn't spiritual, not really, but it had been impossible not to link Wes's actions with Ford's otherworldly handiwork.

She took a deep breath.

"I'm ready."

"I'm not. Seriously, now I think I should have worn my robes instead of the see-through blouse," Liberty said. "What if that pisses off the Catholic God even more?"

"What if it makes him smile?" Sera said. "Sister Edward said God is what we need them to be."

"And today you need smiles," Poppy said.

"I think the Sitwells will too," Sera said as they walked up the steps and into the church.

As soon as she entered, she noticed the open coffin in the center of the altar and she started to cry. She reached for the holy water font and blessed herself, genuflecting as she looked up at the cross. It might have been almost fifteen years since she'd been in a church, but that much she remembered.

This church was different from the one that had been on the same property as the Catholic elementary school she'd attended, but there was a familiarity in the stations of the cross on the wall and the faint smell of incense.

Wes glanced back as they entered and gave her a faint smile. She heard Poppy teasing Liberty about still being in one piece as they walked up the aisle. She'd gone to the viewing the night before and had slipped a little thank-you note into Ford's coffin. Just telling him how much his friendship had meant to her and wishing him peace in his afterlife.

Today as she and her friends filed into a pew opposite the Sitwell men, she couldn't seem to stop the flow of memories of conversations she'd had with Ford. She shrugged out of her coat and heard a gasp from Mr. Sitwell—Wes's dad—as Liberty did. Sera glanced at her friend and noticed she was full on grinning.

Sera elbowed her.

"What? It's not like the blouse isn't covering me from neck to wrist," Liberty said.

"You don't have to let them see how much you enjoy their discomfort," Poppy pointed out.

"They *were* dicks to Sera and let her find out Ford had passed through a douchey letter," Liberty said.

"Point taken," Sera said.

The Mass went by in a blur. She was calm during parts and cried during others. When the priest invited Hamish up to speak and the older man talked about losing his last friend, Sera suspected there wasn't a dry eye in the church. Even Liberty and Poppy were quietly crying.

Sera decided she'd try to meet up with Hamish once in a while, if he wanted to. But the truth was she didn't know the other man well. Just saw another soul who'd lost a friend.

Wes's father got up and talked about Ford, and it was striking because the cadence in Benjamin's voice was the same as Wes's. When he spoke, he talked about the lessons he'd learned from his father. How he'd continue to use them to carry on.

Then it was time for Poppy to go up and read Sera's words. She suddenly felt unsure. Were her emotions okay? Was what she felt the right thing to feel? She was so used to keeping everything quietly inside that this was hard. But she wanted the people who knew Ford to see him through her eyes.

She listened to Poppy's crisp British accent, creating a filter between what she'd written and what she heard. It made the words seem not so raw. She cried and ached at never seeing her friend again and then smiled at the end when Poppy read the last lines she'd written.

Life was richer for having known Ford, reading and discussing books with him and spending afternoons laughing over coffee. She'd carry that with her for the rest of her life. Coffee and books had always been special to her and had brought her family.

She sat back against the pew as Mass ended and the pallbearers carried the coffin down the aisle and out of the church. Ford would be buried in Birch Lake Cemetery near the center of town. It was one of the oldest cemeteries in the US and the Sitwell family had several plots there. She knew Ford was being buried next to his late wife. He'd often spoken of her, and Sera took comfort from the fact that the two of them were together.

His dad was silent as Wes drove behind the hearse following Grandpa's coffin. He heard Oz's fingers tapping on his phone, sending a message. His brother and father didn't have the same relationship he did with Grandpa. Unfortunately, he had become more like them, distant and harsh, at the worst time.

"I don't want us to be like this," Wes said.

He always kept his thoughts in. Why had he blurted that out?

"Like how?" his father asked. "In one car?"

"No, Dad. Like we were with Grandpa. Hamish and Sera really knew him. I don't want to find out stuff about you both when you're dead," Wes said.

"You know me," Oz said.

"I sometimes do. But only what you'll willingly reveal. And I don't know you at all, Dad."

His dad closed his eyes and leaned his head back against the seat rest. "What do you want to know?"

The first thing that popped in his head was why his dad had married his mom. But if he led with that, he'd never learn anything. His dad avoided all mentions of their mom, and whenever Wes or Oz had brought her up, he'd shut them down with an icy stare and then walk away.

"Do you play chess?" he asked. "I don't. Oz, I don't think you do either."

His father turned and looked over at him. "I do. Dad taught

me when I was young and I was in chess club in high school. I play online in a league."

"Are you good?" Oz asked, leaning forward from the back seat and putting his phone away.

Wes kept an eye on the road, but for the first time he could remember he had learned something about his father that wasn't related to how to get something from him.

"I am. I don't know why I never taught you boys."

"We weren't interested," Oz said.

"Yeah," Wes agreed. But he knew the real reason his dad hadn't taught them was because he'd been working and trying to keep his shit together.

"You might have been," his father said. "I really never took the time to see."

Wes felt a pang near his heart hearing his dad open up like this. It was probably seeing his own father in a coffin. Or maybe it was Wes letting down his own guard and inviting his dad to share.

"You were busy working and taking care of things," Wes said, putting into words what he'd thought earlier. It was easy to paint his dad into the villain of his childhood, but honestly, he knew his old man wasn't a monster. He'd been doing the best he could most of the time.

He hadn't turned to alcohol or drugs, and he hadn't beat them—he'd just worked and then sent them to Grandpa in the summer.

"Grandpa didn't teach us either," Oz said. "He just made us go outside... Remember that?"

"I do. And we found that shed in the back of the house with all those tools," Wes said.

His dad started to laugh. "He used to do the same to me. I carved my name into the workbench when I was twelve. Well, started to, and then I cut my finger and Mom freaked out and yelled at him. He said, 'Well, now the boy knows not to do that again.'"

Wes smiled. "He said the same to us when Oz drove his bike off the picnic table trying to get epic air."

"I did get epic air, just sprained my wrist in the process," Oz said.

For the first time in a very long one, Wes felt like his family was healing. There were still cracks and distance that nothing could fill, but losing Grandpa had given them all a moment to share things that usually went unsaid. Wes hoped they could keep this up. Might be nice to feel like they were a family instead of three strangers who shared a bloodline.

He followed the hearse to the Sitwell plot, aware that Hamish's and Sera's cars were behind his. He wondered how Grandpa would have felt about the things they said today. The two of them had known different sides of his grandfather, different to what his family knew. Hamish had talked about a young Ford and the trouble they used to get up to together. The women they'd wooed and finally won and married. The way they had always been there for each other when heartache had struck. Sera's tales of books and laughter had been just as touching. The two of them had shared their memories with everyone at the funeral.

Grandpa had always been so private. Would the stories have bothered him?

Wes didn't know, but he'd read one time that funerals were for the living not the dead, and today he had needed to hear those stories. He wasn't sure if it was arrogance or ego, but a part of him had imagined Ford all alone since Wes had left.

He was glad that hadn't been the case.

"The girl who spoke, is that Sera?" his father asked.

"No. That's her friend Poppy," Wes said. "I'll introduce you if you want."

His father hadn't come to the viewing the other night. He'd privately said his goodbyes and then gone back home. Wes was nervous about Sera meeting his dad. The old man could be a grump who spoke bluntly. This wasn't like Oz meeting Sera because, Wes realized suddenly, he knew his twin loved him and wouldn't do anything to hurt him.

Wes had never been sure of his father's affection.

"Is Sera the one with the party blouse?" his dad asked.

"No. She's the one with curly brown hair," Wes said.

"That's the only one left," his dad pointed out.

"She's coming back to the house with her friends and Hamish after," he said.

His dad nodded. "I'll try to behave. I'm bad at grief."

"I don't think anyone is good at it," Oz said dryly.

His father almost smiled. "Your grandpa would have said the same thing. I just meant I can be an ass. So if I don't talk to them...it's not personal."

Wes had never felt his dad more than at that moment. There had been times when all Wes could do was retreat to his book repair tools, sit in front of a damaged volume and work because he couldn't be with people.

They got out and walked toward the plot as the pallbearers brought Grandpa's coffin. Hamish stood next to Wes's dad;

Wes moved to stand next to Sera. He didn't say anything because he wasn't sure he had the right words.

He just took her hand in his as he watched his grandfather's coffin lowered into the ground. The priest spoke, but Wes didn't hear him. He heard his father's recollection of what Grandpa had said to him. *He learned not to do it again.*

Why was it just now that Wes had realized what he'd learned from Grandpa? Had he not been old enough to appreciate it? Or had it taken the loss to remind him he didn't want to let stubbornness and arrogance cost him, especially where Sera was concerned?

He was tired of trying to figure out his emotions, and he didn't really know how he felt. He just knew he wanted to hold her hand and give and take comfort from her. He couldn't forget their night together, and the more time he spent with Sera, the more he wanted to have her again. But this time actually knowing the woman.

Sera hadn't expected the entire day to be what it was. Wes's dad, Benjamin, pulled her aside when they got back to Ford's house to talk.

"Thanks for your words today. I hadn't really taken the time to know my dad once the boys were grown," he said.

"He was a good friend to me. So funny," she said. "I hope you know I didn't do anything malicious to make him give me those books."

"Having met you, there's no doubt about that. That was Wes's thing anyway."

"Yeah, I had a feeling," she said with a laugh.

"I shouldn't have allowed him to use our letterhead to send that message," Benjamin said.

He was formal and she had observed him enough throughout the day to accept that it was his way. He was a very reserved man, but his tone was sincere. "Why did you?" she asked.

"He seldom asks me for anything. Neither of them do," he said, almost to himself.

All of the Sitwell men had emotional constipation. Something must have caused it. For herself, it was the insecurity of the foster-care system. That fear of starting to care about a place and people and then being uprooted and moved.

Whatever the Sitwells had faced, it had to have been very traumatic and hurtful. There was no way to deal with that type of thing in a good way. No matter what happened, there was always some sort of fallout. They were all, from what she saw, decent men. Each of them so very different but also similar, including Ford.

"I guess I can understand that. But it was a bit scary for me to receive," she said.

"Apologies. We're tax attorneys anyway, so that type of litigation isn't our specialty."

She shook her head. Glad to learn that it hadn't been Ford's entire family that had been upset with her. "Why was he so upset?"

"Books were his hobby with Dad. I can only guess, because he's a Sitwell, that they had a falling-out and he took the gift to you personally. You'd have to ask him. Thanks again for your words," Benjamin said as he turned to go talk to Hamish and Poppy.

Liberty was talking to Wes's brother. She wasn't flirting, so Sera guessed she'd found out he was a tax attorney. Liberty took care of their books and was likely using the opportunity to pick his brain. The surge in revenue from the Amber Rapp event had pushed them into a higher tax bracket and Liberty didn't want to screw anything up.

She left the formal living room, with its overstuffed bookcases and comfortable but worn furniture, to go and find Wes. He was in the kitchen at the table where she'd had tea with him that first day.

He was leaning over a piece of foolscap and had gold leaf in his hand. He was touching up the gold on the pages. She went to stand next to him and he looked up.

"I saw you and Dad talking. How'd that go?" he asked.

"Okay. Why are you in here alone?"

He put down the knife he'd been using to apply the gold leaf and stood up, stretching as he did so. He'd taken off his suit jacket but still wore a black shirt and tie. He'd dressed from head to toe in black for the funeral, which made his blue eyes brighter and his blond hair seem even thicker.

She stood in the doorway, stopped by a wave of lust. No denying it. There was something very sensual about Wes when he worked on books, and tonight, in his formal wear…she couldn't tear her eyes from him.

She swallowed hard as she watched him and tried to remind herself they'd just buried Ford.

Life moved on. Sera knew that more than anyone else. She wanted Wes. This Wes.

The quiet bookbinder who was happier working in the kitchen than mingling. The man who used his hands with confidence and surety to fix broken spines and torn pages. The man who hid away from anything he couldn't fix by turning to his workbench.

"I don't do grief well," he said. "Actually, my dad said that. I borrowed it as an excuse to hide out."

Emotional constipation, she thought again.

"Grief is… I think this is the first time I've really had a chance to let go of someone and share my emotions about it," she said. She'd been too young when her parents died. But each time she'd left a group or foster home she'd missed the people left behind. She'd tried to develop a thick skin where leaving was concerned, but deep down it was another wound that eventually turned into a scar.

"Have you had to let people go often?" he asked. "You mentioned your parents died and you were put in foster care, but I don't know much more."

Normally she'd shrug and change the subject if someone asked her this so bluntly, but being in Ford's house after his funeral made her want to share more about her life. Ford had been the one to encourage her to open up. But she'd never really done it. She had been able to talk to him about books, but that was it.

Tonight, though, she wanted to reveal more of herself. She wanted to have the closeness that came only from sharing something real with another person.

There was the added bonus that she and Wes were only sort of friends. He was leaving in less than six weeks, so whatever she shared would only temporarily link them. And temporary was definitely her comfort zone. Even if she couldn't stop thinking about Wes, even if her heart beat a little faster whenever he was around. She knew no one stayed. No matter how much she liked them and wanted them to.

"My parents died when I was six. I really don't remember them. There was a house fire, so I don't have any pictures of them," she said. "There were no relatives who were close and could raise me, so I went to foster care. Until I was thirteen, I was in a Catholic group home, and then went into an individual foster home and the system. So I moved around a lot and nothing felt permanent."

He tipped his head to the side, staring at her. People did that when they learned she didn't have a nuclear family or even a single-parent family. Most didn't know what to say.

"That sounds rough. Was it?" he asked.

"Sometimes. The houses where I was placed were mostly good to me. No physical abuse. But I always knew I was leaving." She paused, taking a deep breath. "Can I ask you something?"

"You just did," he said with that half smile of his she was coming to like a little too much.

"What happened to your family?"

"I'm not sure what you mean."

"You do," she said, not willing to let him dodge since she'd just been open with him. "If you don't want to say, that's fine. But don't pretend something didn't drive a wedge in your family. Because it's obvious to me there is more to it than distance."

He rubbed the back of his neck and then shook his head. "There is. But I can't today. I'll tell you about it later, when Dad and Oz are gone."

Whatever it was, it weighed on him. In a flash she realized that if she was casual about him, she'd let it be. But she wasn't. She didn't want to think too hard about why helping someone who was bound to leave was important to her.

Eleven

Sera stayed at the house after her friends and Hamish left. His brother and dad got their stuff packed up and headed back to Portland after dinner. Wes didn't really want to be alone. The talk with his dad had been interesting and he'd expected Benjamin to be his usual surly self with Sera and her friends. But he'd been nice, friendly, for him.

"Do you want me to go?" she asked after everyone was gone. "I think I'm hanging around because I feel closer to Ford here. It's like he's going to come in with a cup of tea or a new book he's gone away to look for."

She sat on an overstuffed settee that was in front of an entire wall of floor-to-ceiling bookcases. They were overstuffed as well, with worn books, both antiquarian pieces that had been in his family for generations and hardcovers and paperbacks from the last few decades. One of his favorites was a copy of *Robinson Crusoe*, which had been in their family since the early 1800s; the edition was old and worn and needed repair,

but since it had been shared from father to son in each generation, Wes had always been reluctant to restore it himself.

"I don't want to be alone," he said.

"I get it. Me either," she admitted. She'd slipped her shoes
off and curled her legs underneath her.

For the funeral she'd put her hair into a bun at the back of
her neck. He wasn't sure how, but her hair wasn't curly at all
in the way she'd styled it. "What happened to your curls?"

"I tamed them with super control gel and a comb," she
said. "I have to do it when it's still wet. The hair at the back
of my neck is still wet."

He moved to sit next to her, reaching out to touch her hair,
but hesitated. "Can I?"

She nodded quickly. "Part of it will feel crunchy. Have
you ever used gel?"

He touched her hair; it wasn't whatever she thought crunchy
was. But it was still damp. Up close, he noticed a tendril had
escaped her bun and was curling down her back. He wrapped
it around his finger and then let it go.

He loved her hair. He had spent a lot of time thinking about
it and wishing they'd had more time the night they'd hooked
up. To him, her hair represented that untamed part of Sera.
Though today she'd tamped that down for the funeral service.

Grief. It was the one thing they were both trying to man-
age. His cut through him. Sharing this night with her was
making things both easy and harder.

"Wes?"

She'd asked him something about hair gel. "One time.
I went to a punk party at college. So my roommates and I

spiked up our hair. I put way too much in and it took three days to wash it out."

She laughed. "Rookie mistake."

"To be fair, my hair usually just does this and I'm okay with it."

"You're so lucky," she said.

He'd never felt that way. He was so much a product of his mom's actions that it was hard to see luck anywhere in his past or his present, to be honest. Sera made him almost hopeful he could be lucky someday. He'd seen some changes in his dad in the car, so maybe...

"Your dad apologized for letting you use his company letterhead," she said. "I can't believe I never thought to call the law firm."

"Probably because I followed up the letter with an in-person asshole visit."

"You were a bit of a dick. Asking me if I was your grandfather's lover."

"Well...to be fair," he started, but how was it fair to assume the only reason Grandpa would have left her anything was in exchange for sex? That was outdated thinking and he'd always considered himself a modern man. "It wasn't. I was mad and jealous that Grandpa hadn't left them to me."

"Yeah, it wasn't fair at all. And why do you need those books anyway? Hamish gave them to me today," she said. "They are mostly ones Ford recommended or lent to me. There are a few old journals and some loose parchment paper I could use in my work. But nothing like the books you have in here."

She was right. She had been from the beginning. But it

wasn't easy to admit, even to himself, that he'd wanted those books because he'd thought of all these volumes in Grandpa's house as his. He'd been the one to come and live with Grandpa for three years. Wes had earned them.

"Because I'm a greedy bastard," he said.

"But you're not. I think there is something else going on with you and Ford. Maybe with your entire family."

Yeah, something else. That unspoken thing that even today he couldn't find the courage to bring up. When they'd been six and had been returned to his dad, he and Oz had just been happy to be home. But that happiness had been tarnished by life. Was he really still whining about his childhood? He should suck it up and get over it. But he'd never been able to.

Probably because they never talked about it. And now he *couldn't* talk about it with Grandpa.

"Definitely something else," he said when she turned and put her hand on his forearm.

"Do you want to talk about it?"

No. But yes. He did want to have a big conversation with his dad. To ask why he'd worked so hard to get them back from his mom, mortgaging his house and borrowing money from Grandpa to pay her off. Then, when he got his sons back, why he seemed to regret it.

"It's complicated, and I always feel like a bit of a whiny bitch when I think about it," Wes admitted.

Something about being in this room with Sera made him want to talk. But at the same time, no one wanted to emotionally vomit up their life. Especially to someone as arresting as Sera.

"Stop it. You're not a whiny bitch for saying you deserved

to be treated better in childhood. I used to always qualify my feelings of loneliness and sadness over not having a family by acknowledging I had a roof over my head and didn't go hungry and wasn't molested. But there is more to life than that. And we're entitled to want it."

Sera liked this new side of Wes. She suspected he wasn't going to be open to sharing his emotions for long. Today had been cathartic in a way she hadn't expected, but also draining. She'd never experienced—or maybe she'd never *let* herself truly experience—anything like the grief and love that had flowed through her today.

She felt it for Liberty and Poppy, but the truth was that she never sat in those feelings the way she'd sat in them at the church during the funeral.

And then afterward, walking through Ford's home, expecting to see him in his chair or in the kitchen and instead finding only an empty spot.

Wes was in a worse way than she was when it came to dealing with his emotions. She could sense it in him. The vibes he was giving off weren't comfortable. They seemed all wrapped in thorny vines, she thought. Probably because she'd just finished rereading the Grimm's fairy tales collection Ford had recommended.

Unexpectedly, she felt like crying. Ford wasn't going to recommend anything else to her again.

"Thanks for that. I think…my family doesn't talk about our shit," he said.

"Foster parents want to talk about everything and you get sent to see a counselor who 'is there for you,' but not really,"

Sera said. "I guess that's not fair, but I was never directly helped by rehashing my parents' death or how I felt being moved around from place to place."

"So you're saying I shouldn't talk about it?"

"Dude, you definitely need to talk to someone," she said. There wasn't just one way to solve something; the solution wasn't always easy. But that didn't mean he shouldn't try to talk. "It doesn't have to be me alone."

He stretched his arm behind her, his hand still toying with the strand of hair that hadn't made it into the bun. She was so glad she hadn't noticed it until now. But it was typical of her to feel put together and like she was nailing her look, and then find out her hair was doing its own thing.

"I want it to be you. You didn't have to tell me about your childhood, but you did," he said. "Why?"

She'd always been adept at being what the people in her life needed her to be. Survival instinct maybe, but with Wes it felt different. She was being herself. Maybe that was what he needed. Just Sera.

It made it easier for her to let her feelings develop, if she was doing it for him. If she didn't have to admit she wanted to revel, even for a few moments, in being enough for this man.

"I like you."

The words just came out. She'd been firmly reminding herself that he was only here temporarily, but that didn't matter. She'd cared for people before knowing they were just passing through her life. That was what this would be. A sweet epilogue to her time with Ford. That was all.

Her body's reaction to his closeness told her that *wasn't* all. She wanted him. Wanted to feel him inside her again. Partially because she liked the shared bond it built between them, but also because he was hot and she hadn't stopped thinking about him since that night.

Being the leading lady of her life meant she was allowed to take pleasure and joy wherever she found it. The rest of the six weeks with Wes would be good enough.

"I like you too," he said. "But I suck at relationships."

"Don't tell me what you think. Your actions are different."

She turned so she faced him and felt the tug on the strand of her hair as it was pulled through his fingers. He might think he wasn't good at relationships, but that was because he'd been using some metric known only to him. By her standards, as she'd watched him with his father and brother, he had a good one with them. It wasn't overly warm, but then, not every relationship was.

"You think so?" he asked.

"Do you need me to big you up?" she countered.

"No. I just... I want to tell you about my mom. I wanted to talk about it with my dad, but I knew it would set him off, so I couldn't, but...I can't stop thinking about it, and I know it's because after we were returned to my dad nothing was the same."

"Tell me," she invited, putting her hand on his thigh. She felt the muscle contract. Then he put his hand over hers.

"I'm not sure what happened between my parents, but when Oz and I were four my mom took us, and we didn't see my dad or Grandpa for two years. Then one day she dropped us off—here, and we never saw her again. She sent a single postcard when we were sixteen, but I tore it up and never heard from her again. Dad told us she'd held us hostage until he gave her a lump sum settlement, which almost bankrupted him and Grandpa. But that was all he said."

She turned her hand under his. She wasn't sure how to respond. She was horrified to hear that his mother had used him and his brother as pawns to get what she wanted. But Sera wasn't surprised. She'd heard other stories like that, of parents using their children. And her own parents had died cooking meth in their mobile home. Their life had been hard, and she guessed they hadn't found books to escape into the way she had. Drugs offered another type of escape, and she didn't hold that against them.

She knew not everyone had a loving mom and family the way Liberty and Poppy did. But she wished she and Wes could have that.

"I'm sorry."

He nodded. "Dad had to work a lot when we were growing up and I look like my mom, so I always felt like I was a bad reminder of her."

"I like the way you look," she said. "Even if you resemble her, you are definitely your own person."

"What about you?" he asked after a beat, clearly changing the subject.

"I can't remember what my parents looked like, so I'm not sure if I resemble one of them or not."

"No one gave you any pictures?"

"There weren't any left after the fire," she said.

"God, what a pair we are" was all he said, and then he turned toward her and she leaned into him.

She wanted him. Wanted to feel like they were more than the messiness of their pasts. They weren't perfect at all, and she knew this was probably a grief thing, or at least that was what she was going to call it for now as she shifted on the couch to sit on his lap and twined her arms around his neck.

She pushed her fingers into the blond hair she now knew was from his mom and pulled his head toward hers. His mouth was tentative at first, but then his hands moved to her waist as he deepened the kiss.

Sera had been so sweet, but talking always made him feel too much, so when she kissed him and climbed on his lap his body reacted as it always did around her. He was hard and ready.

The room smelled like old books and the pine from the wood he'd put on the fire. There was the subtle fragrance of lavender, which he knew came from Sera. The woman herself was anything but subtle. In this room that was rooted in so many memories, some good and some bad, most of them tainted with his own anger and grief, it was nice to have her on his lap. Nice to just feel Sera.

She sucked his tongue deeper into her mouth as he found the hem of her dress, pushing his hand underneath until his fingers skimmed along the material of her tights. He had missed this. They had said only one night. But that had been because she'd needed to hear that.

And maybe he had as well. But from the first time he'd kissed her, he'd known one time wasn't going to be enough.

He caressed her thighs and moved his hand higher, cupping her pussy and rubbing the heel of his palm against her. Her skin was soft and supple. He liked touching her. When she got turned on she moved against him like he had just been named the sexiest man in Birch Lake. She widened her legs and he caressed her as she shifted on his lap. He felt her hands in his hair, and she tipped his head back so she could kiss him more intimately.

As his cock hardened, all he could think about was fucking her. Here in this room surrounded by the books they both loved, the fire crackling behind them. The scent of leather and lavender. In his mind he was crude, and he knew the response was a way to balance how soft he'd felt after sharing his past with her.

Her hands moved down his chest, opening the buttons on his shirt; he'd taken his tie off earlier. She rocked back on his lap and reached between them to undo his belt and then the opening of his pants. Her fingers were cold against his and she laughed when he sort of pulled back.

"Cold hands, warm heart," she said.

Then her eyes went wide as if she hadn't meant to imply he was in her heart. He knew he wasn't. They were slowly becoming friends.

He lifted her hands to his mouth and blew on them, and she smiled in a way that made his cock jump. There was a softness in her eyes that hadn't been there before.

Warm heart.

The words echoed in his mind. The emotions he'd striven to keep bottled up threatened. He lifted her off his lap and undid his pants, pulling out his cock.

She reached under her skirt and took off her tights and then undid a few buttons at the top of her dress so the bodice gaped open, away from her body. She climbed back on top of him and the moist warmth of her pussy pushed against his cock. She looked down at him as she slowly lowered herself until he was fully inside her.

Their eyes met and he opened his mouth, wanting to say something, but before he could, she leaned down and bit the lobe of his ear.

"Fuck me."

He was unable to think after that. His cock jumped at her words and he put his hands on her waist as she started to move on him. He lowered his head and used his nose to push the fabric of her dress to the side, until he found her nipple through the lace of her bra. Sucking it deep into his mouth, he thrust up into her using his hands to pull her down on him.

She rode him hard and fast, taking him deep, everything inside him building to a climax. He wanted to make it last, but today he had no control over anything. In this room he felt his best self and his worst self. Books made him the man he was and they'd driven him to be his worst self when he first heard of Sera. But without that jealousy and anger and fear that he'd felt toward Serafina Conte, he'd never have gotten to know this Sera, the woman who set him on fire, who made him hope he could continue to change.

He needed to come, to have that moment where his body was in a null space with this woman draped over him. But he wanted her to come too. He reached between their bodies, flicking his finger over her clit, and heard her breath catch and then tiny moans.

Her pussy tightened around him as she rode him harder and faster, taking him deeper than before. Sensations ran down his spine and his balls felt full and tight and he knew he was going to come; he gently bit her nipple and felt her spasming around his cock as she threw her head back and called his name.

He thrust up into her two more times before he emptied himself into her, and then he kept thrusting as she flexed around his cock, and she rocked against him until she collapsed against his shoulder. He held her in his arms and knew this room would never be the same for him again.

He held her, realizing that once again he hadn't touched her hair. She'd used one of those elasticized hair bands to hold it in place. He pulled at it gently. It came free and the damp strands that had been in the bun started to curl. She had warned him it might feel crunchy but it didn't. It was soft and smooth and he couldn't keep from touching her hair.

He watched them as he held her. He didn't want to let her go. He knew they couldn't stay like this forever, and he hated to admit this even to himself because it was going to make their lives more complicated, but for the first time since he could remember he didn't feel alone.

She opened her eyes and looked up at him. He saw the questions there and wanted to say something reassuring, but all he could think was that he didn't want her to go.

No matter what she'd said earlier, he knew he'd sound needy if he asked her to stay. He was too emotionally unstable.

She gave him a sad smile as she reached up to touch his mouth, running her finger along his bottom lip. "Oh, Wes."

Just then he shook his head and pulled her closer, lowering his head until he could whisper in her ear, "Stay tonight."

He was afraid to hear her response. The change he'd thought he wanted, the change he'd put in place by compromising and letting down his guard, wasn't what he'd expected. That change was pushing him into new territory and he wasn't at all sure he liked it.

But there was no going back.

"Okay."

That was it. Just a small answer. The breath he hadn't realized he'd been holding came out in a long exhalation and he just wrapped his arms around her, holding her and pretending nothing was going to be different even while knowing that everything was.

Twelve

She had no clothes to change into but Wes offered her a pair of his sweats and a Pokémon T-shirt that had been washed so many times the Charizard had started to fade. She left her hair down and didn't let herself worry about it, even though she knew half of it was curly and frizzy while the top was straight. She probably looked like Mia Thermopolis before her makeover.

Wes changed into sweats and a plain black tee as well.

Sera's stomach growled and she flushed. "Sorry about that. I couldn't eat at the reception."

"Me either. I'm starving. Want takeout?"

They ordered from the one place in town that delivered.

"How did you not end up becoming an attorney like your dad and brother?" she asked.

"Uh, well, actually, that's tied to Grandpa," he said as he finished adding wood to the fire in the large stone fireplace.

She'd grabbed some pillows from the couch and together they'd set up a picnic in front of it.

She was drinking merlot since that was the only wine in the house, and Wes opted for one of the beers he'd stocked in the fridge. Their dinner arrived—a chicken burger for her, a veggie burger for him. And a large order of fries to share.

"I want to hear about that, but I'm sort of grossed out by your mayo-and-ketchup combo."

"This is very continental and sophisticated. I'm offended by those plain fries of yours."

She shook her head at his silliness. It was as if when she'd said she'd stay, something had relaxed in him. But at the same time, she could tell he wasn't entirely comfortable with it. There was a lot to unpack when it came to Wes. Something that was making her delve into memories and dreams she'd shunted to the side. Perhaps it wasn't Wes's doing but just Ford's death. Otherwise, it would mean she was getting way too attached to him.

"So you're not an attorney because…"

"Oh yeah, well, it doesn't make me look great, but I figure you know I'm not perfect," he said, taking a big bite of his veggie burger.

She took a sip of her merlot and watched him. Her stomach felt like she'd just drunk seltzer water, all fizzy and excited from looking at him. Trying very hard not to realize that she was living out what was her romantic fantasy with Wes. She started to caution herself and then stopped.

She was the leading lady here. If Wes was what she wanted, she could have him. She wasn't going into anything with half measures. And as afraid as she was to trust anyone, she'd said yes to staying. So she needed to give this everything.

"You're right about that," she said. "But parts of you are all right."

"Glad to hear it," he said with sarcasm.

"You're diverting," she pointed out.

"I am. So when I went to college," he started, and then stopped. "It was like I'd been frozen for all my life. But at college no one knew about my parents' divorce and me being a twin and all that shit. I was just Wes."

In a way, it had been the same for her. But she'd also been scared because she'd truly been on her own for the first time. Tawdra had been nice and offered to let her stay until the state needed her to care for another underage kid. There was no social worker to contact if things went wrong once she left. She'd had to stand on her own.

She'd lost touch with Tawdra after college, but when the whole Amber Rapp thing happened, Tawdra had come up to Birch Lake and told Sera how proud she was of everything she had accomplished.

It had been nice in a way. But Sera had still felt alone. Had Wes felt like that? After having seen the Sitwells in action, she believed her situation might have been better.

"And how did Just Wes handle it?" she asked.

"Drinking, partying, flunking out of classes my dad was paying for," he said. "I was one semester in and then got dropped from most of the classes. Dad stopped paying for everything. I was good in the dorm for the rest of the semester, but Dad was pissed. So I couldn't go home."

He leaned back against the pillows and took a long swig

of his beer. "That sobered me up real quick. I only had one other place to go—here. So I showed up and told Grandpa what happened. He offered to let me stay if I worked for him. He had been repairing books since he'd retired, and that's when he taught me."

"What did he do before he retired?"

"Tax attorney. We're not ones for breaking tradition."

"Except you," she pointed out. "You did, right?"

He turned his head to look at her, and as their eyes met, a thrill went through her. "Yup. Now you know how I avoided being a tax attorney."

"Such an exciting tale."

"I mean, I know when you looked at the nerdy book guy—"

"Hey, book people aren't nerdy."

He shifted over and touched a strand of her hair, tugging on it in a playful way. "Hate to break it to you, but everyone who's not into books thinks we are nerdy."

We. Her heart beat a little bit faster when he linked them together. She reached over and touched his thick hair where it curled at the back of his neck. "That's their problem, not ours."

"Yeah. Fuck off, Oz."

She laughed at the way he said it. "How does Oz think what you do is nerdier than being a tax attorney?"

"I'm not sure. He's seven minutes older than me and sometimes he lets it go to his head."

Wes told her a story of when he and his brother were younger, and she knew then there was nothing nerdy about either of the Sitwell twins. They were intelligent and might not have had enough supervision, but from what she could tell, they'd had to find their own way.

She reached over and squeezed his hand. There was so much about Wes that called to her soul. She had to be careful. It felt like Ford had left a void she was in danger of filling with his hot grandson.

Hot or not, Wes wasn't staying. He was trying to figure out closure with his grandfather and she was helping him. And helping herself too. She'd never even had a long-term boyfriend. She'd never let herself go there, and this time she was considering taking a leap into the unknown.

She thought of the new moon when she'd had sex with him for the first time and all that it meant. A new beginning, even though she'd been focused on the ending of one thing. It was time to let the new moon work its magic on her and in her life. No more holding back.

Wes tossed their trash in the kitchen with Sera following him. "Tell me what you're doing to this book."

He glanced at where she stood near the book he'd taken apart. She was leaning over it, her hair falling forward over her shoulder, seeming much longer and straighter than it did normally. There was something almost magical about his maybe-witch woman tonight. He was having a hard time keeping his mind on anything but her.

Sex was the one place where he could turn his mind off where she was concerned. It was hard to admit, even to himself, but he wasn't sure why he'd asked her to stay. Everything about her made him behave in some way he couldn't explain.

He wasn't logical around her. Loneliness was an easy answer, but he was more used to being alone than with someone.

What was even odder was that it didn't feel weird to have her in the kitchen looking at the book he was fixing. He'd always fixed things when his life was fucked-up. It had made him feel in control when he knew he wasn't.

But Sera made him feel out of control and yet somehow surer of himself.

"Let's see. I've taken the damaged bits apart. There are still some well-bound pages to the volume, so I removed the torn ones. Now I'll see if I can repair them with some matching paper fibers. I have a kit that I usually bring with me on jobs. But since I didn't plan to stay for long, I don't have it here."

"But you brought this leather pouch?" she asked, pointing to his tool kit.

"Yeah. I don't go anywhere without it."

"Nerd," she said with a faint smile.

"Hey, I thought we didn't use that word."

"That was before I saw this," she said with a laugh.

He pulled her into his arms and kissed her while she was laughing, trying to capture the joy of this moment. He had never felt so relaxed around someone. Never felt so free. He'd always felt the burden of his father's and grandfather's sacrifices to get him back from his mom. Always felt as if he couldn't live up to their expectations. Always felt he wasn't doing enough.

But with Sera in his arms, those burdens were gone.

She turned, pulling his capable hands down around her waist, and leaned her head back against his chest. "I know what you were doing with the gold leaf, but the cover... How do you repair that?"

He reached around her to gesture toward the board, which he'd sanded and would be restaining. He talked her through what he was doing, hoping he wasn't boring her, but she kept asking questions, so he moved next to her and started to show her different parts of the process.

"Will you teach me this?" she asked. "I'll give you one book out of Ford's box in exchange."

He looked at her. The books that had been so important when he'd first come back to Birch Lake didn't seem like they were meant for him anymore. "I'll do it, but not for a book. Just because you asked me and I like you."

"I know the books are important—"

"Were," he said. "Today changed that."

She looked solemn. "It did, didn't it? Talking to your dad and brother gave me new insight into Ford and you."

"I bet. Hearing Poppy read your words about Grandpa was an eye-opener for me," he said.

Her words had shown him how closed off he'd become from life. He was a workaholic like his dad and brother. They all focused on doing the best job they could, which was great, except they did it to the exclusion of living. And Grandpa hadn't.

Of course, the old man had been retired and that probably made it easier for him to develop his friendship with Sera. Wes didn't want to wait until he was old to start having a life.

He'd thought he wasn't like his dad, but he'd just picked a different career. Not a different life.

"It was so hard to write. I kept crying. I can't believe he's gone," she said.

He took her hand in his. "Me either. I keep expecting him to stick his head around the corner and tell me a better way to do this."

"Or offer me a cup of tea," she said.

"Do you want one?" he asked.

"No. I have a nice buzz going and I don't want to wreck it. For the first time since you let me know Ford was gone, I'm talking and thinking about him without crying."

He hugged her. He felt the same way. He'd hated the years wasted cutting Grandpa out of his life because he'd been stubborn. Regret was a heavy sweatshirt around him. It was useless to indulge in it, but he couldn't help himself.

What if he'd answered that email Grandpa had sent? What if he'd come back to Birch Lake before Grandpa died? What if he'd met Sera before he'd been an ass to her?

Wes couldn't change any of that. He always had regrets. It seemed he spent as much time looking back as he did making mistakes.

Still, a part of him believed sending that letter hadn't been a mistake. If he'd come to town sooner, maybe she wouldn't have been the woman he'd met that morning in her shop.

"He lived a good long life, and whether he meant it or not, I'm glad I met you through him," Wes said, refilling her wineglass and getting another beer for himself.

"Me too. You are totally not what I was expecting."

"Same."

She was so much better than anything he could have imagined. And that was why she was messing with his head, giving him all the feels. Interfering with that lonely bubble he'd been comfortably living in.

There was a mellow calmness sitting in this house next to Wes. He pulled her more fully into his arms, lifting her up onto the table and moving to stand between her legs. His erection was hard against the inside of her thigh, but his mouth on hers was gentle.

The table behind her was wooden but smooth and it creaked as he hit his hands on its surface next to her hips.

He took his time kissing her, exploring the recesses of her mouth. This kiss touched off small fires inside her. She slipped her hands under the back of his T-shirt, running them up his spine and pulling him closer to her. His hands were everywhere. His fingers found her nipples, circling them as his tongue made small patterns against hers.

She pushed her hands into his pants, feeling the scratch of the fabric as she cupped his butt and shifted around until she felt the ridge of his cock against her center. He tasted like wine and Wes. He lifted her up with one arm and pushed her sweats down her legs. She scissored until the pants were at her ankles and then kicked them off.

Wes pulled her shirt off and tossed it aside before stepping back and taking his off too. She leaned back on her elbows so she could see him better. Running her eyes down his body, taking in the muscles of his shoulders and arms, then moving down to his stomach and his hard-on. He stepped between her thighs and she shivered in anticipation, ready to feel him inside her again.

Him. Not his dick. Not sex just so she'd have an excuse to hold someone and not have to feel. This was all the feels centered around one man. She wanted to find a place to escape and hide to try to protect herself, but looking at him, she couldn't.

He looked at her as if she was the most beautiful woman in the world. Like the heroine of a book that was written about the two of them. All those fantasy heroines she'd ever been while lost in a book paled to what Wes made her feel. No book boyfriend could hold a candle to him in this moment.

But instead, he used his hands to hold her thighs open. She felt the warmth of his breath on her center and then his tongue on her clit. She reached for his head, gliding her fingers into his thick hair.

She rotated her hips, directing his tongue to the spot she wanted. He used one hand to hold himself up as the other moved over her body, fondling her belly button and then inching higher to pinch one of her nipples. She arched her back, everything building to a release inside her.

She shifted and reached lower to take his erection into her hand, stroking him and swiping her finger over the tip. She wanted more. She wanted his dick in her mouth while he was eating her out.

But she couldn't get to it.

"Move around," she said, her breath coming in gasps as his tongue kept flicking against her clit. She was almost coming.

"Not until you come…unless you don't like this," he said, taking the hand that had been pinching her nipple and thrusting his fingers inside her.

"It's working," she gasped out. Her pussy tightened, and as

he thrust in and out she orgasmed around his fingers, tossing her head back on the table in bliss.

He moved over her as she was still pulsating as he thrust into her. He held himself there and she felt her body tightening around him. He brought his mouth down hard on hers, and he tasted of sex and Wes. He kept driving into her, harder and faster, and she wrapped her legs around him, lifting them higher to get him to go deeper.

He put his hand under them, grasping one of her butt cheeks and lifting her at an angle. She held him closer, arching as he ripped his mouth from hers and drove into her with a frantic energy that was different from hers but just as intense, and then she felt him come inside her.

He thrust and she arched against him a few more times until he collapsed against her. He shifted so his head was against her breasts and she wrapped her arms around his shoulders, running her fingers along his back.

He didn't say anything and neither did she. A few minutes later, he stood and lifted her into his arms. "What are you doing?"

She had no memory of anyone ever carrying her anywhere.

"Taking you to my bed. I want to hold your naked body against mine tonight."

She rested her head on his shoulder as he carried her up the stairs and into a room she'd never been in. He turned on the light after he set her on the floor. "You can use the bathroom through there. Want a T-shirt to sleep in?"

"Sure," she said, walking to the bathroom. She couldn't help noticing he had stacks of books on the floor and on the dresser. She saw his open suitcase on a chair near the window.

She washed up, her body still pulsing. The combination of the funeral, wine and sex had left her feeling drained. She wanted to curl up and go to sleep. The scary part was that she wanted to curl up next to Wes. She wanted to sleep with him, cuddled close all night, and then see his face in the morning.

She'd never allowed herself to sleep with a lover. She'd never wanted to get used to sleeping with anything other than a pillow.

People left, she reminded herself.

She looked into the mirror and met her own gaze.

"He's not staying."

As if that was going to make her not go in there and curl next to him tonight. As if knowing he was leaving was doing anything to stop her from caring for him. As if she was going to listen to reason when, for the first time in her life, she didn't want to.

She wasn't making a list of pros and cons where Wes was concerned. One side was going to be way heavier than the other.

But she wanted him. She wanted this thing she couldn't define that was happening between them.

She wasn't about to deny herself.

Leading lady energy…she couldn't find it. This was the one fear and vulnerability reason couldn't really abate. The fear of losing someone at the exact moment you couldn't live without them.

He knocked on the door and she went out into his bedroom. Trying to leave her doubts and fears behind her.

Thirteen

The next few weeks flew by, and Wes found himself enjoying his time in the WiCKed Sisters shop. Merle had invited him to join his D&D group, a game he'd never played. But on a lunch break in the back room of Poppy's tea shop, Merle had explained the basic premise, and honestly, it sounded like something Wes would enjoy.

He talked to Sera as he was creating his character for the game and asked if she'd thought of playing.

"I've never really been much of a joiner," she admitted. She'd been a little bit off today, and once the morning rush had died down from the Amber Rapp–inspired fans, she'd kept to herself as she worked next to him.

"Why not?"

He wanted to know more about her. The few bits of her past she'd shared intrigued him, but really hadn't given him enough information to figure her out. He reminded himself she wasn't an old antiquarian book he'd stumbled upon. But at the same time…figuring her out, seeing the parts where he could help, was what he craved. Fuck. He'd never trusted women, but he was looking for a way to trust her with the feelings he was struggling to deny.

There was a part of him that wanted to let go of the past. He knew his lack of trust in women was rooted in his relationship with his mother and the devastating effect her leaving had had not only on their family but also on his father. Wes didn't want to be vulnerable the way his dad had been.

But Sera, with her gorgeous curly hair, sexy smile and body that made him hot and hard, was difficult to resist.

She shrugged. "Just the way I am."

Her voice was not like her. "What's the matter?"

"Nothing."

"Do you not want to talk, or do you want me to keep asking until you do?"

She shook her head, giving him a slight smile. "Not sure which. This is the day my parents died. January 29. Everything changed in my life on this day."

He put down the signatures he'd been binding, walking over to her. "I'm sorry."

"I know. Everyone is. And I know I sound like a little bitch when I say that. But some years…heck, every year…I can't help thinking about them. I'm just shit to be around when I get like this."

He was shit to be around at times too. "Take the afternoon off. I got this and I can handle the customers."

"I'm a small-business owner. I can't just take the day off," she said.

"You know I run a successful business. I can do this for

you. Just sit in the back if you don't feel safe leaving. Read a book, drink your Earl Grey tea and think of new spells to cast on me."

She stopped pretending to work and turned to fully face him. Her hair was a halo around her head, making her features seem more delicate and her mouth look more fully sensual than usual. Or maybe it was just him recalling how her lips felt against his.

"I haven't cast spells on you. But...are you sure you wouldn't mind?" she asked.

He went over to her and hugged her close. She was so used to being alone that a lot of the time she just retreated into herself when she was faced with a tough situation. But this time he was here.

"I think I established the day we met that I say what's on my mind," he pointed out.

"Yeah, you did. Well, okay then. I'll be in the back if you need me," she said. Then went up on her tiptoes to kiss his cheek. "Thanks. When you're finished with the journals, there are D&D books for creating characters over in the games and role-playing section."

"I totally thought role-playing was something else," he said. "Sexual?"

He nodded.

"I've got a few of those too," she said with a wink. "Maybe we can check those out together sometime, if you want."

He got hard thinking about role-playing with her. Working with her was doing more to lower his barriers than anything else. Just seeing her every day. Watching her react and interact gave him new insight into the man he wanted to be.

There were things about her he wanted to emulate and make part of who he was. But it was difficult. Change was something he'd always fought, and this was no different.

"Maybe I will," he said.

She left a few minutes later and he kept working; the scent of lavender surrounded him. He was starting to associate that smell with a feeling he'd never really allowed himself to acknowledge before. Contentment. Almost like he was tucked away from the real world in her shop.

Surrounded by the lavender and her quick smiles, fast wit and curly hair. She also wasn't shy and cupped his butt when she walked by or kissed the back of his neck. She said she hadn't cast a spell on him, but he was enthralled.

And she reinforced the enchantment with each of those brushing moments in the shop. She had him in a state of constant arousal. She challenged everything he'd always believed about himself when it came to relationships.

He wasn't sure he liked it, but he couldn't resist.

"Where is Sera?" Liberty asked. She wore her red hair straight down her back and had on a pair of wide-leg trousers and a gauzy blouse with stars and moons all over it. She was shuffling a deck of tarot cards.

"In the back," he said.

"Did you do something to upset her?" Liberty asked.

Wes shook his head. He couldn't be angry about the question. Liberty was the mother hen of their threesome and was always ready to defend Sera and Poppy. "It's the anniversary of her parents' death. She just needed some time and wouldn't go home. I suggested she go read."

She looked down her nose at him, then shuffled the cards again. "Want me to read your cards?"

"What does that mean?"

"You seem... *Confused* isn't the right word, but at a cross-roads. And I want to be sure Sera isn't going to get hurt," Liberty said.

He wasn't sure he wanted Liberty to know that much about him or that even he himself wanted to know it.

"Maybe another time."

She walked away, but he knew he would have to figure out why he was here eventually. The reasons he'd thought he was staying had disappeared, replaced by the woman in the back room.

Sera had her legs tucked under her and a cup of Earl Grey steaming gently on the small table. She'd worn leather leggings to work because she'd woken up feeling sexy. She had paired them with a long top made out of tulle and put a sweater-vest over it. She'd always loved contrasting textures and styles.

The day had started out well; it wasn't until she'd turned on the register and the date had popped up on the machine that she'd started spiraling. No matter how much therapy she'd been to or how many times she'd tried to figure out her parents in her own personal journals, she couldn't. She didn't understand how they could have had a child when their own lives were so messed up.

She didn't blame them, as she knew that everyone was dealing with some kind of crap. It all boiled down to certain people handling it better. She was nowhere near ready to have anyone relying on her other than herself. Not a pet, not a man and certainly not a child.

How had her parents not seen that about themselves?

Her father had been an orphan like her, and her mom the only child of much older parents. But Sera didn't know anything else about them. Her dad used to sing to her when he tucked her in, and her mom cut her sandwiches into shapes with a cookie cutter. That was it. That was all she had of them.

And the horrible truth of the way they died.

She couldn't even remember their faces, which most days didn't matter, but today…she'd like to. They were buried in Lake Wales, Florida. A smallish town south of Orlando, in the middle of the state where they'd both grown up. Sera hadn't been back since she'd left for college in Maine.

She didn't want to go back. In Florida she was the product of her parents' deaths and all those foster homes.

Here she was just another girl on her own. No one knew the sordid details or the emotional turmoil. She should have asked Wes for advice on how he kept all his emotions about his family inside. She could use a little of that emotional constipation he did so well.

"Hey, want some company?"

She glanced up to see Liberty in the doorway. She was idly shuffling a deck of tarot cards.

"Maybe."

Liberty smiled. "That means yes. Do you want to talk, or be distracted?"

"I'm not sure?"

"Want me to read your cards?" Liberty asked.

Sera thought about it for a minute. She was of two minds

when it came to tarot. There was pre-Liberty, when she put as much faith in them as she did the Magic 8 Ball, and then post-Liberty, when she learned that the right person could find the words to help her.

"Yes," she said. Shifting her legs out from underneath her, she smiled at the sound of vegan leather rubbing together.

Liberty sat down next to her. "Parents or Wes?"

How like Liberty to realize it wasn't just one thing unsettling her. "Parents first. I want to know why they had me. They were so messed up. I'm not sure your cards will give you the answers to that."

"I've taught you well. Ask something about yourself and them," Liberty said gently.

"Will I ever forgive them?"

For the first time, she allowed herself to say it out loud. She'd always made the most of her circumstances—that was simply the way she was—but in her heart she'd always hated them for leaving her alone. And at six that had been okay, if only because she couldn't fully understand it, but at twenty-six it felt wrong.

Confronting her feelings about her mom and dad scared her. She wanted to just leave them in the past, but there was an emptiness inside her she was tired of feeling. She'd thought she'd dealt with the loss of them, but Ford's death was bringing it all back home.

"I'm going to do a spiritual council spread from my Seasons of the Witch Samhain Oracle deck," Liberty said. "I need you to pick three cards. Let's see what your ancestors have for you."

Sera took the cards from Liberty. She liked the thought of a spiritual council, but had never associated herself as someone with ancestors. Which was ridiculous; she might not know them, but they existed. Someone had come before her.

She shuffled the cards and reached out in her mind to them. She asked for understanding and a way forward. So that every year she wasn't catapulted back to her six-year-old self.

She stopped shuffling and spread the cards out on the table, drawing three cards that spoke to her as she moved her hands over them.

Then she sat back as Liberty flipped them over one by one. Liberty didn't say anything, but it didn't take a genius to realize the answers weren't going to be straightforward. When was tarot ever that linear?

Sera remembered when she'd rushed to Ford's house and had found Wes. Not the books. She'd gone looking for a hidden enemy and had found something more. Maybe she needed to embrace that unknown. Except embracing anything she couldn't figure out for herself had always been next to impossible.

"What I'm getting from this spread is that you need to start accepting your true self and the connections you have," Liberty said.

"Great. So what's that mean? I'm my true self with you and Poppy," she pointed out.

"I wonder…what about Wes? Are you being authentic there?"

"In bed," she said. But sex was easier. Sex didn't mean family to Sera. And family was one thing Wes was stirring a need for in her. And he'd been clear he was leaving in like four weeks.

She wanted to keep her leading lady energy at the forefront of her decisions, making choices for herself. But the old Sera—the people pleaser who couldn't help wanting to make permanent connections from temporary stays—was still there in the background. Still afraid to be herself in case that was the reason she never had anything lasting.

"I think you know what you need to do," Liberty said.

"So answers will come from letting myself fall for him?" Sera asked.

"I'm not sure love comes with letting. I think it's happening whether you want it or not. And the success you'll find there is tied to your past and to Wes."

Sera knew she had two choices: try to face it and see what happened, or fall back on the safety of old behaviors. Take what he had to give and then shove down her emotions when he left.

The leading lady would never go for safety. She needed to be bold like Ford had advised her to be. Take chances. Let someone care about her and believe the emotions could last.

Sera invited him to join her for dinner that night. While they'd been hooking up since Grandpa's funeral, they hadn't really been on a date. They worked together, often had a quickie in the back room, or once in his car when he'd taken her to a book auction and she'd gone down on him after.

But no *dates*.

He'd hesitated asking her out because it would make what they had feel real. Like this temporary thing would have new boundaries and become something unpredictable.

Yeah, he knew Grandpa would tell him to stop sleeping with her until he figured it out. Wes understood that wisdom, though it felt outdated. The more times they hooked up, the harder it was for him to think about leaving in four weeks or so when their agreement was up.

He had never thought about living in Birch Lake. His father had left as soon as Oz and Wes had been returned to him. So Wes's feelings toward the town were split in two. He had his childhood, when he'd resented having to come here. And he had those three college years when he'd learned the crafts and skills that had saved his sanity and given him his career.

Then there was his fight with Grandpa and this new territory with Sera.

"It's just dinner," she said dryly. "I'm not sure why it's taking you so long to answer."

"It's not just dinner to me," he admitted. "If I go…it'd be a date."

She tipped her head to the side, studying him the way she did when he was being an ass. After Liberty had gone into the back room, Sera had seemed to shake the mood she'd been in, and he was glad. He wanted her to be happy.

That was why he was hesitating on the dating thing. He wasn't sure he would make her happy.

Mentally he could tell himself that everyone controlled their own happiness, but he knew he had the power to make her unhappy, and that wasn't something he was prepared to live with.

"Oh, a date. What have we been doing, then?" she asked.

"Hooking up."

"Sure, but what about the talking in the shop and all that? I thought we were becoming friends," she pointed out.

"We are."

"So sex and friendship is one thing, but dinner together is a bridge too far for you?" she asked.

Now he felt like an idiot, because obviously when she framed it that way... He rubbed the back of his neck and tried to find a way to say the things she needed to hear, but the words were all bottled up in the back of his throat and he ended up letting out a groan of frustration.

She started laughing. "God, I keep forgetting you're emotionally constipated. Have dinner with me as a friend if that makes it easier."

Constipated? Maybe. But he didn't like hearing that from her. "I want to date you. But I don't know if I can stay here and I'm not sure you'll want me to, and goddammit, Sera, I refuse to hurt you again."

She put her hands on either side of his face, rubbing her fingers against his cheekbones as she came up on tiptoe and kissed him hard and quick. "I don't want to be hurt or hurt you either. Let's start there."

"Start there?"

"Neither of us, from what I've seen or heard, has successfully figured out adult relationships. But not wanting to hurt each other works for me."

He hugged her close, burying his face in her thick, soft curls, the scent of lavender wrapping around him. That worked. He had been expecting her to want perfection or some sort of surety that was foreign to both of them. This felt right.

"Okay."

She shifted back. "Great. And so you have time to freak out, in two weeks on Valentine's Day I'm going to ask you to come with me to Poppy's annual not-Valentine's party."

"I don't freak out," he said.

"Ha." Her lack of confidence in him was harsh but honest.

"Why are you so sassy now?"

"Don't you like it?"

"You know I do," he pointed out. Her sass teased him out of his own solitude and made it comfortable to be himself with her. To let loose and have a little fun. He liked it. She never let him be overly moody when everyone else in his life had left him to it.

The look on her face was contemplative, and he could tell she was going through a lot. "Everything okay?"

"Liberty read my cards," she said.

"More witchy magic. Did she tell you something about your parents? About us?"

"It doesn't work that way. But, man, I wish it did," she said.

How did it work? He wanted to ask, but he had a feeling even if she explained it he wasn't going to get it. Maybe some things were better left uncertain. So he changed the subject. "Where are we going for dinner?"

"The Bootless Soldier tavern."

Immediately images of the two of them screwing in the dark hallway that led to the bathrooms flooded his mind. She was wearing leggings, so that would make it difficult. "Will you be changing into a skirt?"

She threw her head back and laughed hard and loud, and he couldn't help smiling. On some level he got her, and she got him too. On the surface he could only see the ways he wasn't right for her. That he was too different and too difficult. But this moment gave him hope.

"Perhaps, if you asked me nicely," she said.

He pulled her close again until his semihard cock was nestled against the bottom of her stomach. "Please."

She rubbed herself against him and winked. "Sure."

Fourteen

Sera did go home and change into a taffeta skirt, which she'd bought at Christmastime but never had the confidence to wear out of her house because it made her feel extra. She paired it with a sleek black scoop-neck bodysuit and her favorite chunky boots. She grabbed her bag to head out the door and it felt heavier than usual. She glanced down and realized she was carrying a book from Ford's house.

She'd put it in her bag the day after the funeral. It was one with signatures from Ford, Benjamin, Wes and Oz in the front cover, but it was falling apart from use and disrepair. She wanted to get it fixed for them—Ford had mentioned he'd started looking into restoring it but hadn't made any plans. Now she set it in a basket under a blanket in case Wes came back with her that night. She wanted the restored book to be a surprise.

Grabbing her coat off the hook on the wall, she left her house.

The earlier heavy clouds had given way to snow and she stopped, tipping her head back to let the flakes fall on her face. It didn't matter that she'd been living in Maine for eight years; the Florida girl she'd been still loved the snow. She opened her mouth, catching a snowflake on her tongue.

"I guess you like the snow."

She turned to look at Wes. He'd changed as well. She saw the thick black cable-knit of his turtleneck sweater under the collar of that wool coat he'd been wearing the first day they met.

"I love it. Do you?"

"I guess. Most of the time I don't mind. When I was a kid, I used to pray for it."

"I don't think you're meant to pray for snow," she pointed out as he slipped his hand in hers and they started to walk back toward town.

"Father Tom said we should ask for what we needed," Wes said. "I needed a day off."

She laughed at the way he owned what he wanted. Snow and a day off weren't big asks. She liked that about him. Sera had never thought to take a sick day or ask to stay home growing up. She had skipped class only once and gone to the library because the last *Hunger Games* novel had been released and she'd had it on reserve. Tawdra hadn't been mad when Sera had explained why she'd skipped school, but warned her never to do it again.

She knew Tawdra had her best interests at heart. As a foster kid, Sera had been very aware she had to be good or she'd be moved to a different home.

"I didn't know you were coming to meet me," she said.

"I thought you'd know I would," he said.

"No."

"Why not? We're going on a date, right?" he asked.

She shrugged. "I figured we'd meet there."

"That makes sense, I guess. And that would be fine. I missed you and wanted to see you."

She turned to look at him, trying to ascertain if that was just a line or if there was something more to it. He lifted her arms and looked down at her.

"You're fulfilling a lot of my fantasies with that skirt," he said.

She twirled, and when she was facing him again, she felt silly until she saw the look on his face. She was almost afraid to put it into words. There was something so raw and vulnerable there. It reflected what she felt inside.

"This is my first time wearing it. I'm hoping to make some good memories in it," she said.

"I'll do my best to deliver," Wes said with a wink and a playful smile that went straight to her center. She liked him. Just plain liked him. She wanted to believe she could reach out and take him for herself, but like the lesson she'd learned on that long-ago skip day, she had to be cautious.

When they got to the tavern it was busy, but they found a table toward the center of the room and took a seat. Wes got up to get their drinks and some menus. Sera had taken off her coat and was straightening it on the back of her chair when someone called her name.

She looked up to see Merle waving at her. "Hey, Poppy said to meet here at six, but I guess I'm a bit early."

He pulled out a chair at the table and sat down after putting his coat on the back of it. "I guess Wes is here with you."

"He is," she said. "But I'm not meeting Poppy."

"You're not? Oh, sorry." He started to get up as Wes came back with their drinks.

"Hey," Wes said, putting down a glass of white wine in front of Sera.

"Sorry, dude, I thought this was a WiCKed Sisters dinner." Merle stood up.

"It's cool. Is everyone coming here tonight?" Wes asked, looking over at her.

Sera wasn't sure if he was trying to see if she'd forgotten a meeting, or if she wanted to join her friends. She was still trying to figure that out herself when Liberty breezed over to them and plopped into the chair across from her, still in her coat, snowflakes on her red hair.

"I'm going to need a lot of drinks. I've been doing the books all day and my head is mush."

"Hey, we're not—" Merle started.

"We forgot there was a meeting," Sera said, interrupting Merle. "Wes and I are on a date."

"Do you want us to go?" Liberty asked, looking not at Sera but at Wes.

Sera looked over at him as well, wondering what he wanted. She'd wanted tonight just for the two of them, but her friends were a big part of her life. Would Wes fit in with them? Did it matter since he was leaving in a few weeks? He was taking up too much of her mind and her emotions lately.

He shrugged. "I was planning on asking Sera out again tomorrow night."

"Great. Merle, I'll have a rum and coke," Liberty said.

Merle went to get their drinks. Liberty dumped her coat and ran to the bathroom.

"Sorry about this," Sera started.

"Don't be. If we are going to be dating, I want to know your friends and feel like I'm part of your life," he said.

Those words were both a balm to her soul and a warning. She didn't want Wes to become part of her inner circle until she was sure she could trust him. And she wasn't anywhere near ready to do that yet. She was scared and unsure of what the future between them could be. Grief had brought them together—no two ways about that. But this thing between the two of them felt bigger than just grief or a six-week bargain. Would he like her enough to stay, to uproot his life and move here because Birch Lake was her home?

She was trying to be brave, trying her best to be the leading lady. But it was harder than she had ever anticipated.

Wes hadn't really dated a lot, but even he knew this was unconventional. Her friend group was like her family, and he saw it on full display as he sat across from Poppy, who kept asking him questions about his business and how long he thought he'd be staying in Birch Lake.

However long I feel like was what popped into his head, but he didn't say it.

He liked Sera. He wasn't too sure about her friends at this moment, but he didn't want to come off as a jerk. They were a lot of fun and he respected how they had Sera's back. Because he'd come in like a massive douchebag, they were reserved around him, something that he totally understood. But at the same time, he wished they'd ease up.

"He's here for four more weeks working with me, Poppy—you know that," Sera said. "In fact, Wes and I are going to be interviewing some candidates next week to take a permanent position for when he's gone."

"That's good. So after four weeks you'll be going back to… Where did you say you were from?" Poppy asked.

"I'm based out of Boston," he said. "But I grew up in Portland."

"That's where your dad and brother live, right?" Liberty asked. "Think you could ask Oz a few questions for me?"

He rubbed the back of his neck. "Sure."

This wasn't what he'd expected, and he was ready to get up and bail on this dinner, but then Sera reached under the table and put her hand on his thigh and squeezed. "Wes mentioned he's joining your D&D group. Got room for another person?"

He looked over at Sera and she just winked at him.

"Sure. It's kind of a more-the-merrier session. I'm giving people a chance to try out their characters so they can make tweaks before we start our next campaign," Merle said.

"Great. Liberty was saying not that long ago she wanted to rock—"

"Serafina Conte, don't you dare," Liberty said.

Sera tipped her head to the side and looked at Liberty, then Poppy. "What? Just thought you might want the opportunity. I think I'll try it. Wes showed me the link to the web page where you can create your own character."

The conversation moved to D&D and Wes started to breathe a little easier as her friends debated about spells, classes and character types. When he started to relax, he realized how comfortable the three women were with each other. There were times when they talked over each other, but they seemed to always understand what the others were saying. Merle looked as bemused by it as Wes felt. The other thing he noticed was that whenever Liberty wasn't looking at him, Merle watched her with a thoughtful expression.

Not that Liberty looked away all that often. She needled the other man all the time. Everything he said she had a quip for, and as the night wore on and they all downed more drinks, Merle started to give the sass back to her.

Poppy's reserve loosened, and when Sera went up to get a round for the table, Poppy leaned over. "Sorry I was grilling you earlier."

"That's okay."

"It's not really, but I just don't…"

"Trust me?"

"Not just you… It's your entire gender."

Same. He had never felt so seen as he did when he heard the confusion in Poppy's voice. What did it say about him that he immediately understood her not trusting all men? That he had always felt that way about women?

It hadn't helped that his grandmother had died when Oz and he were eight. They'd never really had a woman's influence growing up. His dad had been gun-shy when it came to dating after his divorce and never brought a woman home. So it had reinforced that Sitwell men might be better off without a woman in their lives. Romance was a risk. Wes glanced over to where Sera stood in line. His heart beat faster. For the first time, he had been tempted into taking a chance.

"I'm trying not to be a dick."

"I think we all are," Liberty said.

"You still have work to do," Merle said.

She punched him on the shoulder. "So do you, nerd."

"Do you have a spell you're going to put on me, witch?"

"Maybe I already have," she said. Her face was totally serious, but there was a spark in her eyes.

Merle raised both eyebrows at her and Poppy started to laugh, then turned back to Wes. "I think Sera really likes you."

"Thanks," he said, not sure how he was meant to respond.

"I just don't want to see her hurt. Ford was one of her few guy friends and I know she's missing him. I'm sure you are too," Poppy said. "You seem nice enough. Just make sure the reasons you're with her are for her. Not some messy granddaddy issues."

"Sure."

"I've offended you," Poppy said.

"You kind of just told me not to be a jackass to your friend…" He held in a chuckle.

Sera set the tray she held on the table, then stepped between him and Poppy. "Leave Wes alone."

He couldn't tell if she was upset that her friends had been butting into her life or not.

"I was trying to help you," Poppy said.

"We are still figuring things out. What's up with you tonight?" Sera asked, sitting down between him and Poppy and putting her arm around her friend.

"Alastair called," she said.

Wes didn't know who Alastair was, but the conversation around the table stopped and everyone turned to Poppy.

For the first time since he'd known the other man, Merle looked almost menacing. "What the fuck did he want?"

"I don't know. I didn't answer the call," she said.

Wes turned to Sera because he had no idea what was going on. Whoever Alastair was, he was a big deal to Poppy.

Sera leaned over, her hand on his thigh again. "He's Poppy's soon-to-be ex-husband."

"Ah," he said. He didn't really know what else to say about that. There was clearly much more to the story, and normally he'd be interested in learning more, but Sera's hand on his leg was making him hard, turning his brain into a puddle. He'd brought her here tonight to have fun.

She was so close he could see the amber flecks in her brown eyes and feel the warmth of her breath on his lips. He parted his mouth slightly and leaned closer, and she licked her lips. He groaned. He didn't care that they were in the middle of the tavern and her friends were talking all around them.

He wanted her more than anything or anyone.

Something indefinable shifted inside him. He was always going to want her. He might not be able to figure out how to trust her, but he was in his comfort zone, and he wasn't going to try to resist her.

Sera took Wes's hand in hers and scooted closer to him. He wrapped his arm around her shoulders. She settled back against him, watching Poppy's face and hearing the anger in Merle's and Liberty's voices. The one time Merle and Liberty would ever agree was when it came to Alastair.

Poppy was being quiet. She had been odd all night. Grilling Wes had been kind of funny because she did it in that polite way she had. And Sera enjoyed watching him squirm. It was so different for Wes not to be confident. Even when he wasn't sure of the outcome, he always came in guns blazing.

She wasn't sure of anything right now. Before Ford's death, she'd had a nice, comfortable, safe life. She'd had the shop where she sold books and handmade journals. She'd had her friends who were kindred spirits. And she'd had her friendship with Ford. It hadn't been exciting or sexy, but it had been hers.

Then everything had changed. Amber Rapp made them famous and the safety she'd found in her shop had been rocked with so many customers and so much demand. Ford had died and his hot asshole grandson had come into her life. And now Poppy's past was coming into focus.

Sera realized she was scared.

The safety she'd thought she'd cultivated was crumbling. She'd been proud of the way she always reminded herself that people left. Thought she was ready for all things to be temporary. But the truth was so much different. She wasn't thinking of anything as temporary since they'd bought the shop in Birch Lake and she'd purchased her house.

She had been building something permanent. And fuck it. She'd been merrily rolling along making journals and acting like this was always going to stay the same.

Then Ford died.

And nothing had been the same since. A part of her was pretty sure it wouldn't be again.

And she wasn't ready. She wasn't ready for this all to go away or change.

Change had always been the one sure thing in her life, but now she wasn't ready for it.

Feeling closed in at the table, she pushed her chair back, pulling away from Wes and going to the bathroom. How many bathrooms had she escaped to over the course of her life? It was the one place in the foster homes where she could lock herself in no matter what. It was the one place she always dashed to when she felt overwhelmed by acceptance from Liberty and Poppy.

And tonight, when her world felt like it was tipping on its axis, it was a place of safety. She made it halfway down the hall before she stopped, hearing Wes following her.

She remembered their flirting earlier, but knew she wasn't ready for sex. She didn't want a hot screw in the hallway of the tavern because sex was starting to mean more than satisfaction with Wes.

Dammit.

"You okay?" he asked.

No. She wasn't okay. In fact, she wasn't sure she ever had been. And the usual facade she liked to pull into place when she felt this way wasn't there. She'd let her guard down with Wes.

Stupid.

She'd started to think of him as more than temporary. Even though she'd mouthed the word *temporary* more times than she could count. In her soul, she was already starting to see him in her future.

"I guess not," he said. "Want to get out of here? Walk in the snow?"

She looked over at him. Maybe it was her own panic that had been rising for the last few minutes, but she noticed the tension around his mouth, the way he held himself.

He had been grilled by Poppy and asked for favors from Liberty. And in his own way, Wes was as much a loner as she was. This had to be strange for him too.

"Yes."

"Great," he said.

He held his hand out to her.

Temporary. She tried to say that in her head loudly, but then shoved that thought away. She took his hand and squeezed— for her subconscious so that bitch knew Sera was going to make her own decisions where Wes was concerned.

They walked back into the tavern and saw her friends still in a heated discussion. Sera would normally stay and be a good friend to Poppy, but she couldn't today. She needed to get out of here. What was meant to be a fun, flirty date with Wes had turned into something more.

And Sera felt like she couldn't breathe.

She reached for her coat and her friends looked over at her. For once she had no idea what to say.

"Sorry, I have an emergency work thing and I need Sera's help. Poppy, I'm sorry about your ex. See everyone tomorrow," Wes said, putting his hand on Sera's back. A shiver of relief went through her at the way Wes had handled this. He had no idea what was going on in her head and in her soul, but he'd done the exact thing she needed. He gave her an out.

He had her back. It wasn't the first time that had happened with someone, but it was the first time with Wes.

It could be the last time, her subconscious warned.

And Sera just ignored that. Instead, she put her coat on and they stepped out into the darkening night sky, under the glow of the lamp where he'd kissed her for the first time. She looked up at him, the snow falling lightly around them, and knew that no matter how many times she tried to tell herself she was ready, prepared for him to leave, she wasn't.

She wanted to see a future with him.

Fifteen

Leaving the tavern with Sera, kissing her under the streetlamp, Wes told himself he was being the man she needed him to be. But he couldn't help feeling like he was playing a part. He had been since he'd come to Birch Lake. He kept trying to tell himself he was changing, but the truth was he didn't want to.

He wanted something he wasn't going to find in Sera's arms. He'd never allowed himself to admit before that as contented as he was with his life, he was lonely. With Sera, he'd found someone who looked at the world in a similar way. He wanted that. He wanted to just let down his guard and trust her.

Something he could no longer deny after seeing her and her friends. He had no real close friendships other than Oz. Hazel, his assistant, was probably the only other person he talked to regularly, and they weren't friends. Sera's group felt like family. Wes had never really wanted a family of his own because he thought they were all like the Sitwells.

Sera, who'd grown up drifting through the foster-care system, had stronger and more meaningful bonds than he did. He was tempted by that as much as he was by Sera herself. She was something different, and though he'd always been arrogant and assumed he could figure out anyone and anything, this time he couldn't.

She broke the kiss and it seemed to him almost as if she were having a crisis too. His dad always said only one person could freak out at a time. That had been his one parenting rule when he and Oz were growing up, and it was the one thing Wes had taken into his adult life.

She was freaking out, so that meant Wes had to get his shit together.

"What's going on?" he asked. She leaned into him, putting her face in the center of his chest and muttering words he really couldn't hear.

But the tone sounded frustrated.

"I didn't catch that. It's okay if I wasn't meant to," he added. He kind of liked her having a crisis because it left no room for him to freak out on his own.

She lifted her head and shook it. "I'm a crap friend. Poppy could really use me right now, but I can't be there for her."

"That doesn't make you a crap friend," he said, linking their fingers together and starting to walk back up the street toward WiCKed Sisters and her home.

"It doesn't? It feels like it."

Their date had turned into something else. To be fair, he certainly had seen a different side to Sera tonight. It was no less beautiful than the other parts of her. She was so raw and honest—and that attracted him. She didn't hide from her emotions; he envied that.

He tipped his head back, realizing he was a little bit buzzed. Also, as always when he was close to her, he was turned on. But she probably didn't want to have sex when she was feeling the way she was.

"I don't know the history between all of you, but I do know Poppy didn't seem resentful you left. Do you want to talk about why we needed to leave?"

She shook her head.

"Do you want to talk about anything?"

She stopped walking and looked up at him. "I don't know how to say this and not sound like an idiot."

He put his hands on either side of her face and stared down into those big brown eyes of hers. "You could never."

"Trust me, I can," she said wryly. Then she took a deep breath and blinked a few times. "I started to feel like I belonged in that group with you by my side."

He dropped his hands. Not what he was expecting. They'd said temporary. He wasn't sure he could trust her; he was trying, but a part of him wasn't sure he believed he ever could.

"I know. This was six weeks—nothing more. And we've wound down almost half of that," she said as she turned from him and started walking up the street without him.

He was tempted to let her go. That he stood there and watched her really pissed him off. He hated this part of himself that detached from emotion and shut down.

But he saw that pink skirt and her curly hair all around her head and knew he couldn't let her leave.

Not like this.

He ran to catch up. He caught her around her waist and pulled her back against his front because some things were easier to say when they weren't face-to-face. "I felt that too."

The words were sort of ripped from deep inside him and sounded like a hoarse whisper, guttural. Tonight in the tavern, drinking and having fun and taking part in uncomfortable conversations for the first time, Wes felt like he had people who he... He couldn't make himself even think it.

"We suck at this, don't we?" she said, putting her hands over his where they rested around her waist.

We.

Just that one word made the tension in his stomach and back relax until he could almost breathe again. She'd made them a team.

"We do."

"So I guess we're going to just keep doing what we have been," she said.

"I guess so. But maybe... Do you want to try staying the night together again?" he suggested. She'd only stayed the night that one time after the funeral. He understood now that maybe it was because they'd both let their guard down thanks to his grandpa.

But he needed her for more than just sex, and he was beginning to think she needed him too. Which made him feel better.

He wanted this thing between them to grow no matter how much the unknown scared him. No matter that he had no idea how to navigate this thing with Sera. No matter how much he wasn't sure if he would ever trust her enough to stay.

★ ★ ★

Wes was asking for more than she had ever given anyone else. Since she'd left the foster-care system, having her own space and her own home had been important to her. And he wanted them to start staying the night together. She couldn't just be like, *Yeah, but only at yours.* That wasn't fair to him or to her.

If she was going to go into the unknown space where her feelings were leading her, she needed to really go there.

"I guess."

They'd gotten up the main road and had crossed over in front of WiCKed Sisters. Tomorrow she was going to have to start changing out the window for Valentine's Day. She had put Wes to work making some love journals and self-love journals. Some people wanted a partner—others didn't.

She wanted a partner. When had that happened? She'd always prided herself on her resilience and ability to just be alone. It had never bothered her. Having her chosen family around her had always been enough. She also never wanted to risk herself by making a mistake like her parents had and hurting those she cared for.

But thinking about Wes staying the night… If it became a habit, would she miss him when he was gone?

Then she shook her head, thinking that making plans had never protected her from being hurt before. Something Ford had said drifted through her mind. *Love is never wasted.*

He'd been referring to his wife when Sera had mentioned it must have been hard to continue living without her. Ford had admitted it was still hard, but he had all those loving memories. They had been a life raft after his wife had died and his son and grandsons had gone away.

Could Sera find memories with Wes? The kind that would be enough to sustain her if they couldn't find a way to last past the time they'd given each other?

"If you're not ready for me to stay, that's cool," he said.

If there was ever a man who didn't sound cool with something in that moment, it was Wes. "You're not cool."

"No. I'm not. I don't understand the emotions that you stir up in me and I'm trying to remember the one good thing my dad said to me growing up—that only one person can freak out at a time and let you have it—but this isn't my comfort zone."

He was so blunt and honest that it was both warming and a little bit hurtful. He didn't want to care for her. Even though she was struggling with similar insecurities, it stung.

"Yeah, I get it," she said.

"I know, which is what makes me feel like a big d-bag. God, it would have been so much easier if you'd just been some floozy trying to swindle Grandpa."

She almost laughed at the way he said it. Watching him try to grapple with feelings that mirrored her own made her feel safer in a way. "Sorry about that."

"I'm not. I like you, Sera. There, I said it. I mean, you had to have guessed."

For a minute she closed her eyes and just let that affection, and the warmth and joy it brought to her, live in her mind and body. He *liked* her. For a moment something she'd never been close to was within her reach.

Wes liked her, and she liked him too.

The complications of that started swarming in her head, circling around, and she shoved them aside, slipping her arm around his waist, starting them toward her house. "I wasn't sure. It is icy tonight, and you might not want to take the risk of driving back to your place."

She felt him relax against her.

"There is that."

When they got to her house, she realized this moment was the one that would change everything. She had no idea if having Wes stay the night would be something she enjoyed, or if she'd never want him to do it again.

She wasn't confident at all in her ability to make this attraction and affection into anything more than an affair. Ford might have been a man who enjoyed decades of loving memories while being alone, but Sera wasn't made of the same stuff.

She'd been born into a life where the only way she survived was by being on her own. Her friendship with Liberty and Poppy had given her a sisterhood and found family, but they each lived alone. No one had stayed in her space since she'd left Tawdra's and the bedroom she'd shared with Milly.

Sera chewed her lower lip between her teeth as she unlocked the door, fumbling the key and dropping it.

Wes bent down, picking it up and unlocking the door for her. "Let's just try it tonight."

He had done it again. The way he had in the tavern, giving her a nice, safe out. This didn't feel like leading lady energy to her. It didn't feel like she was putting herself first at all. It felt like she was once again taking the safe path and missing the spectacle.

She wanted more than the safe path with Wes.

"I want this, Wes. I might not know how it's going to turn out. But tonight, I did some soul-searching, and as much as I'm scared to ever plan for the future, I'm also excited by what it can bring."

"Me too," he said.

She led him into her house and he closed the door behind them. Her house, as always, felt warm and welcoming. She drew her strength from this space she'd curated to reflect the woman she was.

Not the woman she always let the world see, but the true Sera. And that was why bringing Wes to this space felt like a leap into the unknown. But there was no going back. He had already left a mark on her home and on her. She hadn't let herself see it until tonight when he'd asked to stay.

She was making it seem as if not letting him sleep with her in her bed was going to preserve some barrier between them. But that barrier had disappeared the night of Ford's funeral, and no matter how much she mentally tried to wedge it back between them, it wasn't going to happen.

This time he wanted to take her in her bed. Not like they were at the tavern; he wanted sex to feel like it meant something. But frankly, being in the hallway brought him back to their first night together. He remembered the feel of her hot pussy on his cock, and he couldn't think about anything other than getting back inside her.

She'd taken her coat off and her boots and he watched her standing there. He saw in her eyes that hint of vulnerability that made him want to protect her. To wrap her in his arms and make promises he wasn't sure he knew how to keep.

Things like he'd keep her safe and keep anyone from hurting her again.

Even himself.

But he still felt like an edgy bastard deep down, and pro-
tecting Sera wasn't going to be easy since he still felt so out
of control.

Fuck.

She tipped her head to the side, watching him for a moment before she held her hand out to him. He still wore his
coat and boots, and there was no elegant way to take them
off, so he just did it in a frantic moment. When she reached
for him with that look on her face, he knew she wanted him.
And that made it impossible for him to think of anything but
getting her completely naked. Something he hadn't done yet.
He'd settled for clothing shoved out of the way so he could
get inside her as fast as he could. Like he had to capture the
moment immediately or he'd miss it completely.

And this time...with the woman who was letting him stay
the night. Not because they were both grieving and had no
one else to cling to, but because they'd both decided to.

"Wes?"

"Sorry. I'm trying not to be a total horndog and just fall
on you. I want this time to be romantic..."

"In what way?" she asked.

"I don't know. Like in romantic movies? But truthfully,
they always cut away from the couple, and the only people
I've seen doing it are in porn...which I'm not sure counts as
romance."

She caught his hand and kissed his knuckles. "I don't know.
I just know when you touch me, I like it and I can't think of

anything else but how good you feel. And right now…that's all I need from you."

She put his hand on her chest where the scoop neck of her top left her skin bare. It was cold to his touch as he moved his hand over her skin. The moment he touched her he'd stopped thinking, but his feelings weren't as easy to control. When he touched her, he was very aware that this was Sera.

Not some chick he'd picked up in a bar.

Sera.

He kissed her neck, her familiar scent of lavender setting him ablaze, then lifted his head to watch as he drew his finger along the line of her top. Her skin was soft to his touch. She arched her back, thrusting her breasts forward toward him. For a brief moment it was hard to believe he was here with this woman. That he was going to stay the night. Not because of the ice or because he was too drunk to drive home. But because she'd asked him to.

God, he was such an emotional wimp. All he could think about was making this night one they both would always remember. The first night he'd stayed at hers.

He continued to take his time, touching only her exposed chest. She had such soft skin and it was radiant, pale.

He slowly pushed the shoulder of her top down on one arm, letting the gaping fabric expose more of her flesh. He pushed his hand inside and down farther until he could cup her breast. Her nipple was hard, pushing into the center of his palm. He circled his palm over it, making it harder and eliciting a moan.

His erection was hard, straining against his jeans, so he lowered his zipper, giving his hard-on room. He put his hand on her waist and ran his fingers around until he found the fastening at the back and lowered the zipper until her skirt fell to her feet.

He hadn't realized she had on a bodysuit until that moment. She put one hand on her hip and tossed her long curly hair as she watched him. He stepped closer, not sure he could think of anything but getting her naked, but the way she looked tonight was an image he'd always treasure. Reaching between their legs, he cupped her pussy. The fabric of the crotch was warm and moist, and he pushed it aside, touching her intimately. He shifted, reaching up to tug the bodysuit lower until her breast was exposed.

She put her hands on his head and pushed his mouth toward her breast. Then he felt one of her hands moving down, grazing his cock. She wrapped her fingers around his shaft and moved up and down, rubbing her finger against the tip each time she got to the top. She made no apologies about wanting him and needing him. Her confidence stirred something deep and primal inside him.

He sucked her nipple into his mouth and let the sensation linger on his tongue. Her hand was stroking him into sexual oblivion where nothing existed except the two of them. The scent of her body as it got wetter and ready for him turned him on like nothing else ever had.

She was stroking him faster and harder, and he fondled her clit the way he knew she liked it. Her hips rocked against his hand; he thrust two fingers into her pussy and she let out a long, low moan. Using the tip of his cock, he rubbed it against her clit as her walls tightened around his fingers. Bringing her pleasure and watching her writhe against him was addictive. He needed it. He needed *her*—and not just in his arms like this. He struggled to put the feeling into perspective. But right now, with her coming, he pushed that worry aside.

He sucked harder on her nipple, pushing his fingers up as the sensation of her clit against the tip of his cock made him start to come at the same moment she called out his name and he felt her orgasm against his hand. He shifted his hips against her, coming until he was empty. Then he wrapped his arms around her. Not saying a word. Ready to stay for as long as she let him.

Sixteen

Valentine's Day had never really been her sort of holiday. But since she'd met Liberty and Poppy, Sera found herself looking forward to it each year. They'd turned the holiday on its head and made it about all love, not romantic love. This year the party was going to be hosted in WiCKed Sisters and they'd opened it to anyone who wanted to attend.

They'd charged a nominal fee to pay for food and drinks and had created little party favors that included a crystal Liberty had charged at the last full moon with love vibes, Poppy's No Time for Love tea, which she'd bagged herself, and a small 4x4-sized journal with a heart cut out where you could write a love intention.

Sera had hired Greer to help out with the binding and Wes had been teaching them how to make the simple journals. Mostly Greer had started out making the one twelve-page signature for each journal. Sera made the covers and Wes handled the binding. Wes thought Greer would be ready to

start binding soon and they seemed enthusiastic about learning the bookmaking skill.

Greer was tall with a thick silky-looking beard and mus-
tache and hair Sera was envious of. It hung around their shoulders in long, smooth waves. Their eye makeup was always
on point and they dressed as the mood struck them. One day
they were in a long sarong with a thick sweater, the next all
flannel, giving them lumberjack vibes. Sera was happy with
them at work.

And not just because of their help with the journals, which
she was finally getting ahead on. But also because they were
a nice presence between her and Wes. Wes had been sleeping
over at hers and she at his place for the last ten days. Having
a new coworker and friend had cut through the tension and
kept her from overthinking so much, allowing her to relax
and enjoy the passing days.

Sera still freaked out a little bit if she let herself think too
much about dating Wes. So she was trying to go with the
flow. Except that was contrary to everything she was. So
while she was having fun and leaning into being more impulsive, her journal was full of doubts and fears.

She loved sleeping in Wes's arms. He always pulled her close
and she found comfort in both the warmth of his body pressed
against hers and the soft, low sound of his occasional snores.

"Girl, stop staring at him," Liberty said, coming up behind her.

"I can't figure him out," Sera said.

"The cards I drew for you said to resolve the past. Have
you?"

"No." She'd been ignoring that part. She'd just indulged

in having her lover in her life almost 24/7 and let that sensuality take over.

"Do it," Liberty said. "I'm starting to like you two together."

"Me too," Sera whispered and then turned her head into Liberty's shoulder. "What am I going to do? I want to make future plans, but I'm not sure I'd trust them. What if he still wants to leave? Or wants me to follow him?"

Liberty put her hand under Sera's chin, lifting it. "Trust yourself. And figure out what you haven't resolved in your past."

"Wow, is that all. I didn't realize it would be so easy," she said sarcastically.

Liberty laughed and shook her head. "Nothing worth having is easy."

"I hate that platitude."

"It's not a platitude—it's the truth," Liberty pointed out, moving back toward her side of the shop, where she had set up some tarot card reading stations.

Sera walked over to Wes and Greer, who were chatting as she joined them. "I think we're almost ready."

"Definitely," Greer said. "I invited my boyfriend to join us. His train was delayed, but he should be getting in soon."

"Can't wait to meet Riley," Sera said. Greer asked to go and meet him at the station, and she affirmed she'd see them both later.

Wes finished the journal he was binding, setting it aside and turning to rest his back against the workbench. He drew her to him with his hands firmly on her hips. She'd worn a pair of red vegan leather leggings and a frothy white organza blouse that had red hearts all over it. She'd tried to tame her curls into a messy bun, but curls kept escaping at the back, which didn't bother her the way it used to because Wes was always touching them.

Wes wore his habitual faded jeans that fit him in all the right ways and a red sweater he'd explained was his Christmas and Valentine's one.

"Oz is coming," Wes said as he settled her between his legs.

"He is?"

"You sound as shocked as I was. Yeah, I invited him thinking he'd turn me down, but he's on his way. He's staying at Grandpa's tonight with us."

"Are you sure you want me there?" she asked.

"Yeah, I do. If you don't want to, it's okay," he said.

They had been inching toward a relationship, even though neither of them really knew what that should look like. But letting his brother know they were a couple... How was that different from her friends knowing? This was another big step for them.

Or was she making it into something it wasn't?

"I can almost hear the gears in your mind clicking as you calculate the pros and cons," he said.

She lightly punched him on the shoulder. He was getting to know her so well. Not even things she'd told him, just habits he'd observed. "Stop it. So do you think Oz is here to find love or get over a broken heart?"

"I'm not sure my brother has a heart," he said.

"Do you?" The words slipped out and she immediately wanted to call them back.

But Wes simply lifted her hand and pushed it under his sweater until it rested over his heart. "You tell me."

She let out a breath she hadn't realized she'd been holding and leaned into him, tipping her head back so their eyes met. She had to stop waiting for him to leave. She had to stop doubting he was going to stay. She had to start believing she was worthy of love.

Easier said than done.

Wes loved the way Sera looked in her red leggings and watched her as she moved through the crowd at the party. Oz was parking and would be joining them in a few minutes. Sleeping over had added a new dimension to their relationship and Wes didn't regret it. The more time he spent with Sera, the more time he wanted to spend with her.

She might be the first woman in his life he felt that way toward. He had invited Oz on a whim but also because Wes knew while he was alone in Birch Lake it was easy to pretend that he was making strides toward trusting Sera.

But he'd seen through that lie like it was a piece of old, worn paper. It was easy to trust her when he wasn't in his real world. If things went well tonight, he was going to invite her to go with him to New York next week for a big book auction that he attended twice a year.

If things went well… He didn't know how they wouldn't, but it was hard for him to silence the anxieties in his head.

"Wes," Oz called as he walked into the shop and made his way through the crowds.

Sera, Poppy and Liberty were circulating, so Wes was manning the register in Sera's part of the shop. Just keeping an eye on the place and answering questions. He'd sold a good amount of the Charm, Curse, Confluence game after the ladies had led everyone in a round.

He one-arm hugged his brother. "Good to see you. How was the traffic on the way over?"

"Not bad," Oz said. "Dad sends his regards. I think the old man had a date tonight."

"No way."

"Yeah. Not sure with who, because he just said he had to leave early and told me I could as well."

"I can't believe that."

Oz laughed. "Maybe he's finally mellowing."

"Maybe. I think Grandpa's death definitely affected him more than he let on. He actually talked to us in the car, so why wouldn't he be going on a date?"

"Yeah. So...things are getting serious between you and Sera?" Oz asked.

"Why do you ask?"

"Because you texted me declaring that she's staying over and to be cool about it." His brother arched one eyebrow at him.

"Yeah, things are going good. I'm not sure where they're going, but I just don't want anything to fuck it up."

"I won't kill your vibe with her," Oz said, picking up one of the journals on the counter. "Is this what you've been doing?"

"I'm strictly the assembly line for the journals. They're all Sera's ideas," he said.

"What's this one do?"

"Brings you what you desire most," Wes said. He'd purchased one earlier and he wasn't sure he'd use it, but he was tempted. He wanted Sera to be in his life. He might not be able to say the words to her or even express them in his actions at times, but his subconscious was making him keenly aware he didn't want to leave Sera or Birch Lake.

"And people believe that?"

"Oz, there is power in writing things down," he said. "Sera and her friends focused their energy and opened this shop. Then Amber Rapp did the same. So, yeah, I think it works."

Wes had been skeptical when he'd first heard Sera talk about it, but he had started to believe. There was magic—not the fictional witchy stuff that everyone flocked here for, but real mystic energy in Sera's journals, in speaking things into existence. He didn't deny it.

"I'll take one," Oz said, pulling out his wallet. "I've had my eye on the new PlayStation but can't get on the mailing list to get one. Maybe this will help."

Wes wasn't sure Oz believed the journal would work for something so material, but he sold one to his brother anyway. "Poppy's got some special tea for the night and Liberty charged some crystals if you're interested."

"I'm not turning new age or anything. Just supporting my brother," he said.

Greer came over with their boyfriend, Riley, and made the introductions before offering to watch the shop so Wes and Oz could mingle. He took Greer up on the offer and moved through the throngs of people toward Sera.

Merle stood next to her and said something Wes couldn't hear, and Sera threw her head back and laughed. A jolt of desire went through him as he watched the joy on her face and let her laughter wash over him like the scent of her lavender perfume. It was something that affected him deeply.

He stood there for a minute as realization started to dawn. He wasn't taking a chance and easing his way toward caring for her. He already did care. Not the way he'd been defining it, but maybe in a bigger way. In a way that involved the *L* word.

Damn.

He turned away for a minute because he knew that if Sera saw his face, she'd guess something had changed in him. He doubted she'd figure out what he was just now starting to realize. That no matter how much he told himself he was moving slowly, he hadn't been. He hadn't taken the precautions that he'd wanted to. But maybe that was why he'd stayed all along.

He'd long since given up the illusion that it was for the books or anything Grandpa had left her. He was here for Sera. He might tell himself other things and even tell Oz or Sera something else. But the truth was all centered on her.

"Dude, you okay?" Oz asked.

"Yeah. She gets to me," Wes remarked. Letting his brother think it was merely a physical reaction that had him slowing down. Knowing how much he cared for her had made his arms feel empty. He just liked touching her. He always did. But now he knew that it was because she was a fire in his veins. She was a passion he'd never be able to walk away from.

The party wound down and Sera was sitting on Wes's lap around a long table with Oz, Merle, Poppy and Liberty. Oz and Poppy had been talking quietly for a long time. Liberty was annoying Merle as she liked to do, asking him pointed sexual questions about his D&D quests. He'd told her a number of times that wasn't the aim of the game. But she liked to try to rattle him.

Actually, Merle was always so calm and even-keeled that it was fun for everyone to watch him playfully lose his cool.

"Hey. I know you said you don't do gifts on V-day, but I have something for you."

He was more relaxed than she'd ever seen him before, and for the first time since they'd met, she wasn't tense either. The worry that had been continuously dogging her since he'd asked if they could start spending nights together had finally eased.

"What is it?"

"Come with me and I'll show you," he said, lifting her off his lap and standing.

"If it's your cock, I've seen it before," she said.

"Oh, I'll be giving you that later, but I have something else for you now," he said, kissing her hard and quick.

"Are you two leaving?"

"Not yet," Wes said. "Just wanted to show Sera something in her back room."

"If they were on a compaign with us, I'd guess they were going to have sex," Liberty said pointedly at Merle.

"We'd have to roll to be sure," Merle said wryly. "But I'd be tempted to agree."

"So you agree I'm right," Liberty teased.

Wes took Sera and led her away from the group, so she didn't hear Merle's response. Those two were always dancing around each other, and at first Sera hadn't been sure she wanted Liberty and Merle to hook up because... Well, a man would ruin the balance they'd always had, but now she wasn't sure. Wes was making her look at everything in a different way.

Not unlike the way Ford had.

Wes stopped her in the doorway that led to the back room. "I have had several erotic fantasies about making love on that overstuffed couch during the workday. But it would feel cliché now that we know they're expecting us to."

"Maybe. Are you saying your gift is in your pants?"

He shook his head, smiling at her, and her heart tightened. She loved his smile. It didn't happen all that often, and when it did, he looked so open and so caring. She could almost forget that life had her bumping along between so many people and places.

"Later. Here you go," he said, turning and grabbing a flat package wrapped in craft paper with the words *For Sera* written on it.

She took it. Felt that sting of tears in her eyes. Wes was the second man to give her a gift and the first lover to do so. She hoped she wasn't being silly by letting that make her care more deeply for him.

But she couldn't stop it.

She held the package in her hands until he cleared his throat.

"Are you going to open it?"

She nodded, not sure she trusted her voice not to crack. She slid her finger between the paper in the back, loosening the tape until she pulled the wrapping off and tossed it on the bench behind him. She looked down.

The red-and-gold art deco cover of *Mansfield Park* by Jane

Austen. She carefully opened it, gasping when she saw it was a first printing from Thompson, one of her favorite historic publishers. It had been meticulously restored.

She'd mentioned a few weeks ago that she'd been trying to collect first editions of all of Jane Austen's books.

She pictured Wes at the kitchen table in Ford's old house, working the cover, repairing the gold leaf, which would have been patchy by this time. His long fingers carefully using the tweezers to pick up the leaf and then patiently place it on the worn-out patches.

She loved the way his lips parted when he leaned over to work on something that required a delicate touch.

This was something she hadn't expected. "Thank you."

She threw herself into his arms and hugged him tightly. He couldn't know how much this meant to her.

"I was working on it before I came here...before Grandpa's death. I had someone offer to buy it, but I held on to it instead," he said, putting his finger under her chin and tipping her head back. He rested his forehead against hers. "Maybe something was telling me to save it for you."

"Maybe," she said. She wanted to believe that. To believe, like Liberty did, that something larger was at work in the universe directing them to where they needed to be.

She'd seen it with Ford and her friendship with him. So why was she so afraid to trust the signs with Wes?

Fear and nothing else kept her from allowing herself to believe that the universe was pushing them together. Because there were too many signs around her that Wes was right for her and for her life.

Except she'd never believed there was one person meant

for her. She'd seen enough heartbreak in her life to know the chances of this working out were thin.

But she wanted it to. So badly.

"Thank you so much," she said.

"You're very welcome," he said. "Was I out of line with what I said?"

Every time she started to feel safe and secure in their relationship, he seemed to push her the tiniest bit further.

The leading lady in her, the one who'd boldly been wearing all the clothes she'd previously kept tucked away in her closet. The one who took chances and was embracing the life she'd always wanted but was afraid was out of reach. That woman knew there was only one answer she could give him.

No more hedging.

No more just writing about the things she wanted in her life.

No more doubting the fact that she deserved Wes.

"No. You weren't. You surprised me, Wes. And I am liking every second of it."

Seventeen

Wes only had two weeks left of his contracted time with Sera, and now that Greer had taken over making the signatures, Wes had taken on more of the cover making, which left her time to actually design covers with the scraps of paper she collected. He loved watching her work in the afternoons after the morning rush passed.

After Valentine's Day it seemed everything was moving forward too fast. Never in his life had he wanted the days to stretch out. He got a text from his assistant, Hazel, alerting him to a book sale in a nearby town that afternoon. She'd found it on one of her online groups.

"Hey," he called over to Sera.

"Hey," she said back in that sexy way of hers.

Or maybe he just found everything about her sexy.

"Can you take the afternoon off? There's an estate sale about an hour or so from here with a huge book collection. Might be fun to go together," he said.

She chewed her lower lip and then nodded. "Let me check with everyone. You can totally go regardless."

Which was nice of her to offer since she was technically his boss, but he wanted to go with her. Greer had stopped working, not even pretending they weren't listening to the conversation.

"I can handle the shop and the journals we have left to make today," they said. "I'm the master of the Coptic stitch now."

Wes laughed at the way Greer mimed stitching.

"You definitely have a talent for binding stitches," Wes agreed.

"Great. Let me go and talk to Poppy and Liberty," Sera said.

She moved away and Wes watched her go, admiring the swish of her hips in faded jeans. He loved how eclectic her clothing was and how she never wore the same thing twice. The same piece, yes, but she always managed to make it into a different vibe. Maybe the vibes matched her mood, or maybe it was delightfully random.

"Dude, you're staring."

"Can't help it," he said. He'd given up pretending he and Sera weren't a couple while they were in the shop. Everyone had already figured it out after Valentine's Day. "If you get ahead on the binding, use your time to make more signatures."

"Sure thing, boss," Greer said. Wes had been in charge of training and supervising Greer when they'd first started.

They had a real talent for binding, but also a love of books almost as obsessive as himself and Sera. Greer had mentioned wanting to apprentice under Wes to learn book repair. Which Wes was considering...if he stayed.

He had already found a shop just two down from WiCKed Sisters available to rent starting in March. It would make a nice space for him if he decided to set up shop in town. The books he dealt in were different from Sera's, so he wouldn't be directly competing with her.

He'd given this a lot of thought. Even had his accountant run the numbers for him. He could make a go of the shop here. It wouldn't be a hardship, and he'd be closer to Sera.

All pluses.

But it was in Birch Lake. He wasn't sure he was ever going to get the closure he'd once wanted where Grandpa was concerned. He did understand the older man more than he ever had before.

He'd learned more from him through Sera, those stories and the techniques she had gained from Grandpa. His feelings toward the place had changed.

There was something enchanting about Sera that Grandpa would have been drawn to. She was shy and standoffish with most people until she knew them. Wes had skipped the shy part by making her mad, but having come to know her now, he realized her reaction had been driven by hurt.

He'd hurt her, and though he'd apologized, he sometimes wondered if she would ever fully trust him.

He hoped she would.

But hope… His dad said to put hope in one hand and shit in the other and see what you had more of.

Crude, but it did the job. There was no way he could ignore the fact that if he moved here, it would be for her.

He wasn't going to pretend there was anything else drawing

him to Birch Lake. Prior to Sera, he had bittersweet memories of the boy-man he'd been. And that was it.

He had to figure out if he could live this close to Sera if they broke up. Because the other thing he'd come to understand about her was Sera expected everything to end and everyone to leave.

There were times when she struggled to believe Poppy and Liberty would be there. She told him she knew it was silly, but the future just always seemed very much a single-rider line to a roller coaster. And suddenly she had friends next to her.

He'd always had Oz, but that was it. Now he was seeing double and enjoying the ride. Like today, inviting her to this estate sale.

He knew she'd love going through boxes and stacks of books. Finding some things for herself and her store. And he wanted to do that by her side.

Books, which were usually a solitary thing. A lone read was suddenly becoming a communal activity when it came to Sera.

"Okay. The girls will help if you hit any snags, Greer. Are you sure you'll be okay?"

"You know it. Have fun, you two!"

They got their coats and Wes led the way to his Range Rover. He was glad he'd retrieved it from Portland because they'd need the space today if the sale was as good as Hazel thought it would be.

"I haven't been to an estate sale ever," Sera said.

"Glad your first will be with me," he said.

Wes told himself he sounded chill. He wanted this to be the first of many new experiences they had together.

★ ★ ★

The music blasting from the speakers as Wes turned on the car wasn't familiar to Sera. It definitely wasn't Amber Rapp's latest "Rhapsody for a Cheater." It sounded like some kind of grunge style but she couldn't identify it. Wes apologized as he turned the volume down.

"That's fine. What song was that?"

"I don't know. I was listening to 'Take Me Back to London,' by Ed Sheeran and Stormzy, on my streaming service."

"I'm not sure I've ever heard anything by Stormzy."

"He's good. Mostly rap. After I left Birch Lake and told Grandpa I was doing things my way, I ended up in London for six months. Heard him when I was over there."

"What happened with you and Ford anyway?" she asked. "He never mentioned it exactly, just that he had some regrets about you and your dad and brother."

She'd been dying to ask him and better understand the relationship between the Sitwell men, but the timing had never been right. Today it felt—*she* felt—like there wasn't anything she couldn't ask or say.

Wes put the car in gear and headed out of town. "Yeah? I have them too."

"So?"

"You're not going to drop this?" he asked.

"If you want me to. But I think, let's face it, you stayed here for something other than the books."

"Maybe I stayed for you," he said.

"I think partially, after we got to know each other, but at first… Listen, I don't know much about relationships, but I think couples should share things. Poppy said that's one of the reasons her marriage broke down."

"She did?"

"Yeah, and she's better at making things last than I am, so I asked her for some advice."

She wasn't going to say up front that she was out of her depth in this relationship with Wes. She wanted it to last, and she was going to have to use her friends to figure things out. Poppy had been pretty honest with her, and one of the things her friend had said that really resonated was Poppy wished she hadn't pretended to be someone she wasn't.

Sera didn't push to find out more. Probably because Sera herself didn't want to talk about her own shortcomings. She had messed up things in the past and didn't want to repeat her mistakes.

"That was a good idea," he said. "About Grandpa… I don't know how to tell this story without sounding like an ass."

"That's cool. I've seen that side of you before," she said, putting her hand on his thigh.

"That's right. So I started an online used bookstore and repair shop. Grandpa was still helping me get it set up. Since Dad was pissed at me for flunking out of college."

"Did he ever get over that?"

Wes shrugged. "Who knows? We aren't a very verbal family."

"What did Ford do?"

"He wanted me to open a shop here in Birch Lake. Take the stock and set it up. He offered to go with me to get a business loan. And at first it sounded pretty good, but that wasn't my dream. The more he talked about plans, the more I felt like I was losing myself in something I had been enjoying.

"So I got drunk at the tavern and when I came back to Grandpa's he was in lecture mode—to be fair, part of the reason I'd flunked out was drinking and partying too much—and I just said I didn't care what he thought, because drunk me is an even bigger asshole than you've met. Told him to fuck off and that I was leaving in the morning."

Sera hadn't been expecting that. There was a lot to unpack. Losing oneself in trying to meet the expectations of another person. That had happened to her more than once.

But the other part...telling Ford to f-off.

"And did you?"

"Uh, well, I was really hungover when I woke up. And when I went downstairs Grandpa wasn't there, just a note on the kitchen table telling me he wished me luck, he'd be back by five and assumed I'd be gone."

Wes reached up to rub the back of his neck. Of course he was tense. This was one of the worst things she'd ever heard. Neither of them had acted their best.

"Did you leave before he returned?"

"Hell yes. I packed my car and drove out of Birch Lake and never looked back. Grandpa didn't get in contact until that email two weeks before he died."

She was frustrated that these two men she cared about had been unable to resolve this before Ford's death. They were both hurt by the estrangement and neither of them had been willing to put aside their pride... Well, Ford had, but he'd left it too late.

"You were both idiots."

"What?"

"You threw away your family for pride. Not just you—Ford did it too. And you were right not to let him force you into being someone you aren't. But to just say deuces and walk away...that's not what family is."

Wes turned his head and gave her a long level stare. The kind she hadn't seen since that first day in her shop. She had a feeling he wanted her to stop talking about this, but Liberty's tarot reading said to resolve the past. Both of them had to do that if they were going to be a strong couple.

That was her goal.

She held up her hand. "What does the orphan know about families, right?"

He flattened his mouth but didn't say anything. "I wasn't going to say that."

She shrugged at him. "I have seen a lot of people act like family doesn't matter, and until you truly don't have one, you won't understand how hard it is to exist without them. You and Ford are both deeply caring men. It makes me sad you never figured out how to communicate with each other."

"Me too," Wes admitted.

He didn't say anything else on the ride. The past might be harder to let go of than she'd thought. Hers and his.

Somehow he had thought he'd come closer to forgiving Grandpa and himself until he'd recounted it to Sera. He wasn't ready to forgive Grandpa. He'd been drunk and young. His grandfather should have recognized that and let him cool off.

But instead, Wes had gone all Sitwell and told him to fuck off.

Which he'd had a right to do, but that didn't make it easier
to accept. He'd always found it hardest to apologize to people
who mattered to him. He should have stuck around back then,
but he'd been too young and hotheaded to even contemplate
it. He'd packed up and driven to the next town and gotten a
motel room because he was hungover and had just wanted to
stay in bed. But at least he'd left Birch Lake behind.

And that was why he struggled to find a reason to stay that
wasn't about Sera. The first time he'd left Birch Lake had been
with his mom, when she'd taken him and Oz to her family in
California and kept them there until his dad paid her. Then
when his father had them back, they'd lived in Birch Lake
for one summer before he moved them to Portland and the
condo he was renting.

Wes had never left on a good note.

He wasn't sure he wanted to leave the town again. Or Sera.
"Does knowing help you?"

"Not really. Knowing Ford as a friend, I can't imagine
him behaving that way. He and Hamish have had so many
fights but they always forgave each other. Why didn't he do
that with you?"

Wes had no real idea. "Who knows? He and my dad were
on the outs. I think I was making things harder for him."

But that wasn't the reason. Grandpa had shared a craft he'd
thought would be his career as a young man, before he'd met
Grandma and their families had pressured Grandpa to get a
secure job. Sometimes Wes suspected Grandpa had seen a
glimpse of his own youth in Wes.

"That's the thing about relationships I don't get. I mean,
I've seen them get hard. Tawdra's husband worked away for

most of the year, and when he was home, they used to fight. I kept wondering why they stayed together."

"Did you ever ask her?"

"No. I was too afraid to rock the boat. She'd let me use the garage to make journals, and I was selling them at school, so for the first time I had my own money. I didn't want to risk upsetting her and maybe be sent to a different home. It just seemed sad that neither was leaving—so they must have wanted to stay, right?"

"Or they were afraid to leave and be on their own," Wes pointed out. "One of the things I admire about you is how comfortable you are being alone."

She tipped her head to the side as she turned it to study him. Her hair was larger now that they were outside the shop, in the humidity. He again felt that punch of emotion he'd experienced on Valentine's Day.

"We're all alone, Wes. Liberty's mom was the one who made me realize it. You haven't met Lourdes, but she's really... otherworldly. Like a wise goddess. She said to me that people end up disappointed because they're looking outside to find fulfillment instead of looking in."

Wes turned off the highway toward the estate sale. Lourdes did sound wise. But fulfillment was a tall order, and it was never easy to figure out what would make him content. He had thought it was a successful business. That he could find contentment in repairing damaged and torn old books.

And for a short while he did feel something close to inner peace. But it never lasted.

"I'm alone most of the time and I don't mind it. But I'm not sure I've found anything fulfilling about that," Wes admitted.

"Yeah. Same," she said, linking her fingers through his. "It's hard to figure out what fulfillment is supposed to be, you know? It's like, books make me happy. Rereading *The Scarlet Pimpernel* makes me fall in love with swashbuckling romance again. But do I want that in real life? No. So is it just the fantasy life I crave?"

He pulled into the estate and followed the signs to park. Lifting her hand to his lips, he kissed the back of it. "Yeah. I guess we all have to define those things for ourselves. Which might be what Lourdes meant. Maybe there isn't one way to be content."

Which made sense to him in a way. Oz and his dad found contentment in numbers and making everything fit in a spreadsheet. And in the law. Finding statutes that backed up whatever they were arguing. He felt the same way about books and repairing them. Or finding an old edition someone wanted.

Sera must feel that way about the journals she made. He observed the care and attention she gave the covers and how diligent she was in guiding her customers to finding the right intention to put in them. They all had their things and he had to find a way to let that be good enough for him.

Sera seemed closer to it than anyone he knew, except maybe Oz. His brother just got on with things. But Wes never could. This time he had to. He had to figure out contentment and Birch Lake so he could find a way to keep Sera.

Eighteen

The smell of old paper and dust was rife in the air as they were led into a four-car garage. All the books that had once been part of the library in the big house had been boxed and moved here. Wes had scheduled an appointment, so it was only the two of them in the garage.

She closed her eyes. After sharing so much of her past, she ached in a way she hadn't in a long time. Wes made her more vulnerable than she wanted to admit. Realization had been slowly dawning that she wanted something more permanent with him. It wasn't just him staying at her place.

It was him mentioning that maybe in the fall they could go to London and visit the bookseller Ford had worked with on Charing Cross Road. Her heart stopped when he'd casually mentioned it, way beyond the six weeks he was contracted to work for her.

Way beyond.

She tended to plan a month ahead when it came to other

people. Liberty and Poppy were the only two who had ever tempted her out of her safety zone into making long-term plans.

Now Wes.

"Since we both own bookshops, we should probably make some rules before we start browsing," he said.

He had a point. There was a chance they might want the same books. She looked over at him; he had a list on his phone of titles he was hoping to find. And he looked so cute as he was reading over his list, and so serious. She'd never really seen this side of him before.

Impulsively, she leaned over and kissed him. Startled for a moment, he hesitated and then kissed her back. "What was that for?"

"Being so cute," she said. "If there are any books on your list, you can have them. I really don't deal in high-end books, more stuff that will intrigue our customers and fit into genre fiction or the classics, and of course witchy stuff. Which I know you also do. So maybe we can set those aside and then alternate picking so we each get some?"

"You think I'm cute." He stated it, tipping his head to the side.

"Why else do you think I'm always trying to get in your pants?"

"My charm?"

She laughed. "You don't always lead with that."

"We can explore this topic later. We only have a two-hour time slot. Want to start on the left or the right?" he asked.

Since she stood on the right, she indicated she'd take that side. He nodded and they both went to search through the

boxes of books. The estate sale management company had
provided them labels to use for the books they wanted. Sera
had set a budget for herself. Otherwise she'd probably be
tempted to take out a loan and buy them all. The first hour
went by quickly.

She'd found lots of good stock for the shop, and some
weathered books she was pretty sure Wes could repair, which
she stickered in case they ran out of time and he didn't get
to them. She also found a collection of Beatrix Potter books
and remembered her client. Wes was helping her track down
a copy of the specific book, but so far hadn't found one. One
was an early edition, fan folded book that had seen better days.
She stickered it for Wes.

Sera knew some rudimentary book repairing skills, but that
sad little volume needed Wes's care. She'd enjoyed watching him work on repairing books at nights when they were
home together.

She'd sit on one side of the kitchen table when they were
at Ford's old house and Wes on the other. She'd been cutting
papers or making covers for journals. There was something
soothing about being with him surrounded by the bookbinding work they both loved. And that was the only reason she'd
even allowed herself to think about saying yes to his proposed
trip to London.

Wes came over and noticed the book she'd stickered.

"This is for you. I don't think we're going to get through
the room in two hours."

"That's what I was coming over to say. I've marked some
things for you too. There was an entire box of old Western
paperbacks that will be perfect for your shop."

She smiled at him. "Thanks. I'll keep working through this side, I guess."

She bent down to place her sticker on the book and he patted her butt before he walked away.

Were they becoming a couple? Was this what it felt like to be in a relationship? She only knew she wanted to trust that this could last. That Wes was going to be here in the fall. But a part of her, that horrible inner voice she wished would go away, warned he might not. Reminded her that no one stayed in her life forever.

Especially men. Look at Ford.

She shook off those thoughts. She was coming with leading lady energy. She'd stood up to Wes when they first met. Negotiated this relationship with him. She was with Wes because she wanted to be with him.

Which was honestly the most terrifying thought she'd ever had. She had finally admitted she wanted him in her life forever.

And that excited her. She continued working through the boxes, and she and Wes only had one row left when the estate company staffer came to find them. Wes turned to the woman and smiled, asking her if they could have a few more minutes to look at the last row. She granted it since the next appointment was still up at the house looking at the bookcases, warning them they'd have to leave when he was done.

He wasn't afraid to ask for what he wanted. Which of course she'd known from the beginning, but this time...she'd seen he wasn't someone who accepted life as it came. He made it his own.

So maybe—no, definitely—he'd asked her to go to London in the fall because he wanted her there with him. That thought made her feel warm and fuzzy inside.

Wes arranged to have the books sent to a storage unit he'd rented in Birch Lake so they could sort them. But Sera kept the beat-up Beatrix Potter title and handed it to him when they got to the Range Rover.

Of course, as soon as she pulled it from her bag and handed it to him, he couldn't help the feelings that washed over him. She was making it harder and harder to remind himself he was better on his own. He wanted to find a way to show her his feelings. He knew just saying the words would be best, but that wasn't him.

So instead he took the book from her. "Thank you. I got one for you too."

He pulled a copy of *The Scarlet Pimpernel* from his bag. It was a 1930 edition, hardcover, and inside it had an inscription.

May our love be as strong and true as Percy and Marguerite's.
B.

She opened it and let out a soft "oh" as she read the inscription. He knew she'd love it, and she did. He watched as her curls fell forward, as she ran her finger over the faded ink. His gut tightened, and that word he was trying so hard not to say was right there.

Not now.

He couldn't deal with those feelings. He wanted to simply exist in this sunny end-of-winter afternoon with Sera. Just existing was his sweet spot when it came to life. Until Sera proved he might enjoy having someone along for the ride.

"I love it. I wonder who B is?" she asked as they both got into his car. He turned toward her from behind the wheel.

"I'll leave that for you to decide. The couple who owned the estate were Enid and Larry. So I don't think it was them."

She closed the cover, holding the book to her chest and looking over at him. "Maybe Enid had a lover? Kind of cheeky if that was the case for her to put it in their library."

"Indeed," he said, putting the car in gear and heading out of the estate. "Or maybe she left it there for him to find to make him jealous."

"Intriguing. What if B was Enid's first husband who tragically died young?" she suggested.

He loved this game they were playing, and both of them continued making up scenarios until they reached the outskirts of Birch Lake.

"What if they were both book lovers who were searching through boxes and Larry found it and gave it to Enid as a romantic gesture?" she said.

He looked at her. That was the reason why he'd wanted her to have it. A reason that made him so tense he could barely concentrate on driving, so he slowed the vehicle. "That would be…"

"What? Sappy? We've never talked about this, but are you one of those people who is cynical about love?"

He shrugged. He wasn't sure if he was sad or relieved she hadn't jumped to the conclusion that he'd given the book to her for that very reason.

"I don't know that I've ever really thought about it," he

said. "I guess if it was the right person, it wouldn't be sappy. You?"

She leaned back against her seat and opened the book, running her finger again over the faded ink.

Oh, she was a romantic.

He saw it in the way she dressed, in the way she moved through life, the way she took care with each of her journals, trying to bring joy and happiness into the lives of others.

She sighed.

"What?" he asked as he pulled into his parking space behind her shop.

"I want to believe this was a romantic gesture, but life has shown me it was probably more complicated than that. I've never really experienced anything like that. But it doesn't mean love doesn't exist."

He got out and walked around to open her door, but she'd already hopped down and was waiting for him. He wanted to do something big and romantic for her. Something more than finding this book. Something she'd know was romance from the moment she saw it.

Which made his back tighter and more tense. He had never been one to let his guard down and trust a woman. But with Sera it seemed the most natural thing in the world. She made him a better man, made him want to finally leave the past behind and start being present with her.

"I think with the right person it exists," he said.

She gave him that soft smile, the same one she'd worn earlier when she'd mentioned he was cute.

"Am I being cute again?"

"So cute," she said.

He leaned in to kiss her, but the back door opened and Liberty came out. "Thank God you're back. I need to talk to you."

Wes stepped back and Sera cupped his butt and leaned up to bite the lobe of his ear. "We can continue this tonight."

"We definitely will," he said. He watched her head into the shop ahead of him with Liberty, who was pale as a ghost. Her hands were shaking.

He'd never seen the redhead like this before. He hoped everything was okay, but when they entered Sera's back room, he saw Poppy was waiting on the couch.

"Everything okay?"

"Yes. It's a personal thing," Poppy said, but the look on her face told him that it was bad news.

"I'll let Greer know they can take a break and to stay out of the back room so you can have your privacy."

As soon as they were alone, Liberty collapsed on the sofa next to Poppy, and Sera sat down next to her.

"What's going on?" Sera's heart was in her throat. Was Liberty ill? Was something wrong with the business?

"Nan told me the name of my father."

"I thought you didn't want to know him," Sera said.

"I didn't. She thought I was Mom again, and today when I visited her, she called me Lourdes. I corrected her, but she never really… Anyway, when I got up to leave she…she said, 'I'm glad you aren't with that John Jones—you and the baby deserve better.'"

Liberty was shaking and Sera had no idea what to do to

help her friend. "Okay. So now that you have the name, what's next?"

Liberty shook her head. "I really don't know. I mean, I was happy not knowing anything about him. Same as he didn't know anything about me, but now…"

Poppy put her arm around Liberty and Sera did the same, the three of them hugging each other close.

"We've got you, Liberty," Sera said.

"That's right. You are in control here. Do you want to try to find him?" Poppy asked.

Liberty sighed, and then Sera realized her friend was crying. She was trying not to let them see it. Strong, bold and brassy, Liberty was the strongest of them all. She'd never been bothered by anything that happened to them. Even when Sera freaked out, Liberty always had her back. Like when Sitwell & Associates had sent that letter weeks ago.

"We can curse him. I just got a new book in, and I think with your skills we can find a good curse or charm for you," Sera said.

"We totally can," Poppy added. "The next new moon, when the energy is right."

Liberty lifted her head and they all scooted back. "Thanks, guys. Maybe. First, I have to figure out if I should tell Mom I know."

"Why wouldn't you?" Sera asked. Liberty and her mom were super close. Sera envied their bond and admired it. It wasn't like Liberty to keep anything from Lourdes.

"When I was six, I asked her about him," Liberty said. "Mostly everyone at school knew their dads. So I was curious. She told me he didn't want a child, told her to abort it or keep it but he never wanted to know anything about me."

Immediately Sera hated the man. No matter what Liberty decided, Sera was tempted to write about him in her journal and hope karma found him.

"I can't believe your mom told you that," Poppy said. "My mum couldn't even tell me Santa wasn't real."

Liberty smiled, but Sera was still consumed with… *Hate* was too strong, but it was close. She had no family. No one. And she had always craved a connection to the blood relatives who were lost to her. How could Liberty's biological father just walk away from her?

Sera had met other foster kids who knew their parents were alive or even knew their names and also knew their parents wanted nothing to do with them or couldn't handle raising them. But seeing strong, capable, wonderful Liberty like this… Fuck that man who didn't want her to exist.

"I pushed and she was crying the whole time. You know how she is," Liberty said.

Her mom did cry easily. And always came with big feels for everything Liberty did. She'd taken Sera and Poppy in as surrogate daughters. Including them in the shelter of her motherly love. Sera felt bad that Lourdes had to make the decision to raise Liberty on her own.

For the first time, Sera thought her parents' deaths might have been for a bigger reason. If they'd lived, who knew what she would have become. Maybe she'd have turned to drugs to escape life, the way they had. She'd never have met Poppy, Liberty, Ford or Wes. She'd never have moved to Maine and opened WiCKed Sisters either.

"Did she ask if you wanted to know his name?" Sera asked.

"Not at six," Liberty said, rubbing her eyes. "But when I was sixteen a letter arrived, and she got really mad at first and then asked me if I wanted to know anything about my sperm donor... That's how we always referred to him. There was something in my mom's eyes, and I knew the letter had to be from him. But I thought, why now? And you know how I am. I also thought, *Screw you, dickhead.*"

"Thought?" Sera said.

Liberty laughed. "I said it out loud. Mom repeated it and we burned the letter from him, did our cleansing ritual with sage to get his spirit out of our house and our lives. That was it. And I was good with it. I'd made my choice, you know?"

Sera did know. Making a decision like that was what had saved her own sanity when it came to moving on from her parents and from every home she'd ever been placed in. It made the randomness of life feel a little less scary when she'd owned the decision to start over. Again and again.

Liberty had owned not knowing her father, as had Lourdes, but Liberty's nan had officially changed that. Liberty wouldn't be able to keep it from her mom. And she must know that.

"Do you want us to go with you when you tell her?" Sera asked. Because she was finally putting it together. Liberty knew she'd have to tell her mom, and the last time her sperm donor's name had come up, her mom's reaction hadn't been what Liberty expected.

"I don't think so. Oh, I don't know. I'm not sure I'm going to do anything with it yet. But I don't want to hurt her. She's already had to deal with him and she made a choice. She chose me."

Chose. The way Liberty said it made Sera believe her friend was slowly getting her mojo back. She was determined to be in control of her fate.

Sera was too. Liberty shoved her doubts and fears aside and stepped into her normal sassy self, and Sera needed to reach into her own hidden depths. Pulling out her confidence. Because when Wes had given her that book, she had wanted to ask if he'd done so because of the inscription. But fear had kept her silent.

If Liberty could face a man who had never wanted to know she was alive, then Sera could be brave enough to ask the man she was coming to care deeply about, the man she was starting to see a future with, if he felt the same way.

Nineteen

Wes was in Grandpa's house alone for the first time in about a week. It was sort of odd and sort of nice. He liked the relationship he was developing with Sera, but at the same time, his neck itched and his skin felt too tight thinking of how he'd rather have her here with him. He ate his dinner standing up by the sink, which had been his habit before Sera.

Then he worked on the Beatrix Potter book she'd found for him; the book was in sad shape and would require his gentlest approach. As he worked, he thought about Sera. She was with Liberty and Poppy tonight. He envied her the closeness of that relationship, and though he and Sera were sleeping together and sharing their lives, a part of him felt comfortable with that only because it was still temporary.

He had realized it when he'd seen the three women together. Sera was different with her friends. She let her guard down in a way she didn't with him. And until that moment he'd been patting himself on the back for moving closer to her. But now those old doubts and fears stirred.

But what more could she want from him?

Their family had never been dirt-poor, but they weren't the Kardashians either. There was no monetary gain she could want from him the way his mother had wanted money from his father. Did she want him to open up more, or to be the one to make a commitment even though neither of them knew what that would look like?

He heard a car outside and walked to the front door and opened it, sure it was Sera.

But it was his dad.

"Hope you don't mind me dropping by without notice. I still have some of Dad's old clients in Birch Lake. I used to stay with him overnight. Didn't think to let you know," he said.

Wes stepped back to let his dad in. He hadn't realized his father had been visiting Grandpa once a month. Which just made him feel like a shittier version of himself.

His relationship with his dad had stalled out when he'd been forced out of college and Wes had given his dad the bird and walked away. But that was almost a decade ago. Maybe it was time to start again.

This time in a more adult way.

"You alone?" his dad asked as he came into the foyer and took off his coat.

Wes nodded as he grabbed the coat from him. "Sera's with her friends tonight. But she might be here tomorrow."

"I'll be gone in the morning," he said. "So that's going well?"

Wes shrugged. He thought so, but he couldn't shake his

doubts and anxieties. He'd given her a book with a romantic inscription, and she'd seemed happy about it without acknowledging it. Letting her guard down and really counting
on him being around for longer than six weeks was more than
she could do at this moment.

Would that ever change until he admitted he wanted more
time?

"That's not really an answer," his dad said. "Want to talk
about it?"

"No."

His dad smiled and nodded. "I get it, son. I'm dating again."

"Really? I guess hell froze over," Wes said. His dad had used
antiquated sayings like that a lot when they were growing up.

"Maybe, or just a light dusting of snow." His dad walked
down the hall to the kitchen and took two glasses from the
cabinet and then the bottle of Jack Daniel's. He held it up toward Wes, who nodded.

He hadn't thought he wanted to talk, but as he glanced
at the Potter book open on the kitchen table, he decided he
should. "Dad, what made Mom leave?"

His father glanced over his shoulder but finished pouring
the whiskey into their glasses and then turned and handed
him one. "Let's go into the living room. I'm going to need
to be comfortable if we're talking about her."

Wes followed his father into the living room and sat down
in the large leather armchair that used to be Grandpa's. It
smelled faintly of the cologne he'd worn and the cigars he
used to smoke in here.

"What's bringing this up?"

"I suck at relationships." That was enough for the old man

to hear. But Wes wanted to be better and part of it had to be everything that happened in his childhood. His therapist had tried to get him to talk about it more than once. But Wes didn't know where to start.

There was so much he didn't know about his mother.

"I'm sorry to hear that. I mean, I'm not surprised. You've always been a lot like me," his dad said.

The fuck? He wasn't anything like his dad. Oz was his dad's little mini-me in looks and career choice. Wes had always felt like the odd man out.

"Shocked you?"

"Yeah. How do you figure?"

"You keep everything inside, and truthfully, that was probably part of why your mother left."

"But why did she take us and demand money from you?"

His dad shrugged and took a long sip of his whiskey, and Wes did the same, feeling it burn down the back of his throat. His mom had to really hate all of them. And pure hate wasn't an emotion he understood. Being pissed at someone and holding a grudge, yeah. But hatred?

"She didn't say. And frankly, I was pissed off and didn't care. I wanted to see you boys, and she said the only way I'd be able to was if I had sole custody and paid her one hundred thousand dollars. Your grandpa and I scraped together the money. Making it a formal legal battle would have dragged it out, so I just did what she asked. I knew I wanted you back," he said.

Wes had a lot of love for his father and this quiet, truncated confession of his. "Why didn't you act like it?"

His dad shook his head in a slow, almost sad way. "I was

still mad at first about the money, and then too much time had passed and I had no idea how to bridge the gap."

Wes pondered those words after his father went upstairs. He wasn't going to allow himself to make the same mistakes his father had.

"I've missed this," Sera said as she was lying on her back on top of Hanging Hill under a thick blanket with her friends next to her. The full moon looked huge tonight in the clear sky.

They had all been focusing so much on WiCKed Sisters and their own personal lives they hadn't taken time for their friendship.

"Me too," Poppy said.

Liberty was dancing around them and singing the Lizzo song about it being bad bitch o'clock. She only knew those words so kept repeating them. They'd gone through two and a half bottles of white wine and had finally stopped crying and gotten to the numbed-out fun part of their buzz.

Sera turned her head to look at Poppy. "Sorry I bailed the night you needed me."

It had been on her mind a lot. The other night when Poppy had brought up her ex, Sera had wanted to stay, but her mind had been in a different place.

"It's cool. We talked later. I'm not one to hold on to things like that," Poppy said. "I love you, Sera. That's never going to change."

"Love you too," she said.

Poppy rolled over so they were facing each other. "I hope

you and Wes had hot sex after you left. One of us should be getting laid regularly."

"We did," Sera said, laughing. "Oh, Pop, I don't know what's wrong with me. Wes is turning out to be great and I'm still holding back."

"There's plenty of time. Let things develop naturally between the two of you," Poppy said. "Because of how you were raised, it seems like you want connections to happen fast—otherwise you might miss them." Poppy was talking truth right now and Sera realized that she needed to hear it.

"That's so true."

"Hey. What are you two talking about?" Liberty dropped down next to Sera and then poured the last of the wine evenly into their three glasses.

"Me and Wes."

"Toady Sitwell! Actually, I like him. Sometimes I can't stop being mean. I think that's why I'm alone," Liberty said.

"You're not mean," Sera reassured her. "You just have high standards."

"That's Mom's fault," Liberty said, then downed the last of her wine and laced her arm through Sera's.

Sera did the same to Poppy and the three of them lay there.

"When I was little, my mum used to say 'tell your troubles to the moon and they'll be gone,'" Poppy said.

"I like that." Sera wished she had someone to tell her things like that. But it was only her drunk mind going down winding paths to things she'd already sorted in her head a long time ago. Besides, she really didn't have troubles. She had doubts and worries. Wes had given her that book, which she loved, but that inscription. Had he meant it to be romantic?

"We should do that," Liberty said. "Let's stand up and chant, and then each of us can whisper or shout our fear to the moon."

"You know this is why the entire town believes we're witches, right?" Sera asked as they all stood up. Even though she was protesting this, she loved it. She felt the most like the leading lady of her life when she was here with her friends, dropping her guard and being herself.

"Yup."

They joined hands and started singing together. Liberty, who was the most witchy of them, had said the song choice mattered because it set the intention. So when they all busted out with different ones it made Sera laugh.

Then her friends started laughing too.

"We all need something different," Poppy said.

"But we all have each other," Liberty said.

"'We Are Family'?" Sera suggested.

As the words left her mouth, she realized for the first time she wasn't having any of the ungrounded doubts that sometimes swamped her when she thought of these two women as her soul sisters.

"Perfect," Liberty and Poppy said at the same time.

They danced and sang around the circle and then slowed down to tip their heads back and look up at the moon.

"Can Wes love me?" Sera asked. "Do I want him to?"

"Should I agree to pretend to still be married?" Poppy asked.

"Should I find my dad?" Liberty asked.

They all sat in their questions, and the silence at the top of Hanging Hill felt comforting to Sera. The answer wasn't coming into her wine-fogged brain, but for the first time she knew what it was that had been holding her back from Wes.

Did she want him to love her?

Could she love him?

She had never let herself really love anyone before Liberty and Poppy. And even then, there were times when she wasn't comfortable admitting to herself how much she needed the two of them in her life.

Finally, Liberty broke the trance they'd all fallen into. Sera didn't feel any closer to an answer than she had before.

"I didn't do our moon water or charge our crystals to-night," Liberty said.

"It's okay. We need this more," Sera said. "Whatever you two decide, I'm going to support it one hundred percent. I didn't even realize Alastair wanted to stay married."

"We're divorced. He hasn't told his family and they invited us to a family event," she said. "Part of me wants to tell him to fuck off, but we did have some good years and I do like his parents. But then, he's still...him. So it's complicated."

"Men are like that," Liberty said. "That's why I keep things light."

Sera had done that until Wes. And honestly, if she could get out of her own way and admit her feelings, she would be happier with him.

Wow.

Where had that come from?

That might be the beginning of her answer, and earlier she'd pretty much decided to ask him about the book. She'd do it tomorrow. It was time to take this leap and see if she'd finally found someone to share her life with.

She'd always wanted someone in her life, but she'd never wanted anyone to know she did. Stupid, of course, but it had made her feel stronger to try to shoulder her burdens alone. Not anymore.

Wes couldn't sleep and wasn't interested in lying in his bed alone. So he went back downstairs sometime after two. He walked into the living room and over to Grandpa's bookshelves. He'd been slowly going through the volumes, and he'd thought he'd seen their family copy of *Robinson Crusoe*, by Daniel Defoe. Though it had been published in 1719, their family edition had been purchased in the 1800s and had been a gift from father to son. They'd continued the tradition since.

Wes had always thought his dad was the weak link in the father-son lines in their family, but after tonight, hearing the way he'd fought for them, he accepted that his dad emoted like Wes did by burying everything down deep inside. He wanted to read the book again.

He had seen it the night of Grandpa's funeral but hadn't been back in here that much. He and Sera had had dinner in here occasionally, but he paid more attention to her than the books when she was in the room.

His dad and he hadn't talked any more about relationships, but maybe it was because both of them knew they'd have to change to make one work. It was hard to admit things needed to be different. But Wes had slowly been changing since he'd come back to Birch Lake.

"Was this your plan?" he asked the empty room, but he knew he was speaking to Grandpa. He'd always been a little bit tricky, just like Oz. They were good men but they both thought they knew what was best for everyone else and didn't hesitate to push and manipulate Wes.

Of course, there was no answer. But Wes couldn't let the thought go. Sera was the perfect woman for him. He hadn't realized it until this moment, when he thought about Grandpa leading him here. Ford would have known Wes would never be blasé about his grandfather giving away a box of books.

He finished searching the bookshelves and couldn't find *Robinson Crusoe* anywhere. He moved into the hallway where there was a glass-enclosed bookcase, which Wes had emptied last week. He'd put those books into a box next to it. Had the book he was looking for been put in there?

He couldn't find it in there either. His phone vibrated in his pocket, and when he took it out, he saw Sera was video-calling him.

He answered it sitting down on the floor with his back against the wall. He didn't have his headphones, but his dad usually slept like the dead, so if Wes kept his voice low, he shouldn't wake the old man.

"Hey, you," he said when her face popped up on his screen.

"Hey. I have to ask you something," she said.

From having spent a few nights at her place, he recognized she was in her bed. She was still fully dressed and her hair was flying all around her head. Her eyes were bloodshot, making him wonder if she was drunk.

"Ask away."

"You look so handsome tonight. I like it when you don't shave," she said.

She'd definitely had a bit to drink, and he guessed Liberty had needed that bonding with her friends tonight.

"Thanks. You look sexy as fuck with your hair hanging down around your face. Wish I was there with you," he said.

"Me too…" She drifted off for a second, looking happy and a little dazed. He wished he was there to hold her.

"Your question?"

"Did you give me that book because you know I love *The Scarlet Pimpernel*, or because you saw the inscription and wanted me to have it?"

He drew his knees up and leaned his head against the book-case next to him. "Both."

"Both."

"Yup," he said. This was not how he'd imagined this conversation with her. But somehow it was easier this way. He had always bottled up affection. Never wanted to admit to caring for anyone, least of all a woman like Sera. She was everything he wanted and all the things he was afraid to take for himself.

But here on the video call, he could tell her. If she wasn't ready to hear it, her rejection would sting, but he'd be alone to deal with it.

"Oh, good. I hoped so, but then you didn't really say when I was coming up with scenarios," she said.

"Woman, how was I supposed to guess that was what you wanted to know?" he asked her in a teasing tone.

"Read my mind."

"You're the witch, not me."

"I'm not a witch and I can't read your mind. Heck, I'm not sure I can figure out my own," she admitted.

"Me either," he said. That was what had been bothering him. He wanted to tell her how he felt, but he wanted to know how she felt first. And given Sera's childhood, she wasn't going to make that move.

He'd have to be the one to do it. He was going to have to find a way to talk to her and tell her how he felt.

He saw her head fall back against her pillow and then the slight soft sound of that snore of hers he loved. She must have propped the phone up against the pillow he normally used, because it didn't fall over. God, this woman.

"I really like you, Serafina Conte," he said softly. He didn't want to wake her but he had to say it.

He disconnected the call and then went upstairs to bed. He felt lighter after admitting his feelings to her. It didn't matter that she hadn't heard. Now that he'd said it once, maybe it would be easier to say it again when he was with her.

Twenty

Sera wasn't feeling the greatest the next morning and vaguely remembered calling Wes but wasn't sure what she'd said. She showered, took two ibuprofen to help combat her hangover headache and then headed into WiCKed Sisters to start her day.

Last night had changed something inside her and she was excited to be embracing this day with new energy. Dancing under the moon and giving her troubles to it had unearthed how much she was keeping inside.

She had trust in her friendship with Liberty and Poppy. She was always afraid to be the weak link and had been stewing over leaving the tavern the other night when Poppy was trying to figure out what to do with her ex. But Poppy had understood. Which was what friendship should be.

It was a cold, gray winter day, the kind she really didn't love. When she'd been growing up in Florida she hadn't loved the hot, long, almost hundred-degree days in summer either. With her headache, the gray dampened her mood. She was glad she'd dressed in a bright raspberry-pink full-length skirt she'd paired with a formfitting black cropped cashmere sweater to keep her warm and help pep her up.

The store was cold when she entered, so she turned up the heat and went to make herself a cup of coffee. She heard the door open a few minutes later and swiveled to see Wes walk in. His hair was damp from the chilly morning and he still had the stubble she remembered seeing on his face the night before.

So that hadn't been a dream.

"I got here early in case you didn't make it in," he said with a quick smile. "How are you feeling?"

"Ugh, I drunk-called you, didn't I?"

"You don't remember?"

"Sort of. It's hazy. Please tell me I didn't say anything cringey."

"Nah, you just said you thought I was cute and then asked me about *The Scarlet Pimpernel*," he said as he shrugged out of his coat and hung it on the peg he always used.

She looked at his thick wool coat hanging there next to hers. Inhaling deeply as his words sank in. She'd already decided to bring it up today, but apparently drunk-her was all over it like her skin rash after touching aloe. "I did. What did you say?"

"That I picked up the book both because I knew it was a favorite title of yours and because of the inscription."

"Oh."

She hadn't really known what her reaction would be. But

butterflies in her stomach and a turned–on excitement coursing through her body wasn't it. She wanted to sit in the feelings for a minute, but Wes watched her like he was expecting a response.

Luckily the coffeepot finished brewing at that moment, so she turned to pour each of them a cup. She still wasn't sure what she was going to say.

"Sera?"

She turned and handed him a mug after she'd poured a little milk in his as he liked. She added two sugars and milk to hers.

"I'm so glad because I hoped you'd meant that too," she said. "I really don't know what to say next."

"What do you want to say?" he asked as she moved over to the couch and sat down in the same spot she'd been sitting and reading his letter the day they met.

He sat next to her and she closed her eyes, inhaling the scent of his cologne, and then she turned her head toward him. What did she want to say?

I like you a lot.

I might love you.

I'm not sure I can trust you to love me.

None of those were leaving her lips. Not a one.

She took a deep breath and tried to think. She'd be cool and fish and see if he liked her the same way. God, at twenty-six she should be better at liking a boy than wanting to pass him a note that said, *Check yes if you like me.* "I like you a lot."

Fuck.

What was wrong with her?

"I do too."

She tipped her head to the side. Had she heard him right? Then he smiled at her. The smile she had only seen once or twice because Wes was a serious man most of the time.

She smiled back at him.

Her headache seemed to melt away, or at least the pounding in her head was pushed away by the pulsing through the rest of her body. She turned and leaned closer to him. Wes took their coffee cups and put them on the floor next to the couch as she sort of launched herself at him, kissing him long and slow and deep.

For the first time, she felt secure with him in a way she hadn't thought possible. This emotional connection was new and fresh, and all the things she had secretly yearned for but had been afraid to name were ahead.

His hands moved up her back under her cropped sweater. She loved the feel of his hands on her skin. He tipped his head to the side and deepened the kiss, sucking her tongue into his mouth as he rolled them both to their sides so they were pressed completely together from chest to groin.

She lifted her leg, wrapping her thigh around his hips, and felt the ridge of his erection against her center. She ground against him as they continued to kiss. She wanted more.

Wes always turned her on so quickly. She thought she'd gotten used to her body's reaction to his, but this time it felt new. He wasn't just a temporary guy she was hooking up with for six weeks. He was a man who liked her a lot.

Given his history of emotional constipation and her own fears of everyone leaving, that meant more than she'd have ever guessed.

★ ★ ★

Kissing Sera took all his attention, which was a good thing because he was trying not to let the fact that she liked him make him panic. And it did. There were no two ways about that. It was what he wanted, but how could he trust himself to do right by her?

Meanwhile, his cock was ready for him to stop thinking about anything other than how to get her naked so he could slip inside her.

They were in the shop a good thirty minutes before any of the other employees and owners arrived and an hour before it opened. He was fairly certain of their privacy in her back room, surrounded by stacks of books on this comfy couch.

He lifted his head and looked down into her brown eyes. Her hair was a bit frizzy this morning, forming an enticing halo of curls around her face. And as she looked up at him, the word he'd been so reluctant to apply to this feeling drifted into his mind.

He loved her.

He loved Sera Conte.

She smiled up at him in that soft way of hers and he knew he wasn't leaving Birch Lake in a week. Or letting her go.

He pushed the hem of her sweater up until he could see her boobs and then he unfastened her bra as her hands drifted down his body, cupping his ass the way she liked to do.

The fabric was soft but not as soft as her skin. The room smelled of coffee, lavender and books. Everything he associated with Sera.

He took one of her nipples in his mouth, sucking on it hard and deep as he felt her hands moving over the fastening of his jeans. He reached down and helped her free his cock. She pushed away from him and he looked up at her as she sort of awkwardly moved to her knees.

"I'm wearing freaking tights and panties. Give me a second."

He threw his head back and laughed at the urgency in her voice.

She cocked her head to the side, giving him a look from under her eyelids.

"How about I give you a hand," he suggested as he sat up and reached under her skirt to pull them both down. She did a little shuffle until they were off and he dropped them on the floor next to the couch, pulling her back into his arms. Her pointed nipples were begging for his mouth. He loved the sensation of her nipples in his mouth and could suckle her all day.

The material of her skirt felt nice against his stomach as she nudged him until he rolled beneath her. She straddled him and then took his cock, positioning him at the entrance of her body. They'd had sex so many times, but this was different. He was making love to the woman he loved.

She sank slowly down on him and he sat up, holding her close as he slid in deeper. When he was fully inside, she put her hands on either side of his face and started to kiss him in that languid way that made his skin feel too tight and his cock harden even more.

He held her hips to him as he pumped up into her again and again, driving her hard and fast, not wanting to take this slow. He just wanted to take her. Take this woman he loved as deeply as he could, hoping that maybe he could leave a mark on her she would recognize as love.

Because his feelings weren't enough. He needed her to feel them too. He needed her to be so in love with him that the thought of leaving him would never enter her mind.

She pushed him back and then reached behind her, putting her hands on his thighs, as she took control of the tempo. She rode him at her pace, and he saw one of her hands coming around to her clit and he brushed her fingers aside.

He knew the way she liked to be touched. He'd memorized everything about her. He also knew she liked him to pinch her nipple when she got close to coming, and as he did both she moved faster on him. Her head fell back, those thick, glorious curls falling around her shoulders as her breasts bounced with each thrust. As he enjoyed the view, everything in his body started to tighten and he realized he was going to come before her. He put his arm on her waist and turned, taking her under him, driving into her harder and faster.

Wanting her to go at the same time he did.

He felt his cock getting bigger and knew he was going to come any second. He brought his mouth down on hers, pushing one hand under her ass to get her at the right angle so he could drive her more quickly to climax. And then she tore her mouth from his, crying out his name as her pussy tightened around him and he emptied himself into her until he collapsed against her, supporting his weight with one arm so he didn't crush her. But he wanted to hold her tightly so they'd always be together.

"I guess you're not upset I like you too," he said dryly.

She laughed and it was the sweetest sound he'd ever heard. Tinkling like the bells on her front door. His life was never going to be the same after this moment.

He didn't know if that was a good or a bad thing, but it was all thanks to Sera. He cupped her face as he leaned down and gently kissed her because the words *I love you* were right there on his lips.

He wasn't sure she was ready to hear them. She was as relationship shy as he was. Liking each other felt like a massive admission on both their parts. But this wasn't going to be enough. Not for long.

He wanted to make this permanent. Find a way to convince her she should love him too.

Sera couldn't help smiling over at Wes at various times during the day. The crowds weren't waning despite the fact that it had been a good two months since Amber Rapp had tied her success to their shop, which Sera was grateful for. But today, even as gloomy as it was, she realized she felt good about her life.

She'd never really let herself sit in that feeling for long. It had always seemed an elusive thing to her—happiness. It wasn't a priority when keeping her shit together had been what she'd had to do for most of her life. She'd had to be strong for herself, rely only on herself.

But Wes had come in early today to help her out, and not because she'd asked him to. It was one of the few times when anyone had offered unsolicited help. And it was the first time the person was a man.

Greer caught her watching Wes as they came out of the back room with another stack of paper to make more signatures. They came over to her and handed her a journal she'd asked them to bring back for her.

"It's going to be different around here next week without him," Greer said.

"It is," she responded, and Greer moved off as the customer who'd been waiting for the journal Greer had brought up came back over.

Now that they'd admitted they liked each other, was Wes still going to be leaving next week? They needed to have a conversation. She'd have thought that asking him to stay in Birch Lake would be easier now. But her palms started to sweat and her head started to pound again.

She reached down to rub the stone next to the register, but it wasn't as calming as before. Probably because she knew it hadn't been recharged last night.

The afternoon wore on and Wes went to grab lunch for all of them from the deli on Main Street while Greer was in the back, video-chatting with their mom.

Foot traffic in the shop was slow, and when the door opened, she was surprised to see Wes's dad walk in.

"Hello, Benjamin. Nice to see you again. Are you here for Wes?" she asked.

"No, I saw my son last night. I just wanted to check out your shop. What is it you do here? My client mentioned you were a witch."

"Some people think that, but no, I'm not."

"Why do they think that?" he asked.

She wasn't sure where he was going with this line of questions. "Probably because of the vibe of the shop and the fact that I sell journals with intentions bound into them. Not everyone understands the difference."

He reached up and rubbed the back of his neck. In that

moment, despite the fact that he and Wes had different coloring, she saw the resemblance between them.

"I have no idea what that means."

"Well, let me show you," she said, leading him over to the workbench where she had some journals set aside for the next day. She pulled the journal to her, and the book she'd had repaired for Wes was revealed.

She touched the spine of the copy of *Robinson Crusoe* from the 1800s and then turned to Benjamin. But he wasn't looking at her. He looked instead at the book on the tabletop.

"That looks like my father's."

She smiled over at him. "It was."

"Did he give it to you?" Benjamin asked. She heard the worry and maybe the beginnings of anger in his voice.

She totally understood because Wes and Ford had both, on separate occasions, told her how the book had been handed down from father to son, and how each new generation wrote their names on the inside cover. Sera had asked the bookbinder who'd fixed the volume to add a new page so any sons Wes or Oz had could add their names.

"No, he didn't," she said.

"Did Wes?" he asked.

"No," she said. "I took it to have it repaired—"

"You took it?"

"Uh, yes," she said.

"That book belongs to our family," he said.

"He's right, Sera. Why do you have it?" Wes asked, coming up behind her.

She looked at him, and his face was so like it had been on that first day. The part of herself she'd allowed to bloom after their early morning together shut down. He watched her suspiciously, like she'd broken his trust.

She shook her head. She knew she needed to tell them why she'd taken it, but a part of her didn't feel like she should have to defend herself. "I got it fixed for you. I had new front pages added so when you or Oz have sons, they can put their names in it too. I wanted it to be a surprise gift for you. Ford said books are meant to be read and I know you feel the same way."

Wes just looked at her, but his father reached for the book and took it off the table. "That's not something you had a right to do."

"I guess not," she said.

"Why would you take it without saying anything?" Wes asked. "Did you mean to keep it?"

What was it with these Sitwell men? "I'm not a thief. I took it because I knew how much the book meant to you and you said you weren't sure you could repair it because of how much you valued it. I did it for you and your family. It's a gift. Maybe I should have asked, but I wanted to surprise you."

Wes's mouth opened and she shook her head, so hurt and angry that he had immediately jumped to the conclusion she would steal from him. Angry that his first instinct had been to accuse her of something instead of listening to her reasons. Angry that she'd let herself trust him.

"I'll thank you both to leave."

Twenty-One

Fuck.

That was the only thought running through his head. His dad walked next to him but didn't say a word. Wes shoved his hands into his pockets and threw his head back, ready to scream.

"Sorry, son," his dad said, putting his hand on Wes's shoulder. "I wish you didn't have to experience that."

"Experience what?"

"A woman who puts money before you. You asked why your mom wanted money from me to get you back and it's because she was obsessed, thinking I was hiding money from her. After your grandmother died, I inherited a small amount and put it into a certificate of deposit for you and Oz's college fund. But your mom wanted new furniture and a better house and thought I should have used the money for that."

"So she took us?"

"No, she bought all the furniture and drove us into debt.

I don't know if she thought I'd pull the money out and use it on the stuff she'd purchased or what, but I didn't. So one day I came home from the office and you were all gone," his dad said.

Wes saw the anguish and heartbreak on his dad's face. Wes wasn't entirely sure if that was because he was experiencing those feelings for himself for the first time, or if it was just that he was old enough now to see his dad as a man and not just a parent. "I'm sorry, Dad."

"I thought I'd never see you boys again," his dad said, tipping his head back.

Wes suspected his father was trying not to cry.

Wes wasn't sure Sera wanted money. She knew he wasn't wealthy and her stated reasons for taking the book made sense to him. What he couldn't wrap his head around was why she hadn't just asked him.

It wasn't that her actions were totally sus. It was that her motivations weren't clear. Or was his messed-up mind trying to complicate something way simpler than he was assuming?

If he trusted Sera, then there was no issue. She'd taken his book to repair it, as a gift for him. She hadn't taken the book for herself.

Could he let himself just trust her?

"I don't think Sera took it for money," he said to his father.

"You fix books for a living," his father said.

"But I was afraid to fix that one," he said. Suddenly, he knew exactly why Sera had chosen the book and sent it out to get fixed.

"Why?"

"It's the one thing that means something to you and Oz and me. It's the one positive bond we share."

Benjamin shook his head. "Is that what you think?"

"Yes," he said to his father. "We barely speak. It was the same with Grandpa. You and Oz don't even like books, but you do like that one."

Benjamin shook his head. "Kari—that's the woman I started dating—she pointed out that I don't do a very good job of letting the people in my life that matter to me know that they do. I can see now, I've done that with you. I'm trying to get better."

"Great, Dad. I'm glad to hear you're dating and trying to change too," Wes said. And he was. The conversations he'd had with his father since Grandpa's death were good. It made his dad seem more human than he ever had before. Which Wes was grateful for, but what the hell was he going to do about Sera?

"Dammit. I wish I'd kept my mouth shut in Sera's shop. I was trying to get to know her," his dad said.

"Something else Kari suggested?" he asked. Wes was intrigued by his dad's mystery woman, who seemed to be the first person in his memory to make his dad try to change.

"Yeah. She said if I wanted to be closer to you boys I had to get involved in your lives. Oz is easier because we work together. We're having coffee together every morning and talking for fifteen minutes, not about work."

Wes almost smiled, even though he was panicking inside about how he was going to fix things with Sera. He knew she'd expected every person in her life to leave and he'd just walked out the door. But hearing his dad allocating time to spend with Oz was nice, if typical. They'd always seemed to get along.

"So this trip to Birch Lake wasn't just for the clients?"

"I've moved them to an online account so I don't need to see them. But things have always been harder with you, Wes. You're not like Oz, who sees the world like I do."

"And I look like Mom."

"You probably don't remember her, but you look more like my mom," his dad said. "She was the one who made your grandpa get out of the office and live. They met when he was working in London. She always used to get him to take her on adventures, and they weren't always out of the house. We read a lot when I was growing up and I was happy to see you following in her footsteps."

But he had never been able to say it. Wes had followed his father's example down to a tee, even though he'd told himself he was nothing like the old man. Turned out he was actually the mirror image of his dad.

"Want me to go talk to Sera?" his dad asked.

"Not now. I'll tell her you apologize for accusing her of having nefarious motives for taking the book. I'm the one who screwed this up—I have to fix it."

His dad reached out for him and Wes hugged the old man back. It wasn't as awkward as their last hug. Both of them were making strides to move forward.

But how was he going to fix things with Sera? He'd hurt her. And today, when he'd promised himself he'd do everything to build a future with her... He'd self-sabotaged that relationship right into the trash.

★ ★ ★

Sera was fuming, and when Greer came out of the back room, she asked them to watch the shop while she went out for air. She'd known Wes would leave. That was the first thought in her mind.

But this wasn't just about leaving. His reaction to the book had been him not having a clue about who she was. He'd been the one man she'd let spend the night at her place, the one guy she'd finally thought might stay...but she had to admit, in the back of her mind, and in the heart of her soul, she'd been holding her breath.

Waiting for the other shoe to fall, waiting for him to decide she wasn't enough.

She grabbed her coat and headed out the back of the shop, leaning against the wall, tipping her head up to look at the cold, gray February morning.

Liberty's card pull had said Sera needed to make peace with the past. Something Sera had been giving herself kudos for doing when she'd let Wes spend the night. But even then she'd been thinking about the six weeks they'd agreed he'd stay. The stories she'd agreed to tell him about Ford.

He'd had a reason to be in her life. A reason to stay. And now it was over. The fact that he was leaving a few days early shouldn't surprise her.

But it did.

It hurt because in the back room today she'd thought they'd made promises to each other. The kind their souls could understand, and she felt stupid realizing she might have been feeling something that wasn't there.

She wasn't a trust-her-gut kind of person. Her gut had

never told her to do anything but stick to herself as a way to stay safe.

"What happened?" Poppy asked as she came out the door with Liberty behind her. They both had on their coats and Liberty handed Sera a mug of tea.

Sera opened her mouth to tell them, but instead of words, her voice did this crack that sounded horrible, and she started crying. Dammit, she never cried.

"What did he do?" Liberty asked, her voice loud and angry. "This time I'm cursing him."

But Sera didn't want that. There was no curse to make Wes love her or make him want to stay. God, now she could admit that was what she wanted. Now, when he'd accused her of stealing from him in front of his father. Now, when he was gone.

"No," she said to Liberty. "I don't want that."

Poppy moved closer, wrapping one arm around Sera's shoulders. "What do you want?"

"To be trusted. To be enough that he'd want to stay," she said, and the words sounded even more pitiful out loud than they did in her head. She understood that he had his own baggage and the way she'd taken the book was triggering for him. But she wished...that he'd trusted her.

"You are enough. He's the one who is lacking," Liberty said. "What happened?"

Sera smelled the tea Poppy had brought her. Rose hips and lemongrass, one of Poppy's mixes. Sera closed her eyes and took a sip, letting her sisterhood with these two women surround her.

"I, um, I took a book from Ford's house and then sent it

out to be repaired without saying anything to Wes. It's a very valuable book, and more than that, it has a lot of sentimental meaning to Wes and his family."

Wes had shared with her that he didn't want to repair the book himself even though it was almost impossible to read because it was so worn down. He had been afraid to fix it in case he damaged it further.

She'd meant the gift to be a goodbye, for when he left. To say thank-you for his time in her life. But their time together had changed. Those late-night stories and book work had formed a bond between them, she'd thought. It was difficult now to accept that it hadn't.

There was no way Wes could mistake her gesture for anything other than a kind one, if he truly knew her. And the fact that he didn't left her spinning out of control.

"Well, I see why he'd be upset, but he knows you weren't going to sell it or keep it," Poppy said. "That's totally not who you are."

"He *should* know that," Sera agreed. The Beatrix Potter book she'd given him at the estate sale was worth more than this copy of *Robinson Crusoe*. "But he didn't. I mean, I get it. He's emotionally constipated—his entire family is. But I think I fooled myself into seeing something more in him."

"Fooled yourself?"

"It's something I used to do in foster care. Find someone who I thought would be my new sister or mom or dad, and then it turned out they were only doing their job or moved to another group home and we'd lose contact."

Poppy shook her head. "You weren't fooling yourself. He was into you. Is there a chance he'll realize he was wrong?"

"If he does, would you take him back?" Liberty asked.

Maybe. She wasn't sure. Trusting another person to be there for her had always been a big ask. His actions today made her doubt so much about herself.

Which pissed her off. Because the only thing she'd ever been able to count on was herself. She wasn't going to let him steal that from her. If he came back, he would have to prove he was worthy of being in her life.

She was the leading lady, she reminded herself. She'd done a nice thing and he'd hurt her for it. She wasn't going to just say it was okay and welcome him back into her life, her bed and her heart.

Wes knew he couldn't just walk back into WiCKed Sisters. Not today, at least. He needed a plan. Except he straight up sucked at plans. What he was really good at was saying the wrong thing and then walking away. That was exactly what had caused his estrangement with Grandpa and exactly what he didn't want to allow to happen now with Sera.

He needed help. Taking out his phone, he called Oz.

"Hey, bro," Oz said.

Hey, bro? "Oz?"

"Yeah. Sorry Dad texted something was up with you and Sera and he might have played a part in it."

Wes rubbed the back of his neck as he sat at the kitchen table at Grandpa's house. The book he'd started working on six weeks ago was almost completely repaired; all he had left to do was reassemble it.

Normally this kind of repair made him feel like he'd accomplished something, but now it was tinged with regret.

His mind was hounded with images of Sera sitting across the table from him working on her journals while he'd slowly repaired this book. It had been so much a part of his relationship with her. He'd known it from the moment he'd come back here today to try to figure out how to fix it.

"Dad's not to blame. He said some things, but I'm the one who went all in like an ass."

Wes wasn't going to let his dad shoulder any of this. He knew Sera wouldn't be amenable to him saying it was his dad's fault. He was a grown-ass man who owned his actions.

"I can't believe I'm saying this, but it must be down to these new daily chats with Dad. Do you want to talk about it?"

"I'm not even sure what to say. I hurt her, Oz," Wes admitted.

He heard the squeaking of Oz's office chair before his brother said, "Can you fix it?"

"I'm not sure. She's wary of trusting anyone and she started to trust me and then I went all *you stole another book from Grandpa.*"

"Dad didn't mention that," Oz said.

"It wasn't a full-on blowup, just me asking why she would take it."

Oz's chair squeaked again. "I'm not sure what to tell you. Since you flunked out of college, books have been your touchstone. And I have to say, you've used them to keep everyone else away. Grandpa, Dad, me. But Sera uses books the same way, bro. So I think you probably have an idea what you have to do to fix things. It's just, are you willing to do it?"

Wes had a few ideas. He'd have to go to her friends, of course. He had a feeling Poppy might be sympathetic, but

Liberty would rightfully try to curse him or something. He didn't blame her. He'd done something to Sera that he'd hoped he wouldn't do. He'd hurt her.

He hadn't ever been aware of another person's feelings and put them above himself. He'd been aware he'd hurt Grandpa, but instead of staying to try to heal that relationship, he'd given the town of Birch Lake the finger and left.

But with Sera he couldn't do that again. He loved her. He'd been trying to avoid admitting it to himself, but the truth was there in the pain in his heart. How could he hurt someone who mattered so much to him?

He hated that he'd done it. First, he had to ask for help from her friends. Then he would show her how much he loved her.

Because he wasn't sure he'd be okay ever again if she didn't forgive him. Oh, he'd continue to live, but it would be in that same gray world he'd existed in before Grandpa died and Wes had come back to Birch Lake and seen Sera standing behind the counter of WiCKed Sisters.

Her thick brown curly hair around her face, her quirky outfits, quick wit and temper. She'd challenged him, turned him on and woken him up to the fact that he'd been moving through life fixing things instead of fixing himself.

"Thanks, Oz. I think that will work. I might need you and Dad to come up here once I get this figured out."

"Sure. I can do that. I think Dad might bring his girlfriend. I know he wants her to meet us," Oz said.

"I'd like to meet her. Sounds like she's good for Dad and he's trying to be good for her." That wasn't something Wes would have thought he'd say before this point.

He hung up with his brother and then finished putting the

cover on the antique book. He looked down at it, repaired and in working condition. He would have to do the same for his relationship with Sera.

First, though, he had to get her friends on board. That would be monumental, but if he had the right incentive, something they knew would make Sera happy, they might help.

Actually, that was precisely what he needed them for.

Twenty-Two

For the next two days Sera was in a funk and didn't see any signs of Wes. Which almost made her feel she'd been right about him not caring about her the way she'd cared about him.

He'd spent most of his life running from everything when it got complicated. She couldn't help comparing it to the story he'd told her about arguing with Ford.

Sitting in the back room with a cup of Earl Grey, her feet propped up on a stack of books Greer had been unboxing before they went home for the evening, she knew she had to snap out of this.

She was in those same feels she'd experienced the first time she'd been shunted from one group home to another. That first time she'd believed the new home would become her family. That she'd have something permanent. She'd deluded herself then. Had figured out quickly that she wasn't going to have anything lasting until she created it for herself.

Wes was the first man she'd thought seriously about a future with. She'd even downloaded the application for a passport off the internet, sort of hoping they were really going to London in the fall.

She put her head back against the sofa and felt tears welling in her eyes. She hated crying. It was so unproductive, but at this moment she couldn't stop them and didn't even try. She was allowed to be sad when the man she'd thought…

She loved him. She wasn't going to pretend she didn't.

The new moon had given her all the clarity she'd needed. And that morning, making love on this very couch with Wes had pushed the rest of the doubts from her mind. But then he had to go and be the biggest asshole.

Someone cleared their throat, and she lifted her head to see Wes standing in the doorway that led to the shop. He held a box in one hand, which he set on the table where they had eaten lunch together.

"What?"

"Can I come in and talk?"

"Sure," she said. She wished—*wished*—her heart hadn't started beating faster when she saw him. But he was wearing one of those cable-knit sweaters he favored that hugged his chest. His thick blond hair looked rumpled, as if he'd been running his hands through it. His eyes met hers and then he skirted his gaze away from her.

"Are we back to that?" he asked as he took a few steps closer.

He stopped and stood not too far from the couch, his hips canted to one side as he watched her and waited.

"I'm not sure we ever really left," she said. The thing she'd only just realized about love was that it was easy to deceive herself into believing they were both experiencing it. That seemed one of the great injustices of being human—one person could experience all the love feels and the other could just be having fun.

"Sera, I'm sorry."

She shifted a bit so she sat up straighter. Sorry wasn't something he said often, but she knew from the past that Wes was usually sincere when he did apologize.

"For?"

"What I said to you. My dad is sorry as well, but he didn't know you like I did, so he at least has an excuse."

She nodded as she crossed her arms under her breasts and just watched him. "Why would you think I'd take something that meant so much to you?"

"I'm an ass."

"Don't. You're just saying that to deflect. You're not an ass. And your reaction was something deeper than anger. What motivated it?"

He shoved his hand through his hair and tipped his head to the side, watching her and then letting his eyes drift from her to one of the bookcases crammed with books. He nodded as if he'd figured out something inside his own mind.

"Sera, you're like that bookcase over there. It has every adventure a reader could want on its shelves, and all I'd have to do is reach out, pick one up, and I'd be on the adventure too."

"I thought you had," she said.

"I thought so too, but there was a part of me that wasn't fully into the book. I was still thinking of my own empty bookcases. When I get an old book that needs to be repaired,

I fix it and give it to someone else. Like I don't deserve to keep it."

She shifted around again, setting her teacup on the floor by her feet as she got up and walked closer to him.

"You've always had a family and people who loved you, Wes. Why wouldn't you deserve it? Or me? Do you mean me?" she asked. Her emotions felt like she was on a big old-fashioned wooden roller coaster. The kind she'd read about in *Goosebumps* when she'd been a teenager. His presence made her feel like they were being slowly pulled up to the apex and she was holding her breath, not sure if the drop would scare her shitless or make her laugh with pure joy.

"I do mean you. And I don't deserve you because I have always walked away from those who cared for me," he admitted. "So when I saw *Robinson Crusoe* on your table, all I could do was seize the excuse it gave me to protect myself again. To not let myself believe I could care for someone as deeply as I care for you, Sera, and keep you."

What was he saying?

Did he care for her? Did he want a second chance? And if he did, could she trust him to stay?

He had come back. And Wes wasn't one for making gestures without following them up. She needed more answers.

"What does that mean? You care for me enough to want to remain here for good?"

He'd been relieved she hadn't kicked him out and told him to never darken her door again. But that wasn't Sera. From the moment he'd met her she'd been brave; she didn't back down.

Now she stood before him with dark circles under her eyes,

asking him to come clean with his emotions. He had practiced the words at Grandpa's place before coming to the shop.
It had taken a promise that he wouldn't hurt Sera again, and
that he'd leave if she told him to, in order to get Liberty and
Poppy to both agree to let him into WiCKed Sisters after it
closed for the day.

So here he was, and it was time to do the thing he'd been
preparing for since Sera had kicked him and his dad out of
the shop the other day.

He took a deep breath.

"I love you."

The words came out low and gravelly, and he knew that
was because he'd rarely said them. He'd even rarely let himself imagine he could experience that emotion. Love might
have been in his life, but he'd never seen it or allowed himself to believe in it until Sera. She'd done something to him.
Wove her magic—with her books and her halo of curly hair.
With her smile that made him hard and her quick wit that
kept him on his toes. She'd captured him completely and he
knew he was under her spell.

But it wasn't as if he'd gone into it unwillingly. A part of
him believed this was what Grandpa had experienced. That
he'd found in Sera the well of love she gave to the world.
Amber Rapp might have told the world there was witchy
magic in the journal Sera made her. But Wes had come to
realize the only magic was Sera herself. She'd spent a life on
the outside of other families, watching them from a distance
and creating a strength inside herself that came from a deep,
loyal love.

"You do?" she asked.

She dropped her arms and her hands were shaking as she watched him. He had no idea if she loved him too. She didn't have to fall for him the way he had for her. He wanted her to, but he loved her regardless.

He was going to love her for the rest of his life. That future in Birch Lake he'd been unsure of now seemed like the easiest and smartest decision he could make.

He wanted to be close to her. To talk books with her, to sit at the table at night working on their projects and then pull her into his arms and make love to her before she fell asleep, snoring gently in his arms.

That was new. And scary. But he wanted it.

"Yes. I almost told you the other night when you video-called me."

"The night I drunk-called you," she said.

"Yes, and then fell asleep. You're sweet and sexy, and I knew in that moment I wanted to spend the rest of my life with you."

She cleared her throat and twisted her fingers together. "So what happened when you saw *Robinson Crusoe* on my table? Did you stop loving me?"

"No. I just let my past get in my head."

"I do the same thing. No one who loves me has ever stayed. I'm really not sure that, other than Liberty and Poppy, anyone has truly loved me."

"You know they're never going to leave," he pointed out.

"I do. I was starting to think you might stay as well," she said. "Then you walked out that door."

"You asked me to leave."

"I know I did. I couldn't do anything else," she admitted. "I would have been mad if you hadn't left."

"I know. As soon as we walked up Main Street, I knew I'd been a jerk and wanted to come back, but you needed time. And I needed time too. To be sure of myself and what my heart wanted. I had to know I wanted to stay here not just for you, but for myself."

"And?"

"I do. I am staying. But it would be a hell of a lot easier if I knew you still cared about me," he said.

She chewed her lower lip and then reached up to bunch her hair together, as if she were going to put it in a ponytail, and then she let it go. He recognized those nervous gestures of hers. But he had no idea if that was a good sign for him, and his heart, which was beating so hard and fast, he'd think he was having a heart attack if he wasn't waiting to find out if she loved him.

"I do care," she said.

He took a step closer to her. "Do you care a lot?"

She nodded in a series of quick motions and then took a step toward him, throwing herself into his arms. He caught her closer, holding her to him as she put her hands on either side of his face the way she liked to do.

She kissed him hard and deep. He moved so he was leaning against that overstuffed bookcase so he could run his hands down her back. She lifted her head.

"I love you too."

"I was so afraid you wouldn't be able to," he admitted.

"Well, I do."

"I'm not sure how you got past my barriers. But you have been pushing through them since the moment we met."

"Only fair since you did the same to me," she said.

"No way. You're the witch who cast a charm and drew me to her."

"Maybe it was Ford who cast the spell," she said with a laugh. "He knew what he was doing when he gave me those books."

"He might have. Speaking of books... I have one for you."

He went and got the package he'd had in his hands when he came in and handed it to her.

Sera opened it carefully, peeling back the craft paper he'd wrapped it in. He heard her breath catch as she looked at the book's cover. He'd made a photo collage of Sera's family. Liberty and Poppy, Merle and Greer and Grandpa and Hamish. Then, hoping for the best, he'd put himself and his father and Oz on there too. And he'd used the calligraphy he'd perfected in his old manuscripts to write "Sera's Family" and foiled it with gold leaf.

"It's empty, but I did embed an intention in it," he said.

"What did you write?"

"'Sera's family is full of love, laughter and happiness that never ends.'"

She hugged him tightly, burying her face in his neck, and he felt the warmth of her tears against him. "Thank you, Wes."

"For what?"

"The magic of you and me."

★ ★ ★ ★ ★

afterglow BOOKS

From showing up to glowing up, Afterglow Books features authentic and relatable stories, characters you can't help but fall in love with and plenty of spice!

COMING SOON

To discover more visit:
Afterglowbooks.co.uk